TARA TAYLOR QUINN

THE 4TH VICTIM

MIRA®

Recycling programs for this product may not exist in your area.

ISBN-13: 978-0-7783-2835-3

THE FOURTH VICTIM

Copyright © 2010 by Tara Taylor Quinn

For questions and comments about the quality of this book please contact us at Customer_eCare@Harlequin.ca.

www.MIRABooks.com

Printed in U.S.A.

For Penny Gumser, Phyllis Pawloski,
and LeeAnne Williams. The three women who,
in their own ways, introduced me to Big Girl Panties.
I thank God for the three of you. And love you so much!

Dear Reader,

Kelly Chapman really did it this time. She was considering a case, getting ready to open one of her files to me, something to do with her foster daughter, Maggie Winston. She went inline skating while she pondered. Alone. In December. In Ohio. There's this converted railroad track, now a paved bike path, where she skates on a regular basis. During the spring, summer and early fall the path is well traveled. But not in December.

Without intending to, Kelly put herself at risk and there went her plans. That left me with no heroine and a paved bike path as a crime scene. Now, this was a problem for the book—a kidnapped and out-of-commission heroine. It turned out to be a personal problem, too. Like Kelly, I'm an avid inline skater. I skate for peace of mind. For freedom. For health. I love flying across cement with the wind in my hair. I love pushing myself to get up the steepest hills and I laugh out loud when I race back down.

Kelly just so happens to use the same bike path I skate on. And after she came to harm there, I couldn't skate on my path anymore for the months it took me to write this story. It felt like darkness. And danger. Instead of joy waiting for me out there with the wind, there was danger lurking just behind me.

Kelly wouldn't let me give up, though. She pushed herself—to survive. And she pushed me. I'm happy to report a recent fourteen-mile skate. And even happier to report that I can't wait to get back out there. I'm happiest still to bring you Kelly's story. She'll keep you guessing. That's a promise.

I love to hear from readers. You can reach me at P.O. Box 13584, Mesa, AZ 85216, or www.tarataylorquinn.com.

Tara Taylor

1

Chandler, Ohio
Thursday, December 2, 2010

"You okay?" I glanced over at the young woman riding in the front passenger seat of my blue Dodge Nitro. Maggie, whose hair was all one color now—a shade of blond that complemented those big brown eyes—stared straight ahead.

"Yeah."

"No, really." Maggie knew I wouldn't let her hide from me.

"I'm fine."

Some days, being the new and single foster mother of a fourteen-year-old—a girl who'd been sexually active far more recently than I had—was more challenging than sorting out the various personae of a patient with dissociative identity disorder.

I had experience with the latter. And training.

"Are you sure you want to do this?" I asked, making a turn and then another.

"Yeah."

"You don't have to."

"I know."

"You don't owe her anything."

Maggie's head swiveled toward me, and the emotion I could see in her eyes caught my stomach. And my heart. "Don't I?" the girl asked, her voice more mature-sounding than any teenager's should have been. "Whatever else she did, she gave me life."

That was something Maggie's mother did often— invoking the invisible bond of biological family. A bond that was meant to comfort but sometimes twisted insidiously and could lock you into a seemingly inescapable hell.

"And then she stole it from you," I said without a pause. "One fact negates the other."

"So why'd you come back to Chandler and take care of your mom until the day she died?"

I didn't regret telling Maggie my life story. It had won me a measure of her trust, which helped save the girl's life. As a result of the whole mess—what her mother had done—I had custody of her for the next four years.

But all things came with a price. I could have pointed out the differences between her story and mine—if I'd had the time, which I didn't. But it wouldn't have mattered. Maggie couldn't hear me right now.

With a heavy feeling of dread, I turned into the prison complex.

"Maggie?" If she'd still been a client I could've distanced myself.

"Yeah?"

I waited until she turned and looked at me. "I'm here to stay."

The girl nodded, but her solemn face told its own story. Maggie wasn't believing in happily-ever-after at the moment.

With what she'd been through, how could I blame her?

* * *

Even the unlocked halls in a prison were creepy. Gray. Long. Not enough doors. Staying as far as she could from the butch-looking prison guard walking her down to the dining room, where some female prisoners got to sit at the tables to have visiting time with their families, Maggie tried not to think about getting trapped in there. About some wacko criminal breaking loose.

"You been here before?" the gray-uniformed woman asked. Her voice was all sweet and high, like she was talking to a freakin' puppy. Maggie wondered if the guard knew how bad she looked with that inch of gray showing at the roots of her pitch-black hair.

"Yes," Maggie told her. Because being polite was important. "Once."

Kelly had offered to come with her today, like she had the first time, but Maggie needed to be alone with her mom.

Now she wished she'd asked her foster mother to walk with her to the dining room. Kelly had a way of making the craziest things seem not so bad.

Probably came from being a shrink.

Maggie spotted her mom right off—at the same table they were at before. The one in the corner as far away from everyone else as they could get in the too-small room.

Tables here were only big enough for four. To keep down the chances of riots and fights, Kelly had told her.

To keep these freaks from forming gangs, Maggie figured. Like they'd ever be able to prevent gangs. Rape and violence happened in prisons. Maggie knew that. She wasn't a kid.

There were only a couple of other orange-suited women in the room, with one visitor apiece.

"Hey, baby," Mom said as Maggie nodded the guard

away and slid onto the hard plastic seat across from her mother. Her mother in the orange jumpsuit.

"Hey."

Mom reached out her arms, like she was going to hug her. Maggie pretended not to see, staring up at the ceiling until the stupid tears went away.

There were a couple of bruises on her mother's arms.

And—something that had been happening a lot lately—Maggie had a flashback….

She was about six. Wearing a new pink polka-dot dress. She'd tripped getting out of the car, fell in the dirt outside the trailer door and stained her dress. She'd started to cry about her pretty dress, but before she could do more than hiccup Mom was there, scooping her up with both arms, holding her close and telling her everything was going to be all right. That nothing was worth seeing her baby cry. It was only a dress….

Coming back to the present, Maggie blinked. It wasn't only a dress anymore. And everything *wasn't* going to be all right.

"Kelly said you got ten years for child endangerment and solicitation of a minor."

"It's not fair, Mags," Mom said. "I had no idea Mac and you—"

Maggie's face must have shut down because Mom stopped and took her hand. "I'm sorry, honey. It's not your fault. Don't ever think any of this is your fault."

Maggie wanted to shrug off her mom's hand. Because it was warm. And familiar. And inaccessible for the next ten years.

Because her mom had betrayed her. Lied to her.

Her mom's sentence had nothing to do with Mac. Mom had sold her to a corrupt deputy as a drugrunner.

She held on to those fingers for all she worth. "I love you," she told the woman who'd given birth to her at sixteen rather than have an abortion. The woman who'd quit school and kept a job for every single one of the next fourteen years; who'd been able to chase away the boogeyman when Maggie had nightmares; who'd sat with her when she had the flu and thrown up all over the place; who'd always made sure there were presents under the tree at Christmas.

"I know, baby. I love you, too." Mom leaned forward. "You okay?"

"Yeah." Maggie wanted to ask the same, but couldn't. Those bruises... She wondered if anyone had gotten to her mother. Hurt her. She was scared to death of that.

She lay awake in bed at night wondering about it.

"How're your classes going?" Mom had asked every single school day of Maggie's life. Until this year.

So far, Maggie's first semester in high school had been pretty much a nightmare. Living on the wrong side of the tracks in a small town had been bad enough—but being the victim in a major criminal scandal that involved drugs made fitting in at school almost impossible.

"Good. I'm getting all A's." She had to. She was going to college.

They talked about her classes. Her teachers. Mom asked if she missed cheerleading. Maggie didn't. And then she asked if Maggie'd met any cute boys. Maggie didn't bother to answer that one.

What Mom didn't ask about was Glenna. About being at school without her best friend who'd been murdered by the bad cop. The one who'd paid Maggie's mom for access to Maggie.

And she didn't ask about Kelly. About life at Kelly's house.

"She's never going to replace you," Maggie finally blurted out. It was part of what she'd come here to say.

"I know." But Mom's eyes filled with tears. And Maggie

changed her mind about saying the rest of it. She'd been stupid to even hope that Lori Winston would be okay with Maggie's growing feelings for her foster parent.

But maybe Kelly had it all wrong. Maybe it *was* all Maggie's fault. If only Mac would contact her like he'd promised. He'd help her see the truth.

Kelly wouldn't approve of Mac talking to her. She'd freak. Call the cops. But that was because she didn't understand.

Maggie wasn't like other teenagers. She'd grown up fast. And smart. She was mature. Didn't act like a drama queen.

Mac loved her. It wasn't their fault that he'd been born twenty years before her. Or that she was only fourteen.

"Listen, Mags, I've been talking to someone in here." Mom's voice got that tone, like when she was planning to schmooze the landlord out of having to pay rent. Or calling in sick when she wasn't sick at all.

Maggie felt like she might throw up. She wanted to leave. But she couldn't, even though the guard was right behind them, leaning against the wall, watching Maggie and waiting for her to signal that she was done.

"I want you to be careful." Mom's voice got all whispery. "There's this woman in here who used to be an attorney. She says Kelly Chapman can't be trusted. She says Kelly lies to people to get them to tell her things, and then she turns them in."

"The only reason she called the cops on me is because I was a minor," Maggie said. "She had to. By law. And for my own safety."

"You were safe, Mags. What you were doing, delivering that stuff, you weren't in any danger. And we were making enough money to get you to college."

"That stuff was *drugs,* Mom. And we could've gotten

loans for college. I wish you'd talked to me. We could've figured something out...."

It was the same old story. Maggie went over it and over it in her head. And never got anywhere.

"We would've been fine if it wasn't for that woman."

Mom stopped and Maggie knew she was thinking of Mac. Mom didn't get it, either.

"I didn't do anything wrong," Mom said. "I didn't have anything to do with the drugs. Never saw them. Never touched them. I don't take them. And I made sure you weren't in danger. I'm a good mother. And when I got worried about you, I got help. I trusted that woman, Mags. I sent you to her so she could help us, and instead, she took you from me. Took you for herself. Look at her, with her fancy degree and her house and her money. But does she have a husband? Has she ever had a kid? No. She lets people like me sacrifice and do all the hard work and then she takes the rewards of our efforts for herself."

Mom's reasoning was skewed. But not completely.

"I have my rights, Mags. That's what Thea, this attorney, was telling me. They strong-armed me. Scared me about losing contact with you."

Mom was right about that and Maggie felt sicker.

"Thea says I can go back to court. I have grounds to make a motion because of the way they kept yelling at me that I'd never see you again. I'll get a hearing and if Mac won't testify for me, then we'll subpoena your records from Kelly. They'll show that I had your best interest at heart. They'll show how much I love you. *I'm* the one who called the damned shrink...."

Mac was a good guy. They could say anything they wanted about him, but if he was so bad, they'd arrest him. They didn't because they knew he wasn't a criminal. Maggie was sure of it. They said he had another life, a family, but Maggie didn't believe it. They were confusing

Mac with someone else. Mac was *hers*. He would've told her if he'd had a family. He loved her.

And she loved him.

"Mac can't testify for you, Mom. You pled guilty."

"Only because they dropped a bunch of stupid charges. That's why they said I did so much stuff, honey, so they could scare me into saying I did some of it. Thea told me how it works. It's all to save the state from having to go to trial. But with the new motion I'll get a hearing."

Maggie knew what a plea agreement was. She'd done a lot of reading on the internet since Mom's arrest.

"Mags, please, just until I find a way out of here, watch your back, okay? I love you so much…."

"I know. I love you, too." That was always there. This attachment between her and Mom.

"You're my life, Maggie. You're everything good about me. The only good thing I've ever done."

"That's not true. You've done lots of good things."

"Just take care of yourself. I'll get out of here, I promise, but until then we can't let anything happen to you."

"Nothing's going to happen to me." Starting to feel scared again, Maggie thought of Kelly. And Sam. They were keeping her safe. They had to be. They'd made sure she didn't get in any trouble for the stuff that she'd done. They knew she hadn't understood what she was doing.

This was just another one of those things Mom didn't get, right?

And then she thought of something else. Mom had said she was getting out….

Mom, who always figured out how to get around whatever got in their way. Maggie leaned forward. "You aren't planning to do anything that'll get you in more trouble, are you?"

"Of course not."

"Don't, Mom. Please. I'm begging you…. Do what this

Thea says. Make a motion, or whatever. I'll say you can use my records with Kelly." She wasn't sure she could do that as a minor, but Kelly would do it if Maggie asked.

Mom's fingers were soft on her face and Maggie had to fight tears again. She wished she could lay her head against her mom's shoulder and cuddle up and go to sleep. Like she had in the old days.

"I'm going to be fine, sweetie," Mom said. "I don't belong in here. They'll see that. And in the meantime, just sleep with one eye open. Do it for me. Okay? That's not too much to ask, is it?"

Wishing she could change who she was, Maggie shook her head. No, it wasn't too much to ask. She turned toward the guard. And felt horrible about how relieved she was that she could go now. About how badly she wanted to get back to Camy, her new, very bossy, little-sister toy poodle, and the room Kelly and Maggie had decorated together.

They'd had fun. Laughed.

While Mom was in this hellhole.

And maybe she deserved to be.

Still, Mom was Mom. And Maggie was Maggie.

And they'd always be related.

2

The first Friday in December was an unusually warm—for Ohio—forty degrees. That's still cold, though, and I was outside in-line skating. Was I nuts? Judging by the absence of fellow exercisers on the trail, maybe. Except that even in the middle of summer, I was often alone out there.

What could I say? I loved to skate. Loved the sensation of flying with the wind rushing past me. Skating had always been my time to reflect. So, cold or not, I'd gone to my usual place, a section of disused railroad track that had been converted into a paved bike path that stretched eighteen miles or more through several counties.

And it was midmorning, to boot. Most people were at work. Or involved in the business of their day, so I got to be there alone. Not everyone had these random two-hour blocks of time in the early afternoons.

Besides, being out in nature, surrounded by patches of trees interspersed with cornfields, was the reason I came out. To have this time away, just me and the wind. To erase the noise of the world and listen to my thoughts.

I slowed to cross one of several country roads that broke

up the path. Then, bending at the knees and leaning slightly forward, my weight firmly on the balls of my feet, I pushed off again, reaching a decent speed in three strides.

The long undergarments covered with sweats, the extra jacket, didn't slow me down. And I was glad for the gloves, the hat covering my ears, the scarf around my nose and mouth.

I'd be out there even if the extra garments *had* slowed me down. I had a lot on my mind. Regardless of the fact that I lived in Ohio and it was wintertime, I had to skate. It was how I coped. But sometimes life didn't take things like weather into account.

Maggie had headed out the door minus a coat that morning. I'd called her back. Handed her the new jacket we'd bought the month before. I'd driven past the bus stop a couple of minutes later.

Maggie had been there. Standing alone. Apart. But she'd had the jacket on.

I was worried sick about that girl. About my ability to mother her. And was quickly realizing something else. Where Maggie Winston was concerned, I wasn't merely acting out of compassion or my need to nurture every creature that crossed my path.

I *loved* her. Felt protective of her. Felt a sense of responsibility toward her. Like she was mine. My family. My child.

Weird. Scary. Out of my comfort zone, to use a cliché that usually made me roll my eyes. I'm Kelly Chapman. The fix-it lady. (I hated being called that. I'd heard some girls in town say it.) I had three piercings in each ear, but no tattoos. And a toy poodle with a queen complex. I was on call 24/7 to anyone who needed help, mental or emotional. I made my private number public, taking calls whenever the phone rang. I was on the committee to beautify Main Street. I cooked and did dishes at the soup kitchen in town.

I read the entire selection chosen by my book club every month and never missed a meeting. I mentored psychology doctoral candidates.

And I lived alone. Always had. Since graduating from high school eons ago. Okay…I counted back…thirteen years ago.

I was unattached. But one hundred percent involved in life.

And suddenly, there I was, with a bedroom in my home that belonged to someone else. A child living with me. Someone who knew when I went to bed at night. Who knew how little I slept. Someone who needed to eat three meals a day. Someone who was hurting and when she went home, to her family, that was me. She came home to me.

The chills coursing through me had little to do with the sweat mixed with freezing wind as I sped along. I was elated, not only by the speed, the wind blowing against all the clothing I had protecting my skin, but by the thought of Maggie. In my home.

And I was uneasy, too. I had no doubt I could help Maggie. But be a mom? I didn't have any experience with that. Lord knew, I didn't have a great example to start with. And my life since my own mother's death had consisted of helping people help themselves. It was a process I knew. Was good at. Loved.

And I loved Maggie. Full-time.

I took two strides while I let my mind go and just *felt*. Yes, I loved this girl. Two more strides. I avoided a fallen twig with some crumpled leaves. Okay—the absolute truth. I wanted Maggie in my life. Period.

Now what? I skated on. Waiting. For what, I didn't know. For more.

The wind had picked up. I didn't feel it. How could I, mummified as I was? But I heard it. Cutting through the clump of trees I'd just passed.

It was an odd wind. Like a force behind me. On a perfectly blue, sunshiny day. My skate hit a pebble. I stumbled. Felt that familiar flash of fear as the ground loomed closer at a crashing speed. Then with instincts honed to the wheels on my feet, I righted myself. And pushed on. Another stride. It wasn't smooth. I was off my mark. Out of rhythm.

And there was something behind me. Jerking, I glanced briefly over my shoulder, and saw a blur of dark blue.

My first thought was that he'd just drive on by me. Then somehow I sensed that wasn't going to happen. Raising the toe of my right skate, I applied pressure to the rubber brake on the back, slowing to let him pass.

There was a thump. Close by? Or far away? Hot wrenching pain seared through my shoulder and neck. Everything was dark. Silent. I was going down....

Kelly Chapman. Sitting at a table in the FBI resident agency in southwest Ohio, Clay Thatcher stared at the picture he'd just been given. Another one to add to the stack.

Short blond hair.

Blue eyes.

Thirty-one years old.

Single.

A psychologist.

The photo, provided by the Chandler Police Department, had been taken at an antique car show in downtown Chandler a couple of months ago. Head tilted slightly, as though she had a question, Kelly Chapman was smiling.

"Ms. Chapman was last seen leaving her office this morning, just after ten. According to her receptionist, Deb Brown, she was planning to go in-line skating," Scott Levin, special agent in charge of one of Ohio's largest field offices, said. He'd driven down to the office to hand-deliver this one.

"That was less than five hours ago," Clay said. Not really long enough for an adult to be considered missing. Certainly not long enough to bring in the FBI.

"She missed her afternoon appointments. In all her years of practice, that's a first."

"So her receptionist called it in?"

"No, she has a foster daughter." Scott looked down at the pages he held. "Fourteen-year-old Maggie Winston. Ms. Chapman was recently granted full custody of the girl. Maggie knows a cop in town, a Samantha Jones. She called Samantha shortly after the lunch hour when Kelly couldn't be reached. Today was early release from school, and Maggie has to call every day as soon as she gets home."

"What about this Deb woman?" Clay asked. "If her boss had never missed an appointment, why didn't she call someone?"

"I'm not sure," Scott said.

"Which makes her the first person we need to speak to." Clay glanced back at the picture. "If the local guys haven't even done the basics, why are we all over this one?"

He didn't mean to be heartless, but they already had far more work than they could handle. Two young girls who'd been missing for a couple of weeks. A possible terrorist cell in Dayton. And a local businessman they suspected of money laundering. A woman who could very well have decided to play hooky for a day didn't usually come under their radar.

"The locals *are* all over it. Ms. Chapman's briefcase was in her office. Her purse was not. They've searched her home, as well. Nothing was disturbed or obviously missing, other than her purse. And her cell phone. They assume it's with her. They've called it multiple times and she's not picking up. When they do a GPS trace, the phone pings in an area around where the woman skates, but no one's been able to locate it.

"And…" his director continued "…*we* are all over this because Ms. Chapman is not just a psychologist. She's on the national expert witness registry."

Oh. *Shit.*

Clay stared his boss in the eye. "Which means she's a target to who knows how many convicted criminals across the country, and that makes this a major crime."

"Right. And she's a major part of the prosecution in a drug case that's coming up in Florida."

"Do we have a list of all her recent cases?"

"We're working on it."

"I'm assuming someone's searched the area around her usual skating route? In case she fell or something."

"Samantha Jones went to high school with Kelly. They're friends. She knows exactly where Ms. Chapman skates and made a run out there as soon as she took Maggie's call. There are several places to park, but Ms. Chapman's car wasn't at any of them. Detective Jones and the tri-county park security group have already taken a utility cart along the skate paths in case she'd fallen and needed medical attention. They're waiting for you to conduct a more thorough search. Detective Jones didn't want to contaminate a possible crime scene."

"They went along the whole route and didn't find anything?" Clay asked. "Not a piece of clothing? A knee pad? Nothing?"

"Nothing."

"So what about her car? Anyone seen it?"

"Negative. The Fort County Sheriff's Department has an APB out on it."

"Fort County sheriff, Chandler police and park security and she's only been gone a few hours?"

"What can I tell you? The lady's popular. Born and raised here."

"Okay. How many people can I have?"

"Two full-time until she's found. More if necessary. I need you on this one exclusively. The Florida trial, it's a kid who witnessed his mother's murder. This Chapman woman was able to get through to him to ID the killer. We have to find this woman so he'll testify."

"Right." Because of a trial. Not because she had a kid at home who was probably scared to death. Or because her life was in danger. Or maybe even because the kid in Florida needed his shrink. "What about her kid?" he asked. "Who's got her?"

"Samantha Jones, at the moment. They've got the girl and Chapman's poodle, too, out at a farm Jones and her husband have. A guy named Kyle Evans. You might want to talk to them first."

"I'm on it," Clay said, and added, "I'll need the dogs." Willie, the bloodhound, trailed, and Abigale was an air scent canine agent. They each had handlers.

Tapping the picture on the table, Clay stood, saying a mental goodbye to the beer that was waiting for him at home.

Some day. Some year. Someplace.

I was freezing. My teeth were chattering so hard they woke me up. Where was my comforter? And Camy? She was always a warm weight at my back when I slept.

I had to find her, but first I had to sleep some more….

God, it was cold. What made it so cold in here? I tried to move, open my eyes to see, but my arms and legs wouldn't budge. The bed felt like rock. Halfheartedly, really just needing to sleep, I tried to roll over, to get a little more comfortable. I wasn't able to move. More awake, I attempted to straighten my leg. And couldn't.

Panic raising, I lay there. My shivering grew more intense. I didn't seem to be able to control that, either. Had I had a stroke? My pulse beat at my temples; my head screamed with pain.

I'd had a stroke. That was the only explanation. I was dying. Could I open my eyes? Did I want to?

I considered my options for a few seconds. Did I have any?

"Help!" I had to try something.

Miraculously, my voice worked. Sort of.

Maggie. Where was Maggie?

My eyes flew open. And saw more of the same darkness I'd seen with them closed. Was I blind, too?

But no, there was a hint of shadow. A darkening over there. I tried to move my head and the pain was so severe I almost puked. But my arm jerked in the process. It was behind me. They both were. Aching. Stiff.

My head hurt.

I hurt all over. Burned. Was I on fire with fever?

Fever didn't sting. I stung. But I also shivered. Was there any heat on?

"Help!" I screamed the word again and again, sending blasts of pain through my head every time.

When my throat was so dry there was almost no sound left, I stopped. As I lay there, my thoughts slowed. I became quietly, dreadfully aware. Instead of working on my legs, I tried to move a finger. Then two. I succeeded.

And scraped my knuckle against hard ground. Cement or rock. At the same time I realized something else. My hands were bound. The stinging at my wrists was because they were tied tightly together with some kind of rough material. Rope probably.

Tears trickled from my eyes over my nose and dripped

down to the surface beneath me. The pounding in my head made it hard to think.

I'm in trouble.

Serious trouble.

And then I remembered. I'd been skating. The wind was behind me. There was a flash of blue. Getting closer.

And then…nothing.

Adrenaline started pumping. Sending fear in its wake. More alert, I tried to wriggle my toes. They moved. And encountered leather. Familiar leather. My skates.

I was still wearing my skates.

And my ankles were bound together.

Okay. I wasn't paralyzed. I was tied up. And must have been hit in the head.

Was I alone? Was it nighttime or was I in a cavern or a cellar somewhere? Was it still Friday? Friday had been the day I'd gone skating, right?

"Help!" I tried again.

I thought back. I'd had an appointment cancel because my client went into labor. Yeah. And I'd had a free hour before lunch because I wasn't working at the soup kitchen; I didn't work on Fridays since that was the day the Chandler police did their stint.

So, yes, it had been Friday.

Was it still Friday?

Was I still in Chandler?

In Ohio?

And what about Maggie? Oh, God, where was Maggie? Did she know I was gone?

Was she okay? Had they gone after her, too?

Who? Who were they?

Afraid to move, to alert any would-be guard that I was conscious, I forced myself to breathe deeply, to think of blue skies and a meadow, the smell of roses, to focus on my abdomen, my center…

It didn't work.

"Help!" I cried.

"Please, oh, God, someone help me!"

I had to do something! I couldn't just lie there and let them hurt me. Or worse. I lurched forward. Wrenched my shoulder.

And got so dizzy I saw stars...

3

Clay sent Barry Rosnick, accompanied by the canine crew, out to the skating trail, to talk to people who lived in the area, organize the search and traverse the entire eighteen miles of converted railroad track.

Abigale probably wasn't going to be much help because the sun was out and there was no wind. Besides, there'd been other people on the path and she detected any and all human scent in the air, as opposed to Willie, who would be given something of the victim's to smell and would try to trail her that way.

Once the dogs were finished, if they hadn't found the missing woman, and there was still daylight, Rosnick would send ground crews to search until dark.

Rosnick was an avid biker and familiar with the track, so that helped.

JoAnne Laramie, thirty-four-year-old veteran agent, was dispatched to the home of Deb Brown, Kelly Chapman's receptionist and the last person known to have seen her.

Clay headed first to join the FBI forensic team who were searching the home of their missing person.

He'd been to Chandler many times in the ten years since he'd taken the job with the Bureau in Ohio. The town, with a population of close to twelve thousand, was the seat of Fort County, and, as such, was home to the courthouse.

Chandler was also the site of a historic fort dating back to the Civil War—a fort from which the county drew its name. The city held a yearly celebration to honor the soldiers, brave men who'd sacrificed their lives. The celebration—a weekend-long series of events, demonstrations, entertainment and lectures—attracted tourists from all over. It also brought in well-known country music stars. Clay attended whenever he could.

He wasn't thinking about celebrating now, however. He pulled up in front of one of the smaller homes in the elite neighborhood. Obviously custom-built, Dr. Chapman's home, with the beige siding and dark brown brick, spoke of understated success. And warmth. In December, with everything in hibernation for the winter, the landscaping on her half-acre lot was still nice, peaceful and welcoming with the paths of river rock forking through the front grass and the year round shrubbery interspersed with gardens that were probably filled with flowers in the spring.

An oasis. He made his way past the caution tape, up the walk and through the front door.

From the soft peach-colored leather furniture in the living room, to the beige-and-white solid wood table in the large kitchen eating area, the home welcomed him with a sense of peace and beauty. There were pine cabinets above and below the granite countertops that framed the oversize sink.

The kitchen island, with its handwoven mats, had two bar stools and a perpetual watering bowl for pets tucked be-neath it.

The floor in the kitchen was ceramic tile so a guy wouldn't have to worry about dropping an egg, while the rest of the home had a mixture of hardwood floors and plush beige carpet.

"We've been over everything, sir," Beth Lacrosse, the agent in charge of the forensics team, said, joining him in the kitchen. "We'll look at her computer files, of course, and do some more in-depth checking, but at first glance this looks like a nice home belonging to a nice woman who has a nice, undisturbed life. There wasn't even so much as a prescription bottle in the medicine cabinet." Medication use sometimes elicited unpredictable behavior, even if taken properly. "A bottle of acetaminophen, some partially used cold medications, some bandages and antibiotic ointment and that's it."

Clay made notes as he walked slowly through the rest of the house. The room that obviously belonged to Maggie, based on the butterflies on the wall, the clothes in the closet and the books on the shelf, had been painted not long ago. There wasn't a single nail hole or smudge on the off-white and butterscotch-colored walls. He looked at the drawers, pulled out a couple.

"Check these," he said to Beth. "Get fingerprints and read everything you find." Kelly Chapman had just recently gained custody of the teenager, he'd been told. He needed to know more about that situation.

Wearing white gloves and carrying a department-issue plastic evidence bag, Beth nodded and called out to a member of her team.

"Look carefully for any hint of gang affiliation, drug use or anything else that could be a problem," Clay said.

"Got it."

Clay moved on to the second bedroom—an office with an antique white desk and mauve microfiber couch and armchairs, arranged to face an antique white coffee table. The wood floors from the hall continued into this room, broken up by a large off-white throw rug with mauve flowers.

Beth's team was already in the office, going through

files and disconnecting the computer to take it into the office where they could use state-of-the-art software to examine the hard drive.

If Maggie Winston had a computer, he needed to get hold of that, too.

And then came the master bedroom suite. Clay almost stopped in his tracks as he walked into the room. From the plush off-white carpet to the porcelain tile on the bathroom floor, every step he took felt as if he was trespassing on something so personal that he—

He was being ridiculous, he told himself. He was working. Looking for a possible kidnap victim who could very well be dead. He'd been through people's dirty underwear more times than he could count.

And still, being in Kelly Chapman's bedroom felt like an invasion to him. The woman's home depicted her taste, her love of beauty. But it also represented success. And a sense of certainty, of strength, that was calling out to him.

Shaking his head, Clay moved over to the French doors on the bedroom's far wall. Opening them, he stepped out onto a deck that overlooked a large backyard filled with trees, a little pond with a waterfall landscaped into one corner and flanked by the woods behind it. On one corner of the porch itself was a covered hot tub.

When he started to visualize the woman in the tub, Clay quickly left.

The bedroom. And the house.

He drove straight to the farm outside town where Samantha Jones lived with her husband, Kyle Evans. Clay was as interested in speaking with the foster kid, Maggie, as he was with the deputy, recently promoted to detective, and her new husband.

As he drove, his victim's house played through his mind's eye. Until he realized something. With all the beauty, the artwork, the decorating—even the personal items in her bedroom and office—there hadn't been a lot that spoke of Kelly Chapman's personal life. No pictures of family. Or friends. No personal photos at all. And no obvious vacation mementos.

He knew, from examining her kitchen, that she liked Diet Coke and ate frozen dinners. He knew she used high-end makeup, though not a lot of it, and took rose-scented bubble baths, but he knew nothing about any relationships or memories she had.

It took him ten minutes to reach the Evans farm.

The fact that it was Friday night, that Samantha and Kyle might have dinner plans, or that Barry and JoAnne had loved ones waiting for them, didn't factor into Clay's decisions. A woman was missing and, if there'd been foul play, every second counted. Statistically, the chances of finding Kelly Chapman alive lessened with every hour that passed.

His phone rang just as he was driving by land that showed the remains of harvested corn. He turned onto the drive that led up to the farmhouse.

"This is Clay," he said, recognizing JoAnne's number.

"I did some checking, on a hunch, before heading out to Chandler. The farm you're going to, Kyle Evans's place—now Samantha's, too—it's the one that was involved in that methamphetamine superlab bust a couple of months ago."

Chemicals from the farm had been used to make the meth. And the toxic waste landfill had been found at the back of the property.

"If I remember correctly, the farmer was cleared of any wrongdoing."

"Right."

Which didn't mean that he was innocent, only that he hadn't been charged. "Maybe sleeping with a cop has its advantages," he said, thinking out loud as he did with the few agents with whom he worked most closely—and most often. The agents he'd trust with his life.

"Maybe," JoAnne said, then added, "Maggie Winston, the girl in this Chapman woman's custody, was one of the drugrunners."

Similar to Dickens's Fagin, the slimeball drug lords, aka a Fort County deputy and possibly some Chandler city officials, had used kids to do their dirty work.

"So you figure Kelly Chapman's disappearance has something to do with the drugs."

"I don't like coincidences."

"I'm with you there. Check the status of everyone known to be involved."

"I've got Greg doing that."

Greg Gilmore, college student, part-timer and researcher extraordinaire.

"Ms. Chapman recently worked on another local case, too, but I haven't been able to track down specifics yet. I'm sure it'll be in her files."

"Why do I get the feeling that this case is going to have more suspects than we have time to investigate?"

In missing persons cases, time often meant the difference between life and death.

Sometime later

They were there. Shivering, I slowly came to. My eyes were closed. More time gone. How much more?

Cold.

Too cold.

Dangerously cold.

Was it dark out there, too?

Was someone sitting there? Watching me?

Was I dying?

Going to die?

Maggie.

Opening one eye just a crack, very slowly, I let it fall shut again. Nothing. Except darkness.

You have nothing to fear but fear itself. A client of mine had used FDR's words as her mantra. I tried to listen to them now. To understand. To do what they wanted me to do. I wasn't sure what that was.

Clearly, Franklin Delano Roosevelt had never been an abducted female held captive in a dark place.

Whoa. I'd had a lucid thought. Hadn't I?

Sort of. Roosevelt had been president during the Great Depression and World War II. He'd introduced the New Deal.

Assorted facts ran through my mind. They seemed important….

Except I was too cold to concentrate. Was I going to freeze to death?

I ached everywhere. The pounding in my head drowned out coherent thought. I'd never been in so much pain. Didn't know the body could hurt so badly and still be alive.

Tears squeezed through my closed eyelids when I tried to move my hand. It hit against something and I froze, afraid the noise would reverberate in the silence around me.

Alert my captor.

I was still alive for some reason.

Was someone watching me? More than one someone? I stayed completely silent. I didn't want them to know I was awake.

Why was it so quiet? Shouldn't there be outside noise?

The blockade behind me seemed like a wall of some sort. With excruciating effort I moved my hand along the ground. An inch. Maybe two.

Solid rock. Smooth rock.

And I was exhausted. Just wanted to sleep. Sleep.

If you sleep you'll die.

Had Roosevelt said that, too?

No. That couldn't be.

Think, Kel. Think of Maggie. That girl needs you. More than she knows. She's starting to trust you. She can't afford to be let down again.

Maggie. A child with so much promise. So much life ahead of her.

I opened my eyes. Both of them.

And waited for them to adjust to the blackness. My face felt swollen. I couldn't tell if I was bloody or not.

I was still bound. Still wearing my skates.

And as I lay there, powerless and terrified, I wet my pants.

"Look, I've told you everything I know. Please, go out and find her...."

Samantha Jones's statement was just short of an order. With a raised eyebrow, Clay sat across from the couch the detective shared with her husband, Kyle Evans. Maggie was sitting on the edge of a recliner on the other side, holding a small poodle.

"We're doing all we can, Detective," he assured Samantha. "Forgive me for saying so, but you're too closely associated with the situation for me to be sure you've told me everything you know. I might find something pertinent, the one clue I need, in some little fact you consider irrelevant." Clay glanced at the fourteen-year-old blonde in jeans, a T-shirt and tennis shoes who had, as yet, to say a word. Even to ask a question.

Kyle Evans took Samantha's hand. Clay wasn't writing that guy off as easily as his wife and the townsfolk appeared to have done. The guy was too quiet. In Clay's experience, the so-called strong, silent type usually had something to hide.

Still, dogs were good judges of people and Kyle had a large one lying at his feet.

"I'm sorry," Detective Jones said, bowing her head and then raising it to look him in the eye. "This is just so hard. Kelly, she's…she's the one who takes care of everyone else. Anything I can do to help, I will. Anything." Dressed in jeans and a button-down oxford shirt, the woman looked more like a teenager than the thirty-one-year-old he knew her to be.

Clay, who mòre times than not was spot-on with his assessment of people, accepted her at face value.

"Tell me about this lawyer, David Abrams."

Maggie stiffened.

"You want facts or personal opinion?"

"Facts first. And then opinion."

"He grew up here. Graduated a few years ahead of Kelly and Kyle and me. He's always been involved with the town. Has a reputation for being generous. And a sweet wife and four kids with another on the way. He seems to dote on them."

The teenager, staring at the floor, wrapped her arms around the small dog on her lap.

"The superlab bust was yours, right?"

"Yes."

"What part did this Abrams guy play?"

"We have no proof of anything…."

"I was kidnapped by the deputy who was running things." Kyle Evans spoke up, looking him straight in the eye. "He told me Abrams was his partner. He also gave me details on the running of the operation. They'd stolen chemicals from my farm. And were running the lab on the farm of a family friend who'd just died of an overdose. Sam was getting close to finding them out and the deputy lured her to the farm where he was holding me hostage. His plans were to kill Sam and then me."

"Except that when I arrived, Kyle tackled the man. The deputy's bullet went astray and I managed to get a round off before he could take a second shot. Unfortunately, my shot killed him so we had no firsthand testimony. But every single detail of what Kyle said checked out," Samantha added. "Other than Kyle's hearsay testimony, though, there was nothing to tie Abrams to any of it."

"And your opinion of the man?"

"He's the kind of criminal you most dread. Highly intelligent. Educated. Well liked and well respected. And completely without conscience. I believe the man is a serious danger to this town."

Maggie moaned, seemingly unaware that she'd done so, her fingers working back and forth, back and forth, in the little dog's fur. Clay raised his eyebrows, glancing from her to Samantha. The detective shook her head and he knew there was more.

And that he'd have to wait for answers.

"Have you vouched for Abrams's presence today?" he asked over the teenager's bent head.

"Yeah. He was in court all day."

Maggie rocked forward, over the dog in her lap.

"Odd, isn't it? To have an attorney in court, pleading cases, when you know he's guilty of a heinous crime?" Clay watched the girl as he spoke.

She didn't seem to have heard him. No one else responded to his comment.

"Maggie?"

The girl's gaze was wary as she looked up. He had to get past that wariness. Earn her trust. He had a feeling he was going to need her. "What can you tell me about Kelly? Anything that strikes you?"

Her fingers still busy along the dog's back, she mumbled, "Kelly's addicted to pens and pencils."

"What?"

"It's true." Sam nodded, her pretty face pinched-looking. "Kel takes notes a lot. And when she's not writing, she's usually chewing on a pen or a pencil. It's just…I don't know. It's just Kelly."

"What else? Who does she spend her free time with? Has she been seeing anyone?"

"She spends her time helping other people," Maggie explained earnestly. The girl rattled off the volunteer work and other activities Scott Levin had already told him about.

"And as far as I know, she hasn't had a real date in years," Samantha said.

"Either of you know of anyone in town who had a problem with her? Any quarrels? A neighbor, maybe?"

"With Kelly?" Samantha asked. "Not unless it has something to do with one of her cases, and I don't know much about them. Although there was one that was a big deal about six months ago. I already told Agent Levin about it. The guy was a bigamist…."

"Right." Clay referred back to his notes. "James Todd. He was recently sentenced to prison on domestic abuse charges."

"Yeah, but he'd been charged with murder. Of his second wife. The defense convinced the jury it was a suicide."

"Is that what Kelly thought?"

"I have no idea. We rarely discuss her cases. I'm not even sure what part she played in it. I just know she testified in court."

"But you're sure this Todd guy is still locked up?"

"Positive," Samantha said. "I checked myself. This afternoon."

Clay wasn't surprised. The woman was thorough. The kind of agent he liked to have on his team.

"There's been no report of any ransom call. Have you checked her home phone?" he asked.

"Yes, and we had it forwarded over here."

"I'll get someone to put a tap on the line, just in case." Sam nodded.

"What about her mood?" He looked over at Maggie. "Did she seem upset about anything?"

"No. Just…maybe…" The child looked down.

"Maybe what?"

"I think she worries about me." The girl looked up at him. "But I swear I'm not doing anything wrong. I had nothing to do with this."

Until that second Clay hadn't thought she had.

"Anyone else you can think of who'd want Ms. Chapman out of the way?" he asked the two adults sitting across from him, anxious to get back to JoAnne. To find out what was in the Chapman files.

Maggie Winston's in particular.

"No." Samantha shook her head. "Like I told you, she's the one everyone goes to for help."

Great. He had a possible missing saint who ate pencils.

And pissed off criminals for a living.

Clay got a call from Barry before he'd even started his department-issue black sedan. "We've got something," the agent said, his voice terse.

"What?" Sitting on the drive on the Evans farm, Clay stared at barns and fields, but imagined a path paved with black asphalt, preparing for the worst.

"Willie caught her scent at the parking lot Detective Jones reported as the one Dr. Chapman used most frequently. He followed it a good ways up the path—maybe

a ten-minute skate depending on how fast she was going."
Willie had been with the agency a couple of years. He was
the best.

"And?"

"Then nothing."

"What do you mean, nothing?"

"She just disappeared, boss. One minute Willie's on her
and then he loses the scent."

"Chapman turned around and went back to her car."

"Maybe, but why go all the way out there and just skate
for a few minutes?"

She could have remembered something she had to do.
Or found the day too cold for skating. The could-haves
were innumerable. But the fact that she was missing made
the short skating time suspect.

"I assume Willie checked the path going from the car
in the opposite direction?"

"Yeah. He didn't find anything."

They had to come up with that car. Period.

Without putting down his cell after disconnecting with
Barry, Clay speed-dialed JoAnne.

"Did you get anything out of the receptionist?"

"Besides the fact that our missing person can't be without a pen or pencil?"

"Yeah, besides that."

"Deb seems truly fond of her boss—and had no problem taking me to the office and turning over Chapman's
files. Deb thinks there could be a lot of possible suspects
there."

"So you've got the files?"

"I'm on my way home with them now."

"Great bedtime reading."

"Looking at the crates in my backseat, I have a feeling
I'm not going to be getting any sleep tonight."

Clay knew that feeling all too well.

* * *

Kelly Chapman's credit cards were not used on Friday. Her Blue Dodge Nitro turned up in Knoxville, Tennessee, Friday night. Clay was at home, in sweats and no shirt, having just padded in from a shower. He was sitting at his kitchen table, poring through electronic phone records, credit card receipts and bank statements when he got the call from the Tennessee state police at around ten.

Knoxville—five hours away.

"It was left in a mall parking lot."

"Any obvious indicators?" He ran his hand through hair that probably should've been cut weeks ago. But that would probably wait weeks more.

"It's in good shape. No obvious dents or scratches. It's clean inside. Maybe too clean."

"In what way?"

"Not so much as a gum wrapper, leaf or spot of dirt on the floor. Nothing personal. Not even in the console."

"Her purse wasn't there? What about the trunk?"

"No purse. And other than a spare tire and jack, the trunk is clean."

"How about writing implements? Any pens or pencils?"

"Nope. Nothing."

Which was the first real indication to Clay—who, during his fifteen years in the business, had seen just about everything—that Ms. Chapman's disappearance involved foul play.

"No blood anywhere?"

"Not that we could see. You want us to take the car in? Have it gone over?"

Ordinarily, he'd insist it wait until he got there. Sometimes the turn of the wheel was a clue.

But he was five hours away. Five hours that could make the difference between life and death.

"Please. But make sure you take pictures first. Inside and out. A lot of them. Too many of them."

"Yes, sir," the trooper replied.

And Clay rang off, already on his way to get dressed. If he left now, he could be in Knoxville in time to catch a couple hours' sleep before sunup.

4

Day
December 2010

I have to keep track of time. That thought reverberated. Over and over. I didn't want to open my eyes. I couldn't remember why, but I knew I didn't. I didn't want to move, either.

Something hard was digging into my rib. I tried to adjust my position enough to relieve the pressure and came in full contact with the rocky cement bed upon which I lay.

And then I remembered. I was in captivity.

Slowly, so if someone was staring at me they wouldn't notice, I opened one eye slightly.

And saw a sliver of light coming in from outside.

I'd passed at least one night here.

That realization changed everything. I didn't have to endure for just a few hours. The police, my friends—they would've known I was gone a long time ago and hadn't been able to find me.

Carefully, through my lashes, I took in my surroundings, such as they were. As soon as I was able to determine that there was no one directly in view, I opened my eyes fully.

The light wasn't much. A beacon in the distance? Light at the end of the tunnel?

Was I in the same place I'd been in the last time I was awake? And the time before that?

I had no idea.

It didn't smell like the bike path, though. There was a sweet odor, easily distinguishable even in the cold. And it *was* cold.

My head still hurt, the pain sharp, but my thoughts seemed clearer. I wasn't as tired.

Had I been drugged? Hit on the head? Both?

Was that why I couldn't stay awake?

I didn't know if I'd been out for hours or days. It must have been at least eighteen hours, I figured, based on the fact that I'd gone skating on Friday morning and now it was a different day.

Okay, so I had to keep track of time. Keep my mind working.

And I had to move. I was cold. But not as cold as I'd been the day before. Thank God I'd worn my hat under my helmet to go skating. Hats helped stave off hypothermia.

But where was my helmet?

Although the pain was excruciating at first, I moved my feet. They were heavy and for a second I panicked, my heart thudding heavily. And then I remembered that I still had my skates on. They'd helped keep me warm, too.

And I was in some kind of enclosure. A natural one, from what I could tell. A cave, maybe. There were some pretty famous caves about thirteen miles from town. And I remember, when we toured them as kids, they'd told us that the temperature always stayed around fifty-five degrees. No matter what time of year it was. I hoped I was in a cave. I'd be protected from the worst of December's cold.

December. I knew the month.

And I knew one day had passed. So…this was Day Two.

That recognition felt good. Positive. I was in control of something.

I was so stiff it hurt to breathe, but I couldn't afford to worry about pain anymore. Or let it stop me.

I had to get up. See if I was being watched and what to do about it if I was. I had to get out. Find something to eat and drink. Somehow. I had to pee again.

And then I could worry about where I was. How I'd come to be there. Who'd brought me. What plans my captors had for me.

And figure out how I could thwart those plans.

One thing was becoming abundantly clear—if I was going to live, I'd have to save myself. No one had found me.

I lifted my head. I could tell that I was alone in my prison. Some kind of cave but not entirely in its natural state. There was cement on the floor. And the opening—indicated by the glimmer of light in the distance—was mostly blocked.

My shoulders, twisted behind me, throbbed. But my hands had gone numb. I welcomed the lack of pain even as I worried about my circulation. About losing the use of my fingers and toes.

I tried to sit up and was consumed by a wave of nausea. Waiting, holding myself suspended, I made up my mind that I was not going to lie back down.

I was not going to *die* lying down.

With that thought pushing me, I shifted my weight and shifted again. Several minutes later I was on my butt, leaning against a rock wall.

At which point I did the only thing I could.

I started to cry.

* * *

"An Ohio psychologist is missing this morning."

The man standing at the old, greasy, two-burner stove frying bacon turned toward the small television set.

"Kelly Chapman left her office in Chandler, Ohio, to go in-line skating yesterday and hasn't been seen or heard from since."

The bacon sizzled, cracked, spitting grease over his arm. The man noticed, but didn't care, his attention focused one hundred percent on the local news.

"The vehicle she was driving, a 2009 dark blue Dodge Nitro, was found last night here in Knoxville…."

The man stared at the picture on the screen.

His whole wasted life, this hole he lived in, the booze, it was all because of her.

"If anyone has seen this woman, or saw the vehicle yesterday, or knows anything about the whereabouts of Kelly Chapman, please call the number on your screen."

He glanced at the number. He wasn't going to call. He wasn't stupid.

"The FBI and Chandler police are offering a ten thousand dollar reward to anyone with information…."

So she was worth that much. He wasn't surprised.

Putting the spraying pan on the back burner, the man grabbed the control that had come with the free box the government had offered the public when the national television signals had gone to digital. He could get twice the channels now.

Which meant there'd be more news.

He wanted to hear it all. From every source. Every opinion. Every supposition. He'd stay a step ahead of them. Show every one of those legal eagles just how much power he had.

He'd show her. No more begging.

Yeah, he had a plan. His ship was finally coming in.

But first, he needed to eat. He took a long, gratifying swig of the beer he'd opened as soon as he'd stumbled out of bed.

A man had to keep his strength up.

Rubbing the gut protruding from the tails of a flannel shirt he'd found in someone's trash a couple of years ago—a perfectly good shirt except for the fact that it had been a size too small even then—the man grinned, his blackened and broken teeth a sign of his past.

A sign that didn't matter anymore. He was looking forward to the coming days. And a future that was shining bright.

The SUV gave him nothing. Not one goddamned thing. No fingerprints. No blood. Not even a smudge of dirt.

Whatever had been there was now gone.

Clay needed the girl. Maggie. Needed to know if Kelly Chapman was obsessive about keeping her vehicle spotless or if the evidence he was looking at had been tainted—in this case, wiped clean.

He wasn't sure the kid was going to help him. She'd seemed unusually calm about the disappearance of her foster parent.

But sometimes kids in the system learned young not to care too much about anything.

He understood that. You did what you had to do.

Unless you chose not to.

"Jones." The detective answered his call on the first ring.

"I need to speak with the girl," Clay said, not bothering to waste time with pleasantries. If Samantha Jones knew something she would've called.

He'd been on the road most of the night. Asleep in his car for the rest of it. He was no closer to finding his victim. And he wasn't in a great mood.

"Yes, sir, one moment. She's still in bed. I'll get her."

So what if it was before eight on a Saturday morning? The kid had all day to sleep.

"Hello?" Maggie Winston didn't sound as though she'd been sleeping.

"Maggie? This is Agent Thatcher."

"I know. Did you find Kelly?"

The hope in the girl's voice struck him. In places he didn't like to feel. Which meant Clay had to adjust his thinking.

He was oddly glad to know the kid cared.

Like it mattered to him that this psychologist was important to the people in her life. That she had people who loved her.

Of course she did. Everyone did. If you looked hard enough.

"No, not yet, but we're getting closer." He gave the rote answer. Even if they never found her, they were one day closer to that conclusion. "I need to ask you some more questions if you don't mind."

"She's on speakerphone, Agent Thatcher. Go ahead," Detective Jones said.

"Maggie, when was the last time you were in Ms. Chapman's car?"

"Yesterday morning." The girl's answer was quick. Certain. Clay nodded, accepting it as truth. "She came by the bus stop after I left the house and gave me a ride to school."

"Why didn't she just take you from home?"

"I don't know. I guess she got ready sooner than she thought she would. Or else got a call and had to go in early."

"Do you remember anything in particular about the interior of the car?"

"It's gray. With leather seats. They have heat controls. I didn't turn mine on. Kelly turned hers on…."

He was beginning to like this kid.

"What about things in the car?" he asked more specifically. "Trash, or maybe a smudge on the carpet?"

"She keeps it really clean," Maggie said. "I remember her briefcase. And her purse. She moved them for me to sit down. And there's the little license-plate luggage tags. She keeps them in the tray on the console. They're from Michigan. She bought them when we were up there for her work. They have our names on them."

"When were you in Michigan?"

"In October."

"And do you know anything about the job she was there to do?"

"No. Just that she interviewed some guy. But I met the attorney who hired her. We were supposed to stay with her but her office got broken into, so we stayed at a bed and breakfast."

The girl wanted to help. That meant a lot in his book.

"Do you remember the attorney's name?"

"Erin Morgan."

"Good. That's good," he said, scribbling in the pocket-size notebook he never dressed without.

"Anything else you can tell me about the car?"

"Just the little beanie dog she keeps on the dash."

"What does it look like?"

"Two or three inches tall, I guess. Light beige with a brown spot. Its ears are kind of cockeyed and it has this pathetic expression."

The girl had obviously spent some time noticing the stuffed toy.

"Do you know if the dog had any special significance?"

"No."

"If you think of anything else, have Detective Jones give me a call, okay?"

"Okay."

"And, Maggie?"

"Yeah?"

"You've helped a lot. Thank you."

"You're welcome."

He had to hang up. To check on ten things at once. Continue the search. "Don't worry. We're going to find her," he said instead.

"I hope so." The teenager's voice broke.

"You can count on it," he said. And then, shaking his head, clicked off his phone. He'd broken one of his cardinal rules. He never gave his word unless he knew he could keep it.

5

JoAnne answered before the phone could ring twice. "Morning, boss."

He preferred her not to call him that. Which was why she did it, he was sure. His second-in-command seemed to have made it her life's calling to annoy him whenever she could.

"What've you got?"

He'd showered at a truck stop—not the first time he'd done so in the ten years he'd been an agent—and was back in his black, government-issue Taurus, the gray corduroy suit jacket his only concession to the cool December Tennessee morning. He'd decided against a tie, since he was on the road, but had one on the seat beside him if he needed it.

"Get this. The foster child..." JoAnne started right in. "The girl's mother brought her to Kelly because she was afraid her daughter was sexually interested in an older man."

"The mother who's in jail for selling her kid to the drug trade?"

"Yeah. She didn't have a problem with making money off the kid, but not for sex. She didn't want the girl ending up like her, pregnant and quitting high school. But that's not all of it, not by a long shot. Kelly Chapman found out that this girl had never even been kissed, but she fancied herself in love with someone Kelly believed to be in his thirties."

Kelly. Not Ms. Chapman. Or "our missing person." Obviously spending the night with Kelly Chapman's files had had an effect on JoAnne.

Staring at the five-by-seven photo taped to his dash, Clay tried to get inside the mind of the woman he was seeking. He'd stuck her picture up there the night before. So he could work as he drove. Or so he'd told himself.

There was something about those vivid blue eyes that called out to him. Something that was different from the hundreds of other pictures of missing persons he'd studied over the years.

JoAnne continued with what she'd learned. "Hoping the girl's crush was just adolescent transference, but afraid it was more than that, Kelly called her friend Samantha Jones to help her find the guy before it was too late."

Two determined women looking out for a young woman in trouble. The kind of thing fairy tales were made of. Maggie was one lucky girl.

"She called Samantha Jones, the detective Maggie's staying with now," he said.

"Right. But they didn't make it in time."

Clay frowned. The young girl he'd just spoken to had been—

"What does that mean?" he asked abruptly.

"She had sex with the guy. In a tent outside town. He'd planned the whole scenario." JoAnne's tone took on an unusual bitterness. "Get this, the dude brings chocolate like a guy might if he was seducing a woman, but in this case, he brings chocolate cookies with white icing. They were Maggie's favorites. He brought *cookies,* Clay. To a seduction. He knew damned well he was having a liaison with a child."

"I take it he's in jail?"

"Nope. They know who he is, although there's no evidence to prove it and Maggie isn't saying. She calls the guy Mac. But she doesn't say anything else about him. According to Kelly's notes, Maggie is in trauma-induced denial. Apparently she's so emotionally fragile that she has to believe in him, regardless of what anyone tells her. She believes he loves her. The alternative, to know she'd been abused in the worst possible way, is too much for her to handle right now. Her conscious mind can't accept that Mac isn't who and what he claims to be."

Nothing was ever as it seemed.

"Find out everything you can about this Mac guy."

"He's that lawyer, David Abrams."

"You said there was no evidence."

"Not admissible evidence." JoAnne sounded weary. Clay understood. "They know that the man who had sex with Maggie was the one who gave her the drugs. That's how she met him. And that deputy who was killed, he told Kyle Evans that Abrams was the one who gave Maggie the drugs to deliver. They showed Maggie a picture of Abrams but she's adamant that he's not her Mac."

"And since the deputy is dead, Kyle's testimony is only hearsay. I'm guessing the confession wasn't taped."

"Right."

"So this lawyer who's so well liked, well respected and still practicing law in Chandler is a pedophile."

"You got it. And he's also the devoted father of four kids with a fifth on the way. There's no suggestion of any misconduct, either with his own kids or anyone else. His weakness seems to be specifically Maggie, not young girls in general."

"Does he know that Kelly and Samantha are on to him?"

"Yep. Detective Jones told him in no uncertain terms that he'd better be watching every step because they were going to get him."

"Unless he gets them first."

"There is that."

"Put someone on him."

"Done."

If Abrams was behind Kelly Chapman's disappearance, his chances of finding her in time weren't good.

Clay studied the picture attached to his dash, trying not to envision that sassy short blond hair matted with blood. Dark images came with this business. Probably some kind of subconscious preparation for what might be ahead.

Because if he found her dead, he'd still have paperwork to do. Still have to get up the next day. And move on to the next case.

"What about the other files?" he said now, parked at the truck stop where he'd purchased the foil-wrapped reheated breakfast burrito he had yet to eat.

JoAnne had the gift. She could trudge through seemingly unending evidence and ferret out the strongest leads. He trusted her judgment implicitly.

"That bigamy case… James Todd, the bigamist charged with murdering his second wife, caused several injuries to a woman named Jane Hamilton, the first wife, but she'd convinced herself she simply was accident-prone. Kelly helped her come to terms with her past and the woman's testimony as a result of that put the man in prison."

Those blue eyes gazed out at him. The hint of a smile made him want to smile back.

"And we're sure he's still there."

"Yes, but that doesn't mean he hasn't sent someone else to do his work."

"Have Barry check out all visitors Todd's had. And any friends he's made inside, as well."

"Got it."

"What else?"

"A case in Michigan… She interviewed a guy, a Rick Thomas, who believed he was an undercover ops agent working for the Department of Defense, but it turned out his army sergeant had sold him out and he'd been heavily involved in underworld crime. The sergeant's dead, but he had a network about as big as AT&T. Any one of them could think Kelly knows something that could implicate them."

"We're talking millions of dollars here, right? Not small-scale dealing?"

"We're talking national security," JoAnne said. "And billions. There's a napkin in the file from a place called Roselane Inn in Temple, Michigan. I recognized Kelly's handwriting on it. It says that Thomas's attorney, Erin Morgan, thought there was a mole in the Department of Defense. It's not clear whether or not that mole was the sergeant or someone else."

"Who might still be in the office…and worried that this psychologist knows more than she should." He studied the woman he'd spent the night with. "Except if that's the case, why do *we* have Chapman's files? If someone was going to be bold enough to take her, why not take her files, too?"

"They had to kidnap her when the chance presented itself. And then go for the files. Her office is in downtown Chandler, right across from the courthouse. There are law enforcement vehicles up and down the street. Anyone expecting to break in and get away with a bunch of files would have to do it at night. Because we were called in on the case so early, we had them by then."

"I'll call Erin Morgan and see if I can speak to this Thomas guy."

"Good. And then there's the Florida case. The perp the kid's set to ID is a member of the Oils." A nationally organized street gang.

"Who's the prosecutor on the case?" Clay wrote the name and number—another call he'd be making.

"There are several local cases, too," JoAnne said. "A woman whose gay spouse came out of the closet as a result of counseling with Kelly. There was a threatening letter to Kelly from the ex-wife in the guy's file. And then there's a man who lost custody of his kids after Kelly got them to tell her how he'd lock them in closets when he drank so he couldn't hurt them like he'd hurt their mother. And a man who'd had an affair and was divorced by his wife after she'd sought help from Kelly—"

"I get the picture," Clay said. He had the picture, all right. He was looking at it. Short blond hair. Blue eyes. Head tilted slightly as though she had a question. Smiling.

This was no ordinary woman.

Clay had to find her. He had questions, too. Way too many of them. Like could he get to her in time? Or was he already too late?

Still Day Two

Now that it was fully light I could make out my prison and there was nothing but rock walls leading to the rock floor where I sat, with some kind of hardy vegetation protruding in a couple of places. A smaller area led upward to the sliver of light. There was no way I could make it up that tunnel with my hands tied behind me, my legs bound, my feet encased in skates.

I was still sitting. Making myself stay awake. Trying to

figure out what to do. I leaned my head against the wall, but didn't stay in that position. I'd fall asleep if I did.

I'd been throwing my feet apart over and over for a long time now. Maybe an hour. Maybe three. I didn't have my watch. I never skated with my watch.

The weight of my skates helped. Instead of being bound tight, the rope around my ankles had stretched a couple of inches. And it was beginning to fray where it rubbed against the skate buckle.

My hands were making even more progress than my feet. I was rubbing them along the sharp rock at my back. Over and over.

The rope was giving.

My blood was warm against what was left of my skin. It had caked to my sleeve, too, making it sticky.

"Sleeves are good." I tried to speak, but my throat was dry and raspy. I'd been talking to myself for most of my life. Until Camy arrived, that is. Then I started talking to her.

Either way, the sound of my voice wasn't new to me. Neither was hearing my thoughts out loud.

Was that strange?

I couldn't decide. Couldn't get a feel for what *strange* might be. At the moment, strange didn't matter.

Freeing my hands did. If I got away, and they ever traced me to this cave, they'd have a sample of my blood to prove I'd been there.

They'd tell my story—about how I rubbed my hands against the wall for hours, scraping away my skin in the process, to break the ties that bound me.

I'd tried to sing earlier. It hadn't worked.

"But I don't need my voice to survive," I said softly, then swallowed against the dryness.

At least the shivering had stopped. I imagined that the sun was shining, but I couldn't see much through the brush at what I assumed was the opening of the cave. I was warm enough, anyway.

I'd wet myself again, too. Not much comfort in that. No good crying about it, either. But I couldn't help it.

It wasn't likely to happen too much more if I didn't get out of there and get some water. I was becoming dehydrated.

No telling what was outside my cave, but at this point, I'd suck dew off the grass.

A teardrop hit my lips and I touched it with my tongue. Tasting salt.

Scared to death, I rubbed harder against the rock. Threw my feet faster. And drank from my own tears knowing as I did that they'd be soon gone.

Clay canvassed the immediate vicinity of the location where they'd found Kelly Chapman's car, while Tennessee state and local police knocked on doors, checked reports and investigated gas stations from the Kentucky-Tennessee state line to Knoxville.

Either Kelly still had a full tank from the last time she'd used her credit card to pay for gas—which had been Thursday morning—or someone else had fueled up someplace other than Tennessee.

Or…another alternative. Someone was lying to them.

Ohio and Kentucky law enforcement were on the hunt, as well.

There was no sign of Kelly Chapman's purse or anything that might've been in it. Her credit cards hadn't been used yet.

And her cell phone no longer pinged. Probably dead.

Clay prayed that wasn't an omen.

He had calls to make, possible suspects to eliminate, but the more pressing concern was to find any physical trail before it got too cold to follow.

Since her car was in Tennessee he was going on the assumption that his victim was there, as well.

Detective Jones called just before nine. Clay pulled his phone out of the holder at his belt.

"We got a ransom call on Kelly's line." The detective had arranged for all calls to be forwarded to her home. Her voice was shaking with urgency. "It came in one minute ago. I tried to keep the guy on the line long enough for a trace, but he didn't give me a chance. He knew what he was doing."

"What'd he say?"

"Just that if we wanted to see Kelly Chapman again, we had twenty-four hours to collect two million dollars."

"Collect," Clay said. "He knows she doesn't have that kind of money—and that enough people care about her to be able to raise it."

"And he's giving us time to do it. Which tells me he's serious. He believes he's going to succeed."

"Where does he want us to leave the money?"

"He didn't say. Didn't mention a time that he'll contact us again, either."

"We've got nothing to go on. No intelligence at all."

"Like I said, he knows what he's doing."

"We need to check records on kidnappings in the Midwest and any successful ransom pays over the past ten years," Clay said.

"I can do that."

Normally he wouldn't want a friend of the victim on his team, but nothing about this case felt normal.

"We need every situation in which money was successfully collected," he said. "Whether the victim's life was spared...or not."

"I understand."

Clay was sure she did. And, hand in the pocket of his slacks, he stared out at the blue horizon.

"I'll put in a request for the money," he said after a brief silence. "Get back to me." Clay clicked his phone shut, blocking any remaining image of the female cop back home in Ohio who knew the woman in the picture attached to Clay's dash. Knew her and cared about her.

He was there to work. And not to care.

Emotion clouded judgment. Clay couldn't afford to feel any.

6

The trees were barren, tall trunks and dead-looking branches with no leaves to offer protection from prying eyes.

But the woods were thick, and just yards into them the road could no longer be seen. Making anyone walking among the fallen leaves and twigs invisible from the road. Invisible to anyone passing by.

The area was government-owned. Protected land. Part of a battleground dating back before 1776. He'd walked among the trees as a boy, having ridden his bike out here with plastic cowboy and Indian figures in his pockets.

When he was younger, he'd spent a fair bit of time in the cemetery in town, too. Pretty much everyone he'd known who'd died was in that cemetery. His parents. His grandparents. A friend from high school who'd been killed in a car accident. A friend from recent years, Bob Branson.

Even his brother-in-law, the deputy he'd thought so clever but who'd really been a stupid, greedy man—Chuck Sewell. He'd been shot in the chest, killed with one bullet, by the female cop who'd outsmarted him.

But that cemetery held other graves, as well. Graves of men who'd lived long ago, soldiers who knew the true meaning of bravery. Of sacrifice. Men who'd done what it took to protect their own. Patriots. Men who'd inspired him, who'd taught him where he'd come from, what he could be. He'd read the tombstones so many times he could recite the words by heart. Didn't matter that the stones were old, some fallen and crumbling, worn almost to the point of illegibility. He'd made out the words. Born August 19, 1776. Died October 12, 1802. Aged 26.

And the children. There were children, so many of them. Little headstones with lambs or angels on top.

And the young soldiers. Aged 19 years, 6 months, 14 hours. Aged 17 years, 4 months, 10 hours. Aged 24 years.

They went on and on.

The one he stopped at most often, the one that called to him, had a man's name across it—*Jonathan Abrams. Born June 1799. Died February 1892.* And then, lower down, *Elizabeth.* That was it. Just a first name. Followed by *Wife of Jonathan Abrams. Born November 1818. Died January 1892.*

They were his great-great-great-grandparents. Jonathan had been nineteen years older than Elizabeth, his second wife. And he'd loved her so much he'd died one month after her passing.

Nineteen years older. Jonathan had been a celebrated war hero. A soldier. A God-fearing, country-serving man who'd helped found Chandler. A man of honor and distinction.

And he'd been in love with a woman nineteen years younger than himself. There was nothing wrong with that. Elizabeth had been fourteen when Jonathan married her. Had children by her. Who'd had children, who'd had children, and so on, culminating with David and his sister, who had children of their own.

David had been born to serve. To do whatever it took to keep Chandler and her people safe and thriving.

He was a smart man. A quick study, his parents had been told when he'd started school. And he was a principled man.

Many might not understand. He accepted that. Just as he understood his destiny.

He was a patriot, walking the same ground as his forefathers, fighting the same fight—the battle to preserve freedom and the rights of the individual, to uphold the Constitution of the United States. But while the fight might be the same, the means were different. Because the times were different. They weren't just warding off arrows anymore. And they weren't merely trying to maintain control of their land.

Walking through the now-barren woods in the quiet of a December Saturday morning, David thought back to that Saturday afternoon not so many weeks ago when he'd made a difficult choice. He'd made a mistake.

If he could take back that afternoon, he would. He couldn't. So he had to move forward. He had to meet his obligations.

Leaves crackled beneath his boots as he walked. He was grateful for the silence around him and craved the right to live as his ancestors had.

David knew he didn't have to stay in Chandler. He had it easy. But others weren't as affluent—or as aware, as acutely aware, of the lives around him. There were those who could remain blind to the degradation. The fear and the poverty. He could not.

So he walked among century-old trees that had been witness to life's battles. In woods that had sparked his imagination as a child and his soul as a young man.

And far back in those woods was a small clearing. He knew. He'd created it himself. Perhaps there was danger in being there.

Danger for him. And for those he served if anything happened to him.

He wouldn't linger. Wouldn't jeopardize everything that those who depended on him stood to lose. But he was obligated to come here. He'd started something. And he had to see it through.

He was a man of honor. And like his forefathers, he would go to any lengths to see that he fulfilled his responsibilities. That the good in which he believed was preserved. For his children. And their children. And the children who would come after them.

Sucking cold air into his lungs, David slowed his pace.

Timing was critical. He must be patient.

And life was precious. Sometimes lives were sacrificed for the greater good. His time among the ancient headstones had taught him that lesson well. One or two people could not be allowed to bring down a nation, a society or even threaten the health of one small town.

Sometimes people had to die.

But he would always pay his respects. And mourn the losses.

David started to breathe a little heavier as he neared the clearing. Would she…

After all these weeks would he finally get to—

Breaking through the trees, he looked everywhere at once, took in every inch of that eight-by-eight-foot sacred place where he'd shown his sweet Maggie how very much she was loved. Just as Elizabeth had been loved by Jonathan…

The area was empty. And yet…

Noticing the red nestled securely among the leaves, David stepped forward and stared.

A silk rose, it's long stem tucked under the brush upon which it lay. A red rose. Just like the ones he'd given her.

There was no note. She'd know the risk. And she'd understand that he couldn't take her gift. But with the handkerchief he pulled from his pocket, David lifted the rose, then tucked it back in place, facing the opposite direction.

She'd understand. And be comforted.

She was still his. He knew that now.

Because she'd been here.

By 9:30 on Saturday morning, a little less than twenty-four hours after Kelly Chapman had disappeared, Clay had turned over the physical search for Kelly Chapman to local police forces, FBI agents and volunteers in Tennessee, Kentucky and Ohio. Another crew was going over the bike trail again, headed up by Barry. They were expanding into neighboring areas, as well. And all ditches along the roads between the skate track and Tennessee were being scoured by volunteers.

Barry and JoAnne were coordinating all these efforts, monitoring incoming information and poring over personnel records.

Before heading back to Ohio, Clay visited Kelly's Nitro one more time. He didn't expect to find anything. An FBI forensic team had already processed every inch of the car, inside and out. But he had to look anyway. Twenty-four hours, more than a hundred people on the search, and they hadn't found so much as a shoelace.

Sitting in the front seat of her car, gazing out over the secured parking lot where the vehicle would be kept until further notice, he tried to put himself in her place. To imagine her life as a small-town counselor and national expert witness. She'd experienced a lot of the trauma that his days contained. But probably not as much death.

He hoped to God not as much death.

What did she think about? Hope for? Want? Would any of those things drive her now?

He had to think how she thought. Know what she knew.

Rubbing his hands along the leather steering wheel, Clay imagined her hands there. Her grip was sure. Firm. But not too tight.

It was as though he could *feel* her.

And she could be dead.

He reached for his cell phone.

Clay dialed the Michigan exchange and the number JoAnne had given him that morning—a home number for defense attorney Erin Morgan, gleaned from Kelly Chapman's files.

She answered on the second ring. Erin Morgan hadn't seen the news. And was clearly upset about the reason for Clay's call, speaking of an affection for his missing person that didn't surprise Clay. Kelly Chapman was obviously a woman people were drawn to.

"We're reviewing all of Ms. Chapman's recent cases," Clay told Erin, sitting in the now-impounded vehicle Kelly Chapman had driven to Michigan for her meeting with this woman. "I need to know anything you can tell me that might point to a possible suspect in her disappearance."

He'd already been in touch with government officials and did not believe they were dealing with an issue of national security—at least, not one that was officially recognized. He'd gained sympathy from the higher-ups at his agency in Washington, but no help other than an offer to keep eyes and ears open and to inform Clay immediately if anything turned up.

"I'm not really the one you should be speaking to," Erin said, sounding calm—but worried. A combination he'd learned to respect. And hate. It usually meant there *was* something to worry about. "I involved Kelly in this, but my fiancé is the one who'd know anything that could help."

He waited, thumb rapping against the steering wheel, while the woman spoke in muffled tones to someone in the room with her.

"Rick Thomas here, sir. What can I do for you?" The voice came strong and clear over the line a couple of seconds later.

Clay recognized the name. Thomas was the rogue undercover agent JoAnne had told him about. She'd failed to mention that the man was engaged to his defense attorney. Clay hoped to God these were people he could trust. He knew he was out of time and was going to have to take some chances.

He told Rick Thomas only that the woman who'd interviewed him several weeks before was missing.

"Erin said she went skating and didn't return." Thomas's reply was succinct. Almost curt.

Clay replied in kind. "That's right."

"What clues do you have?"

"We found her car in Tennessee." That much was on the news.

"So whoever has her took her out of state immediately."

"Correct."

"Have there been any hits on credit cards?"

"No." Not that it was any of Thomas's business, but the information wasn't classified and he needed the man's cooperation.

"It seems she vanished without a trace," Thomas said.

"We're working on some leads." Working on hunches and supposition was more like it.

"I wish I could help, Agent Thatcher, but I hardly knew her. My one conversation with her was brief and touched primarily on a murder I'd been charged with—a local Homeland Security officer—and have subsequently been cleared of committing."

"Do you know of anyone who might feel threatened by what you told Dr. Chapman during that meeting?"

"No. The man who committed the murder confessed right before he was shot in self-defense by the county sheriff. His accomplice, a deputy sheriff here, also confessed and is in jail."

Something wasn't adding up. A local murder didn't equate with national security. Or undercover agents—legitimate or not.

JoAnne had said Kelly Chapman's file referred to a rogue undercover agent. Not just a local murder.

"I'd like to leave a number with you to call if you think of anything," Clay said, his mind racing as he rattled off the Ohio office number.

"You're in Ohio, then?" Thomas asked. Clay almost didn't answer. But Erin Morgan was a woman the missing psychologist had trusted. And Erin, in turn, obviously trusted Rick Thomas.

"No, I'm in Tennessee," he said. "But my office will find me if you need me."

With a quick apology for not being more help, Thomas was gone, the line went dead and Clay was left wondering if he'd just hung Kelly Chapman out to dry. A covert ops agent would certainly have the skills to make a woman disappear without a trace. A rogue agent, even more so.

And Clay had let the man know where he was currently focusing his search.

Clay hadn't mentioned the ransom call. Neither had Thomas or Morgan. Might mean something. And might mean nothing at all.

Still Day Two

I heard footsteps. A single set of them. Heavy. Clomp. Clomp. Sticks broke.

Thank God. I started to cry out but my throat was so dry it hurt and I gagged.

And scraped my wrists on the rock behind me at a faster pace.

And then, as the sounds came steadily closer, I stopped all movement. And listened.

Shivering from the inside out.

Why wasn't someone calling my name? If these were searchers, looking for me, they'd be calling my name. Wouldn't they? Searchers always called names.

No one was calling my name.

Were they?

I couldn't tell. Was that my name I heard in the distance? Very faintly?

They'd have to call my name to find me. They wouldn't know exactly where I was.

The footsteps were almost upon me.

They'd walked straight at me.

Oh, God.

My captor had returned.

If those were really footsteps I was hearing.

Were they?

I tried to swallow and my lips cracked open. I could taste blood.

Was my captor bringing me food? Or water at least?

Did he want me alive?

Or was he coming to see if I was dead?

Was he going to hurt me now? Rape me? Or maybe just kill me since I hadn't died yet?

I was scared. So scared. My heart pounded way too fast and I wondered if this was where I'd die.

I pushed my feet together, resting one skate against the other. The chafing of the skate buckle on the rope was still visible. But only from the inside edge of one skate.

But maybe my efforts hadn't made any difference at all. Maybe I'd just dreamed they had.

Using energy I didn't know I possessed, I did the one thing I'd promised myself I wouldn't do.

I lay back down on the cold hard floor and closed my eyes, my arms beneath me as they'd been when I'd first woken up.

It felt good to lie down. So good.

Just before I lowered my lashes, blocking out the world, I saw the toe of one black boot. At least, I thought it was a black boot.

If I'd had a little more time, I might've had my hands free.

7

The prosecutor in Florida, Jeff Hayden, had just read about Kelly Chapman's disappearance on the internet when Clay phoned him Saturday morning. Back in his own car, Clay listened as the man told him he'd put a call in to a local FBI acquaintance.

And he stared at the picture on his dash, at the short hair and vivid blue eyes, gaining additional understanding of the many lives Kelly Chapman had touched.

"Our defendant is incarcerated without bond." Jeff Hayden spoke with the rush of an adrenaline surge and Clay had to fight not to join the man in his emotion-driven energy.

"But he's got loyal gang brothers all over the state—any number of whom would feel it's their duty to take care of business for him. These guys don't play around. I'd lay at least a dozen deaths at my defendant's feet. Ordering one woman killed would be nothing to him."

"I assume you've got people watching the key players."

"Of course. They're being brought in for questioning as we speak. We've been after these guys for two years and finally have something we can pin on them. Everything rests on that little boy's testimony. Without Chapman there, Camden Baker won't testify and Miguel Miller's going to walk again."

"Have your people send a list of Miller's associates to my office," Clay said. "We need to find out who he might know in Ohio, Kentucky and Tennessee. And who might have left Florida in the past few days." Clay gave the man JoAnne's cell number and hung up.

"What have you walked into, pretty lady?" he asked the photo on his dash, surprised to hear the softness in his voice. He didn't even talk to his mother with such affection.

She looked so small. So fragile. Far too open and trusting. And just plain…vulnerable, considering the company she kept. The fights she took on. One of the nation's most violent street gangs. Underworld threats to national security. A slick lawyer with power and money to spare. And God knew how many other mentally disturbed individuals who could be deranged enough to take pleasure in her death.

Could she survive those odds? No matter how much energy she might have?

How he knew Kelly Chapman was a woman filled with energy Clay couldn't say. But he did know. And a woman who never lacked for energy would not lie calmly down and die. If she'd been left alive, she'd do all she could to survive until he found her.

Which might give them a few more hours. Depending on her condition.

Twenty-four hours had already passed. His chances of finding her were diminishing. And Clay couldn't accept that.

Think, man. What are you missing?

In that second, Clay's phone rang. The local FBI agent had something for him. Something he couldn't discuss over the phone. Putting his car in gear, Clay sped off.

Emotion wasn't going to find Kelly Chapman. Only focus would do that.

* * *

Maggie had just been to visit her mother on Thursday, but she had to go again. She was only supposed to see her once a week. But she'd learned a lot in the six weeks she'd been "in the system." She was a kid, and if she needed to see her mom and it was a visiting day, which Saturday was, they'd let her go.

Detective Jones was at her office working, trying to find Kelly, so Kyle was the one who drove Maggie to the prison not quite an hour from town late Saturday morning. Maggie wasn't sure about Kyle. He didn't talk much, which was kinda weird, but he'd tackled Chuck Sewell barehanded the night he'd been about to kill Detective Jones. Kyle had also been there later that night when they'd come to tell Maggie about Mom.

And to tell her other things, too. Like that Mac was a criminal. Kyle was the one who said he'd heard the dirty cop say Mac was some kind of drug lord. And a lawyer with a wife and kids, too, who was just after Maggie because he was into young girls. He was wrong. That David Abrams guy—he might kind of look like Mac, but that was all. They were two different men. Mac wasn't married. He was hers. He'd told her so. Just like his great-great-great-grandfather had belonged to his fourteen-year-old wife, Elizabeth.

Mac had told her they'd lie to her about him. She'd promised she wouldn't believe them. Any of them. He'd said she was his angel. Sent to him from God. He's said he'd protect her. Which was why he hadn't told her what he did for a living or anything else about himself that they might try to get out of her. He wanted her to be completely innocent, no matter what happened. If they came after him with their lies, he didn't want anything to connect Maggie to him. Anything that could get her into trouble. Because he loved her that much.

And he was right about the lies. People believed Kyle. Including Kelly. Which meant Kelly didn't think Mac loved Maggie. She thought Maggie's Mac was that Abrams creep. She believed Kyle, so she didn't understand.

And because of that, Maggie couldn't see Mac right now. Because he was older and could go to jail for loving Maggie. If they so much as smiled at each other he could be in big trouble. Which meant she had to be without the one person who loved her more than anyone else at the absolute hardest time of her life.

And it was all Kyle's fault.

"You want me to go back there with you?" Kyle spoke for only the third time during the whole trip as they pulled into the prison drive. The first time had been to ask her if she wanted to talk. She'd politely declined. And the second time had been to ask if she wanted to stop for something to eat or drink or to use the restroom. Like she was a little kid. Like she couldn't make it less than an hour without eating, drinking or peeing.

"No, I know the way," Maggie said. And then, remembering last Thursday, added, "but you have to sign me in, and if you want to wait in the hall, that would be okay."

She didn't want to be in that place alone. Even if it was just Kyle waiting for her.

She didn't want to be pregnant at fourteen, either. She wasn't ruining her life like Mom had. She was going to college. To be someone, like Kelly was. But still, she'd cried so much when she'd had her period and knew she wasn't having Mac's child.

If she was pregnant with his baby, she'd have someone of her own to love—and to love her. And she'd have part of Mac with her always. Their love would be alive and the baby would keep them together forever.

Kyle signed Maggie in and then stepped back. "I'll be right here," he said, looking her straight in the eye.

The way Kelly did.

She liked that, when someone looked at her as if she was a real person, not just a kid.

Nodding, Maggie followed the guard through the series of doors that led to the dungeon where Mom lived now.

He'd driven fifteen minutes to the local downtown FBI office for a phone. Glancing at the cheap-looking cell, Clay drove to a nearby park and, moving at all times as he'd been instructed, he headed toward a large deserted grassy area and dialed the number he'd been given. It wasn't like he had to worry about other park-goers this morning. It was December and barely fifty degrees outside.

"Agent Thatcher? Rick Thomas here." The voice that picked up on the first ring didn't completely surprise Clay. It did relieve him, though. "Sorry about all the paranoia here, the scrambled phone, but I can't afford to take chances. We were hoping my past was over, that I was free, but with Kelly Chapman missing we can't be sure. Consequently, my fiancée and brother and I are leaving this morning for a new life under government protection. After this conversation, we won't be speaking again."

Goddamn. What kind of vicious case was he into?

"Who's after you?"

"I've made a lot of potential enemies within the world's crime population—drugs and illegal arms, mostly—but my fifteen years of staying alive in that world tells me that if Dr. Chapman's disappearance has anything to do with me, you're either looking for a man named Hernandez Segura or for a mole in the United States Department of Defense."

Holding the phone between his ear and shoulder, Clay walked and wrote in his pocket notebook at the same time.

"In either case, if they have her, chances are they aren't

going to kill her right away. If someone from my world is behind this, that means they think I've told her something that can put them at risk."

"What could you have told her?"

"Nothing. I've already given up everything I have, which is why I thought the past was behind me. But if they've determined that she could have information that puts them at risk, then they're going to do whatever it takes to get it out of her."

"And if she tells them she knows nothing?"

"They aren't even going to ask her at first. You don't get your best answers when someone is fully cognitive and functioning at their best. Even when they're initially scared. They'll weaken her, physically and mentally, and then they'll start to question her."

Clay got the picture, but asked, anyway. "And if— when—she has nothing to give them?"

"They'll keep her alive a little longer. But they'll step up their attempts to get her to talk. When they're convinced she knows nothing, she'll be killed."

"We've had a ransom call." Didn't sound like the people Rick Thomas had dealt with would need extra cash.

"Could be to throw you off track. Or it could be that your kidnappers have nothing to do with me. I'll pray for the latter."

Clay would, too. Meanwhile… "Tell me about this Segura guy."

"He's into illegal arms. He runs things from an island off Costa Rica. He's got at least eight men that I know of who could get Kelly Chapman out of the country without a trace."

Thomas named the men. Clay wrote.

"Segura's business was brought down by my team, but he walked away because he had a government contact. Since then, he's built the business back up bigger than ever. The guy we know he was working with is dead, but we could never be sure if there was only one government man involved. We *are* certain there was a mole in the DOD. Whether it's the man who died or not is anybody's guess. All intelligence has gone dark on this one."

Scribbling the name of the dead man—a U.S. career military official—Clay rapidly wrote down other details from Rick Thomas's covert life as the man dictated them and then, thanking Thomas, Clay destroyed the phone as he'd been instructed and tossed the remains in a trash bin on the way back to his car.

He had more leads than he had time to follow.

And only one question at the moment.

How the hell was he going to bring one woman out of this clusterfuck alive?

"You look good, Mags. Nice. No makeup. Your hair in a ponytail. I like the sweater. It matches your jeans. Are they new?"

"The sweater is," Maggie said, ashamed. Mom would feel bad that someone else was buying Maggie nice things when she couldn't ever have. Maggie'd thought about not wearing the soft pink pullover. But Kelly said the new sweater brought out the light streaks in Maggie's hair and complemented the deep brown of her eyes. Besides, it was Kelly's favorite and right now, with Kelly missing, Maggie just had to wear the sweater.

The jeans were new, too. Just not as new. And Maggie had paid for them with money she'd saved from the paper route she'd had over the summer. Money she'd saved in the account Mom had helped her open.

"They said you asked to see me," Mom told her now, her eyes all warm and soft-looking, like she got when Maggie had a bad dream or had cramps or was puking or something. It was the Mom she loved more than anything. And missed so much she hurt thinking about it.

Which was why she tried not to think about Mom too much. Or about what Mom had done.

Some days it all still seemed like a huge mistake. Someone was wrong. Except that Mom had written it all down. She'd pled guilty so there wasn't even a trial.

And she was in here, sitting at the stupid, old, scarred, dirty table wearing an orange suit thing that didn't look good on her at all.

"Mags? What's wrong, sweetie?" Mom's hand covered Maggie's on the table and Maggie turned her hand over, grabbing the softness of her mother's, and held on. She tried to talk, but she was going to start crying and she couldn't do that.

She had to be strong.

To grow up.

That was the one thing she knew. Mac was counting on her to be a grown-up.

"Kelly's missing."

"I know. And I guess that's scary to you right now, but in the end, it'll be fine."

No. Maggie could hardly breathe. She couldn't look at Mom. And then she did. Because she had to.

Maggie leaned forward. "Tell me you didn't do this," she whispered.

Mom leaned in farther and she didn't smell good at all. Like sweat and cigarette smoke. And her hair was greasy, too. "Do what, Maggie?"

Mom talked just as low so they wouldn't be heard.

"You know, get rid of Kelly." Maggie didn't want to think about that. It was bad enough knowing that Kelly was missing. She couldn't think about her being hurt.

Or worse.

Her best friend, Glenna, had been murdered. Kelly couldn't be, too. Maggie would just die.

"Oh, Mags, you're so young."

Maggie gritted her teeth. She hated when Mom said that.

"Just tell me you didn't do it."

"How could I, sweetie? Look at me." Mom held up her hands that were handcuffed for the visit, even though a guard stood right behind Maggie. "I'm locked in here. You know that."

"Tell me, Mom." Although why it was so important to make her mom admit something, Maggie wasn't sure. It wasn't like she hadn't lied to her before.

She had. A lot.

"I'm telling you, Maggie. I didn't do it. I didn't do anything."

"Do you know who did?"

Mom didn't say anything. She just looked at Maggie and shook her head, like this was one of those things Maggie was too young to understand.

But she wasn't too young. She'd been sold into the drug trade. One of her close friends had died of leukemia and another had been murdered. Her mom was in jail. She was in love with a man who was at least thirty. And she'd had sex. There wasn't anything left that was young about her.

Mom rubbed Maggie's palm with her fingers, and the chains at her wrist clanked against the table. "Listen, Mags, this isn't stuff you need to be worrying about, okay? I'm going to get out of here soon and we'll be together again. Just you and me. Like it used to be."

"They aren't going to let us live together again," Maggie said. If her mother was behind Kelly's disappearance, which was what Maggie was scared of, then she had to realize it would all be a waste.

She had to tell them to let Kelly go.

"You admitted that you allowed Chuck Sewell to trick me into delivering drugs when I thought I was helping sick kids. You're guilty of child endangerment. They were going to take me away from you no matter what."

Mom's face got stony-looking. "You were never in any danger, Maggie. Not from the deliveries. I made certain of that. And the money was going to pay for you to go to college."

So Mom said. "Then why isn't there more than the couple of hundred dollars I got for my paper route?"

"Because we were just getting started." Mom looked her straight in the eye and Maggie could tell how much she loved her. She loved Mom, too. But...

"You were buying drugs and using them," she said now. No one had ever told her that for sure, but she knew. She wasn't stupid.

"I wasn't doing much. Only enough to get me through sleeping with that Sewell creep so he'd stay away from you."

Maggie didn't want to think about that. Didn't want to think about Chuck Sewell doing to Mom what Mac had done with her. It was...wrong.

And gross.

She had to go. Kyle was waiting. And the smell was making her feel like she was going to throw up.

"Mom, please." She took both of Mom's hands in hers. "Just tell whoever took Kelly to bring her back. Please."

"I can't, Mags. I told you, I had nothing to do with it." Mom slid her hands away and the knot of fear in Maggie's stomach grew into a huge lump. "And even if I could, I wouldn't. That woman's taking you away from me. You think I can't see that? You're changing already. Look at you here today. You didn't come because you missed me and needed me. You came to get that woman out of trouble. To get her back. And I can't be part of that."

Mom stood and Maggie sat there and watched as the guard came forward to take her away.

"Everything I did, I did for you, Maggie," Mom said just before she left. "I'm in here because of you. Because I love you this much. Don't forget that."

Like she could. Or would.

And if something really bad happened to Kelly, if she died, that would be because of Maggie, too.

8

Clay took the highway back to Ohio. Given the amount of time between Kelly Chapman's disappearance and the discovery of her car in Tennessee—adding in time for Dr. Chapman to be moved someplace else and for the Nitro to be thoroughly cleaned—he figured the kidnapper hadn't bothered with side roads.

He was looking at someone who wanted to blend in rather than hide out. Someone right under their noses?

Did that mean Kelly Chapman was right under their noses, as well?

He pushed the gas pedal a little closer to the floor as he phoned JoAnne on his hands-free device.

There hadn't been any positive ID on Kelly Chapman in spite of the three-state search. From which he deduced she hadn't been taken very far.

"I have names for you to check out," Clay said the instant his second-in-command picked up, listing off the names of Segura's men, already committed to memory.

"I'll get Greg right on it."

"No." Clay passed a van. And then a couple of trucks. "I want *you* to do them." He needed her instincts on these. "And there's one more, a Randall Wyatt. He's ex-military.

A higher-up who died in October. See who he was connected to."

"I'm on it. I also got the list from Florida. You want me on those, too?"

"Give those to Greg." They were fact-finding only at this point. "I want all known Ohio, Kentucky and Tennessee associations with any of those names. And whether anyone associated with *any* of them have left Florida in the past few days."

"Got it. Barry went out to the prison to see James Todd. And to check records there. The man's a model prisoner. He's convinced some of the other inmates to attend an unofficial literature class and even managed to get books sent by one of his old college associates. And yes, it's all been monitored. His only visitor has been his wife, who hasn't missed a visiting day since he was incarcerated. Barry said he's completely confident the guy didn't know Chapman was missing until he told him."

Clay considered that. And drove too close to the back of a yellow sedan that was barely doing the speed limit in the fast lane. The car moved over. And he sped on.

Kelly Chapman's photo watched him. Begging him to get her home. To get there in time.

"I was just going to call you." JoAnne's words pulled Clay's focus back where it belonged. On the road—and on her conversation. "Barry questioned everyone in the vicinity of the bike path. There's a lot of farmland out there, but some homes, too. And there've also been several calls on the information line. By all accounts the only person anyone saw on that path yesterday was a city worker in a four-wheel-drive utility cart. The city issues them. They have small beds on the back to carry tools and things. Barry tracked down the worker and had him brought in. He'd been on the trail cleaning up debris. He saw Kelly Chapman putting on her skates, but that was it. He checks the trail a couple of times a week. He starts at one end and goes to the other. He doesn't go back."

"And he didn't think to let us know he'd seen her when he heard she was missing?"

"He went fishing with his son up at Alum Creek last night. A tackle shop in the area has him and the boy on video. He hadn't seen the news."

Alum Creek covered miles of camping and woods a couple of hours northeast of Chandler.

A perfect place to dump a body. To lose a body.

"I'll call the Columbus office and get a team there. They can organize volunteers to help."

"Levin already made the call. They've got a hundred volunteers combing the area."

"What about the cart?"

"They're going over it now, but preliminary reports say there's nothing there. No sign of blood, no hair, no scraps of ripped clothing or obvious marks from skates. But then, that cart's used for hauling trash and debris and tools. It's pretty beat-up."

"So several people saw this worker, but no one saw a lone female skater?" Clay asked.

"Makes you think she wasn't out there very long, doesn't it? That would explain why Willie lost her scent so quickly."

Clay glanced at his traveling companion. "Yeah." *What happened to you, pretty lady?*

"There's more," JoAnne said, her tone matching the urgency raging through Clay. "David Abrams, the alleged pedophile lawyer, was in court all day yesterday as he claimed. Mercy Littleton spoke with several people who interacted with him in person."

So the lawyer was out.

"But she just called," JoAnne continued. "Abrams left his house alone early this morning and got in his car. Based on the number of seemingly unnecessary turns he took, it was pretty clear to her that he was making sure he wasn't being followed."

Mercy had been with the bureau a little over five years and was a good detective. "I take it she wasn't seen."

"She doesn't think so. He drove out of town, parked in some brush that all but hid his car and then walked about half a mile into a thicket that would've been nearly impossible to get through if there'd been leaves on the trees. He ended up in a clearing. Walked around for a bit, picked something up, set it back down again and then left."

"What'd he pick up?"

"A silk rose."

"Did Mercy leave it there?"

"Until she followed Abrams back home. She went back out and brought the rose in for fingerprinting. After that, Barry returned it. He's combing the area now."

"And?"

"No fingerprints at all."

Shit. One break. All they needed was one fucking break. He glanced at Kelly Chapman again.

And almost felt the need to excuse his language.

"Mercy's back on Abrams. I've got Ken camping out near the clearing," JoAnne said.

Ken Sizemore had survival training. And Clay's team of three had doubled in less than twenty-four hours.

"Do you think Abrams knows where the woman is?" That was all Kelly Chapman was, he reminded himself. A woman. A missing person. Like all the others.

"Nothing yet, but I think we should stay with it, Clay. That man has a stake in Kelly's disappearance. I can feel it."

"You think someone took her out there?"

"I don't know, but Barry and Ken are searching for any recently dug graves just in case."

Clay could not consider graves. And he couldn't look at the picture on his dash, either.

"In-line skates, a purse, zipper pulls, a beanbag dog—those things have to be *somewhere*."

"Or they've been destroyed."

It bothered him that, right now, the best alternative was that arms runners or DOD moles had abducted their missing person. She might be in pain, but at least chances were good she was still alive.

"What else have you got?"

"I've reached most of her current clients and will be going through recent past ones next. The gay man's ex-wife who sent the threatening letter moved to Colorado six months ago. The guy who lost custody of his kids for putting them in a closet is in jail in Wisconsin on domestic violence charges. He's been there for a couple of months. The guy whose wife divorced him after seeing Kelly is here in town. I met him this morning. He and his new, young blonde girlfriend. They'd just returned from a gambling trip along the Canadian border. I checked on James Todd's wife, too, just to be sure. She owns a couple of local businesses, purchased with money she inherited from her father. Before she married Todd, she lived alone. She's clearly devoted to him. *More* than devoted."

"What do you mean?"

"I'd say she's obsessed with the man. But while she doesn't seem all that fond of Kelly Chapman, she has nothing to gain from her disappearance."

He had miles to go. Listening, thinking, working on the case made them less unbearable. He'd hoped, when he'd made the trip down the night before, to have his missing person with him for the return journey.

"There's one guy I'm watching, though." Clay sat up straighter. "Marc Snyder, a soldier recently back from a second tour of duty in Iraq. According to Kelly's files, he's suffering from pretty severe post-traumatic stress disorder. She can hardly keep him in the office long enough to have a conversation. She actually chased him down the street once to get him to keep an appointment. A good thing she did because he had a bottle of pills he'd been planning to take and she managed to talk him out of it."

"Why's he a threat?" Other than the obvious—he was unstable. Maybe noteworthy in another case, but they were on the hunt for a psychologist, who presumably dealt with people like this all the time.

"When I told him about Dr. Chapman's disappearance he didn't show any emotion at all. He'd heard about it on the news, so the information wasn't a surprise, but as I spoke with him, I sensed relief. I called him on it and while he said that he had absolutely nothing to do with what happened to her—said he was working out at the Y at the time of her disappearance—he wasn't sorry to have her gone. Said she meddled too much. Pushed too hard. Said she didn't know when to quit and leave people to their own lives."

"Maybe she pushed him over the edge."

"He said that if she'd pushed any harder he was going to have to push back."

"Verify his alibi, get a search warrant for his place and keep an eye on him."

"There still aren't any hits on her credit cards or bank accounts."

He hadn't expected there to be. Particularly not with a ransom call. But it would've been nice.

"Greg's got nothing on Kyle Evans or anyone else to do with the meth superlab that was discovered and dismantled on the farm outside town last summer. All the indications are that drug use has dropped in the county—and in

Dayton, too—in significant enough numbers that it doesn't look like there's a major dealer left."

"Were any outside sources involved?" Anyone with an ax to grind due to loss of revenue?

Someone who wouldn't shy away from taking whatever action was necessary to protect his interests.

"No. It was a wholly local operation. So whoever supplied the area before the locals took over would be pleased to have return business, not angry enough for revenge. All the money from the lab stayed right there in Chandler, supporting city services, if you can believe it, via so-called donations. Other than David Abrams, the two main players were killed. The distributors were high school kids. Greg's found all but one of them. All clean."

"Find the one," he said tersely. One was all it took. And teenagers were unpredictable. Especially if their lives had been changed in ways not to their liking.

"Levin said to tell you the ransom money's been approved and is ready."

"I'll call Detective Jones and fill her in." He wanted to know more about Abrams and figured Jones, with her personal vow to get the man, was his best source.

"You okay?"

"Fine. Why?"

"Your voice. You sound…engaged."

They didn't get emotionally involved with their cases. They couldn't. They'd never survive. And neither would their victims.

"And you aren't?" Clay asked, glancing again at the photo on his dash. This case was different. And not just because so many people wanted the woman found.

"I hope I get a chance to meet her someday," JoAnne said.

Which neither of them would if they didn't stay focused on the job.

Day/Night

Night? Couldn't be sure. December? Dark early in December.

Or eyes closed.

Head pounding. No pillow.

Side hurt.

Move.

Soon.

Sleep first.

Sam's head hurt. Pushing at the clip holding her long hair up, she attempted to ease the pain. Didn't work. Her bun wasn't the problem.

Oh, God, Kel, where are you?

Sam had been exposed to the seedier side of life for years now. Her grandpa had been a cop. Her dad had been a cop—killed in the line of duty when she was only ten. Her mom had been raped before she was born. As a cop herself, Samantha had been on the phone with a man when he committed suicide, right after he'd killed his wife. She'd seen her town slowly traumatized by an infusion of illegal drugs. Had held a young girl who'd been murdered. And just this past summer, she'd shot and killed a fellow officer.

And through it all—through every last incident—she'd had Kelly. First as a kid at school who always seemed able to get to the real point and, in doing so, helped Sam see things clearly, too. And later as a friend who happened to be a shrink.

They hadn't been bosom-buddy close, not like some girls were. Neither of them was the bosom-buddy type. But they'd been there for each other.

They'd been born the same year. In the same small town. They couldn't help but be there for each other. It wasn't like there were a million kids in Chandler, Ohio, thirty-one years ago.

Focusing on her computer screen in the private office Kyle had set up for when she'd moved out to the farm after her promotion, Sam read lists. Statistics. And tried to wall off the emotion crashing in around her.

She'd gone to the office briefly, long enough to sign out the files she wanted, and was now connected to her work computer through a secure network. Camy was on a chair beside her and Kyle's German shepherd, Zodiac, had curled up in the open doorway about half an hour ago. Probably listening for Kyle's grandfather, who lived with them.

Kyle and Maggie had been gone longer than she'd expected. They should've been home more than an hour ago. She'd fixed Grandpa's lunch. Fed him. And helped him into bed for his afternoon nap.

She'd stared at the phone hard enough to make it ring a dozen times over if she'd had any telepathic power at all. Ransom instructions would give them leads.

Still looking at the computer screen, Sam called Kyle from her cell phone.

"Are you guys back in town yet?"

"They let Maggie stay longer with her mother. We're in town now, getting hamburgers. Her choice."

"Is she right there?"

"She's using the restroom."

"How is she?"

"Too quiet."

Sam's heart sank. "I was afraid of that. She knows something." She and Kyle had discussed the possibility several times during the night that had just passed.

"I'm not convinced of that," Kyle said. "She's shaken, that's for sure. But Kelly's that girl's lifeline. It would be more disturbing if she *didn't* show signs of distress."

"Did you get anything on her mother? Why Maggie needed to see her today after just having been there?"

"No. I didn't ask."

Because he wouldn't. Kyle didn't push. But he listened more carefully than anyone she'd ever known.

"Did she seem better or worse afterward?"

"About the same. Upset. How are you doing?"

"Fine." He'd know what that meant, based on an understanding that came from being best friends for most of their lives—and lovers for more than half of them.

"You'll find her, Sam. You always get your man. Always."

"Alive?"

"Maggie and I are buying a burger for you. We'll be there in a few minutes."

"Watch her like a hawk, okay? Kelly'll kill me if anything happens to her."

"Of course. Even if Abrams is behind this, there's no way he's getting near that girl. I can promise you that."

Sam nodded, although he couldn't see her, and tried not to lose hope. David Abrams had been a friend to all of them. Had represented Kyle in his divorce. Played darts out at the farm. Gave generously of his time, money and services all over the county.

Sam's phone beeped an incoming call and she recognized Agent Thatcher's number.

"Gotta go." She wasn't even sure she got the words out before she clicked off.

9

Samantha Jones had collected a shitload of history on Midwest kidnappings. And compiled the information into many different lists based on all kinds of different factors, from age of victim to sex of kidnappers. As Clay beat the speed limit by fifteen miles an hour, he listened to Samantha. Time of day. Number of people. How much time elapsed between kidnapping and ransom call versus how many successful recoveries. Amounts of ransom. She even had statistics for numbers of stranger abductions versus people taken by someone they knew.

She'd already followed up on known kidnappers who'd committed random crimes. Most of them were either dead or in prison. Another had an alibi. And one had disappeared without a trace a couple of years before. And two she had addresses for but had been unable to reach.

"This could be a random abduction," he said. That had always been a possibility, of course, which was why they'd searched her home, the skating trail, her car and anything else for clues as to what had happened. But until they had some clues from the day before, they had to look for and eliminate suspects.

"It could be," the detective acknowledged. "But I don't think it is."

Clay didn't think so, either. "Why?"

"Because the hit was too clean. We know Kelly Chapman was on that trail. The dog followed her scent—and then…nothing. She just disappears into thin air. There's no sign of a struggle. No blood on the trail. No evidence of her having been dragged. Kelly's too smart not to leave a trail if she had any chance to do so. If some unknown person grabbed her and kept her alive long enough to rape her, we'd have found something. The dog, Willie, would have followed the scent. And even if he hadn't, Kelly would've made sure there was *something* for us to find. She's in court regularly. She's heard evidence in a million cases."

He weaved in and out of a small traffic clog caused by two semis nosing along side by side; as he did, he received confirmation from Samantha of what he'd already determined. "You're confident that all the ground between her home, office and the bike path has been thoroughly searched." If the trucks didn't move he'd pull out his bubble and turn on the siren.

"Absolutely. I was out again myself this morning. I don't think Kelly ever finished skating."

"Why not?"

"Because she usually made a call when she got back in the car. Any time she skated alone, she let someone know where she was and always checked in when she was back in the car. Not officially, mind you. She didn't always call the same person. Or tell us she was checking in. But she always called someone. It was like an unspoken ritual with her."

No calls had been made from the psychologist's cell phone since she'd left her office the previous morning.

"So," Samantha continued, "I was thinking that maybe she never made it to the path. Maybe the dog caught a scent from the day before."

"We know for certain that she got there," Clay said. "A city worker was on the trail and saw her."

"Who? When?"

Clay filled Samantha Jones in on the details he'd just received from JoAnne.

"So now we know for certain she was taken from there," Samantha said. "Which means we're looking at a professional hit. They got her off the path and out of there without a trace, with in-line skates on her feet, no less. How do you stop someone on in-line skates without there being any blood?"

"Maybe by knowing that someone? If she saw a person she knew—if that person called out to her and she stopped of her own accord—maybe she went willingly."

"She would never have taken off without telling someone. Not ever."

"So she stopped willingly and was then abducted," Clay amended, agreeing with the detective's assessment at this point. And then he asked, "What do you think about David Abrams? Could he have arranged something like this? If, as you allege, he's a pedophile, he stands to lose everything if Kelly can convince Maggie to turn on him…."

"Maggie's suffering from some kind of deep-seated denial where Abrams is concerned," Sam said.

"And the longer she lived with Kelly, the more chance that Maggie's loyalties would shift," Clay muttered.

"Right. Kelly said that as soon as Maggie felt secure with her, she wouldn't need 'Mac' anymore…."

"Poor kid."

"Personally, Agent Thatcher, I think the man is capable of anything. He's duped an entire town. Saw his partner in crime buried without even flinching. Had sex with a child. And dares to walk around as though he owns the place. His partner, the deputy I shot, was his brother-in-law, did you know that?"

"No." Clay's blood turned colder. With the road in front of him free he pushed harder on the gas.

"Chuck Sewell was Abrams's wife's brother. And he continues to lie to her about what happened. To play the loyal, dedicated husband and father."

Samantha's emotions were getting to him. He couldn't allow that.

"One of my agents followed him to a wooded area outside of Chandler this morning—" Clay said, and was surprised by the abrupt "Where?" that cut off the rest of his sentence. He told Detective Jones what JoAnne had told him.

And listened to the words that flew over the line with empathy—and professional interest. So they were on to something.

"That's where Maggie Winston lost her virginity," Samantha said. "I've been personally keeping a watch on the place since it happened."

Maggie Winston. The girl again. Kelly's new foster daughter. The only major change in Kelly Chapman's life in the past ten years.

"Were you there yesterday?" Clay asked.

"No. I was out at the skate path."

"Abrams picked up a silk rose and then put it back. Any ideas about what that might mean?"

"You think there's a grave." A statement. Not a question.

What he thought didn't matter. "I've got two agents out there," Clay said. "Agent Sizemore will be camping in the area, and Rosnick is combing the area. If there's newly disturbed earth—or anything else that suggests a human presence out there—we'll soon know about it."

"It could be a message for Maggie." Samantha's tone of voice was deadly.

"I wondered." He thought about his next suggestion.

Briefly. There wasn't a lot of time for deliberation. They had too many suspects to investigate. Too many possibilities. "Let's give the girl some rope. See if, when she thinks she's alone and unobserved, she goes out there. And then see what happens when she does."

"You want me to put a fourteen-year-old girl at risk?"

Hell, no. He didn't want that. And he deliberately kept his gaze firmly on the road and nowhere near the photo on his dash.

"My agents will be all over that place. You can set up your own surveillance, as well—as long as your people know not to interfere and understand that my people are in charge." It wasn't a territorial issue but a practical one. Too many bosses put lives at risk. "I'm not suggesting we let Abrams near her, only that we let her go far enough to show us what's going on."

"And if he's there? If they've arranged to meet?"

"We arrest him and you've got what you wanted four months ago. Proof of their involvement. Four months ago you didn't have this opportunity. He was staying away from her. The fact that *now* is when he's returned to their meeting place is significant, don't you think?"

"Maggie asked to see her mother today."

"Does she have regularly scheduled visits?"

"Yes."

"And this wasn't one of them?"

"No."

"You think her mother's involved, as well?"

"I'm not sure. Maggie's been through so much and probably feels pretty alone. It could be that Kelly's disappearance upset her so much she just needed her mother."

"Or it could be that her mother and Abrams are still somehow connected. Or that they've reconnected since the mother's incarceration."

Samantha's silence prompted him to say, "We have to do something."

"What exactly are you suggesting?"

"Can it be arranged to leave her alone? With a way out to the wooded area?"

"I can have Kyle drive her into town to get some of her things. He could drop her off at Kelly's place and then get called away—maybe to the hospital. Kyle's grandfather is failing pretty fast. Maggie knows that. She's helping us take care of him. We could make up some story about needing to bring him to the Emergency Room. I hate to use Grandpa that way, but I know that if he was lucid he'd insist that we do it. If it could help get rid of the threat of a pedophile in a young girl's life… Kyle could tell Maggie to stay at Kelly's until someone comes for her."

"So how does she get from Kelly's to the woods?"

"Her bike. It's how she got there before. It's at Kelly's."

"We'll need to coordinate times. I want agents in place outside Kelly's and in the woods before Kyle leaves that girl alone."

"I'll have him come straight back here to take over the phone and then I'll head into town, too," Samantha said. "I need to be there."

She made the statement as if she expected Clay to argue with her. He wasn't about to do so. Detective Jones had proven herself a more than capable cop. And Maggie Winston would need someone she knew close by, in case things got difficult.

"I have an agent on Abrams already," Clay added. "I'll keep her there."

The number of man-hours he was burning didn't faze Clay. How could it? There were lives at stake.

"I'd like to wait until I'm back in Chandler to bring this down, but we can't. It's going to be dark before then, so you'll have to go ahead without me. JoAnne Laramie will be in charge."

They discussed details and then Samantha asked, "What if Maggie goes out there, and we catch the two of them, but neither of them owns up to knowing what happened to Kelly?"

"Then we bring them both in, put them in different rooms and hope we can either find some kind of conscience in Abrams when he sees the kid in handcuffs, or we get Maggie to tell us the truth."

"I don't want her arrested."

Thinking of the timid fourteen-year-old girl he'd met the night before made it hard for Clay to do his job.

"If she's involved in kidnapping, she's breaking the law," he said. "And it's still possible that kidnapping is all we're dealing with. We need to get Maggie to tell us the truth before she's also a conspirator to murder."

The kid was hiding something. Clay had realized that last night. For her sake, they needed to figure out what that was. Regardless of what she knew, or thought she knew, the girl was carrying far too great a burden on her young shoulders.

"My agents are good, Detective," he said. "They'll take care of Maggie, no matter what she has or hasn't done. She's a kid. No one's going to forget that."

Clay trusted his team. This wasn't the first juvenile they'd dealt with. Not by a long shot.

"I don't know whether to hope she stays put at Kelly's or that she leads us to Abrams," Samantha Jones said as they were ending their conversation.

"Let's just focus on keeping her safe," Clay said, and drove onto the shoulder of the road to pass a car as he put up his bubble and turned on his siren.

10

Day/Night

I was awake. My eyes were closed, but I was fully awake. I'd been awake for a few minutes. I'd opened my eyes briefly. The rock enclosure had grown darker. Not black, but gloomy and dank.

My head was still throbbing. I was pretty sure I'd taken a blow to my right temple. I could feel the swelling now and knew I'd been sleeping too much. I should stay awake. I also knew I was going back to sleep.

That was when death came easiest.

I was mostly okay with dying now. Inevitability had a way of convincing you of the rightness of things. Or at least it brought a certain kind of resignation, of peace.

Even if I broke the bindings at my ankles and wrists, and could climb up to the thin slash of light, I'd still have to get through the barrier covering what I believed was the opening to the cave. I'd already been without water for at least a day. Could be three for all I knew.

Still, I was awake. I had to try.

Forcing myself up enough to free my arms, which had gone numb again, I started to rub them against the wall. And my feet instinctively started to move, too, to scrape one against the other in order to fray the bindings, although they might not be affected by my movements at all.

I opened my eyes. And quickly shut them.

I could keep them closed. I allowed myself that. The starkness out there was far more eerie, more frightening, than the darkness behind my closed lids. I could see anything I wanted to see in here. The flowered couch in my office. The bright fuchsia bougainvillea that bloomed out in my backyard. Maggie's grin when she was lying on the floor playing with Camy.

My little Camy with her pert black nose and big, chocolate-brown eyes. Those long apricot-colored ears as she tilted them at me in question.

Or were the ears red? They weren't brown.

I couldn't really see them. I couldn't really see anything.

I rubbed. And scraped.

Rubbed and scraped.

She couldn't believe her luck. Not that having Kyle's grandpa sick was luck. It wasn't lucky at all. But it fit right in with how things happened in Maggie's world. The only way she could get a break was because an old man had to go to the hospital. She told herself it wasn't *her* fault that he'd fail today of all days, just when she needed time alone.

Still, after Kyle drove away, leaving her all alone at Kelly's, Maggie couldn't stay there like he'd asked. She'd go crazy staying there. The place was too big and way too quiet with Camy out at Kyle's farm with Samantha and Zodiac.

Strange how the great big guard dog let a little princess like Camy make herself at home. Maggie had been afraid to put Camy down at first. Kelly would never forgive her if she let something happen to Camy. The dog was like Kelly's kid or something.

But Zodiac just watched Camy and let her do whatever she wanted. Even when Camy snapped and grabbed a piece of Zodiac's face. Kyle's big dog let little Camy hang on to him.

Maggie had scooped her up then and taken Camy to the room Samantha and Kyle had given her to use. But she hadn't had to. She'd just wanted to.

What she had to do was get out to the woods. She might not have another chance. She had to leave a message for Mac. Had to see him. Things were really bad—worse than they'd ever been—and he'd promised her he'd take care of her. He'd told her that if she was missing him too much, she should leave a flower in the woods. In their special place. She'd done so on Thursday after Kelly took her to visit Mom. He'd told her he'd know from her signal that she needed him and would figure something out. Seeing him would make her feel better; surely he knew that. She had to get out to the woods. To see if he'd been there yet. If he'd found her flower. Maybe he was in the woods right now. Or would come while she was there…

Kelly was the only one who knew about their spot in the woods. Maggie had told her during a session back before everything had gotten so screwed up. Back before that slimeball Sewell had murdered Glenna. And because it was during a session, the information was protected under doctor-client privilege. She didn't have to be a lawyer to know that.

Their spot was safe. It was the only safe place in the world for Maggie right now. At least until she saw Mac. Until she figured out what to do.

Maybe they could run away together. Start a new life where no one knew about Mom, or the drugs, or that Maggie was only fourteen. They could say she was eighteen. With her hair up and makeup on she could pass for eighteen. Her breasts were big enough.

Mac had liked them. A lot. They were one of the first things he'd noticed about her.

He loved her. He'd love the idea of being with her forever. Besides, running away was the only answer.

Avoiding the hallway that led down to the room Kelly had fixed up for her, avoiding the reminder that for a few weeks she'd actually dared to hope she could be a real part of Kelly's life, live in a home that was pretty and clean and had floors without holes in them, a yard that wasn't filled with trash and an adult in residence who came home every night, Maggie headed for the garage. She stopped only long enough to check the mailbox attached to the front of the house.

There was a bill. A couple of junk-mail things about insurance and a preapproved credit card waiting for Kelly. That was all. No letters for Kelly. Maggie wondered if the man who'd been writing her, who cared about Kelly from afar, was aware of her disappearance.

Five minutes later Maggie was sailing down a country road as fast as her feet could pedal, the wind whipping her hair against her face and anticipation brewing up feelings deep inside her.

Soon everything would be okay. Just as soon as Mac knew she needed him.

Clay made it back to town before dark. Forgoing the rest followed by a shower and change of clothes that he really needed, he went straight to the office. He'd called JoAnne. Agents were in place in Chandler watching the Winston girl. She'd flown the coop exactly as he and Samantha had expected.

She'd been sitting alone in that little clearing in the woods for more than two hours. Just sitting there. With the temperature dropping down to the thirties, she had to be getting pretty damned cold.

"She had a hat and gloves in her pocket," JoAnne had said. As though Maggie had known she might be spending an extended period of time in the cold.

Or maybe she always carried them. Hard to say.

What Clay knew was that Kelly Chapman wasn't as likely to have a hat and gloves to keep her warm. And with the temperature falling, if he didn't find her soon, she'd die of hypothermia if nothing else.

With everyone either out on assignment or off for the night, Clay had the office virtually to himself—the way he liked it best.

The top of his desk, like his dining room table, was cluttered with piles of papers, file folders—and probably a dirty coffee cup somewhere, too.

He used to keep a picture of his father there. Until the old man's complacent smile and sad eyes began to wear on him too much. They'd been almost constant companions while Clay was growing up. He'd been an only child, his father's son. In between caring for his mother, who'd suffered from severe depression since being diagnosed with multiple sclerosis years before, Clay's father had coached his Little League teams, taught him to fish, fix things around the house and to study hard. They'd played video games and watched old war movies together. And they'd chosen Clay's career path together, too, and from that point on, until the day he died, Edward Thatcher had lived his own life vicariously through his son.

It was the only life the old man had ever really lived.

Funny, his chronically ill mother was still alive, but his healthy parent—his father—was gone. Dead from a heart attack.

Clay had retrieved the Kelly Chapman open case investigation notes from his agents' desks. Sometimes a fresh look, especially reading everything at once, told a different story than the one they thought they were reading.

At the moment, since they thought they had nothing, anything new would be good.

Clay's eyes were tired, his mind buzzing when his cell phone rang. An hour had passed and he hadn't noticed.

"Yeah," he said, his gaze still on the page in front of him. Testimony from someone who'd seen the city worker on the path. There was something…

"It's JoAnne."

Clay dropped the sheet. "What's happening?"

"Nothing. It's getting dark and she's still sitting there, Clay. Are we going to let her stay there all night?"

Abrams might be waiting for darkness. "Have you talked to Mercy?"

"Yeah. She says our suspect is at home with his wife and kids, where he's been all night. At last glance, through a window above the front door, he was in pajama pants and a T-shirt with a kid on each hip, going up the stairs."

"Give the girl another few minutes and then scare her out of there. Make her think there's some kind of wild animal. Ken'll know how to do that."

"Got it."

"And make sure someone tails her home. I don't want so much as a scrape on that kid's knee."

"And if she doesn't go home?"

"Call me back."

Hanging up, Clay picked up the paper in front of him. And, leafing through the others, pulled out a few more. He placed them carefully, side by side, on top of everything else on his desk, reading them as one page, all together.

They were different reports from different agents. Different pieces of information. But they all had to do with the timeline of Kelly Chapman's disappearance.

Chapman's secretary's testimony. Deb Brown. She'd been loyal to Chapman, so JoAnne had said.

Samantha's testimony.

Witnesses from the skate path.

The city worker.

Kelly Chapman had an appointment cancel, which was what had allowed her to be out skating in the middle of a workday. Did anyone think to check on that? To hunt down whoever canceled and make sure that the reason for cancellation was legitimate?

He thumbed through JoAnne's notes for Deb Brown's testimony. Kelly's Friday-morning client had canceled because she'd gone into labor.

A few more pages and he had the name of the newborn.

So...the psychologist's appointment cancels. And instead of lounging around, going for coffee or gossiping with a friend, or even staying in the office to catch up on paperwork, she decides to go skating. She changes into skating clothes in her office—Clay's kind of woman, one who keeps an extra set of exercise clothes at work just in case—and heads out to the skate path. And then disappears into thin air.

She was seen there at 10:05 by a city worker who was often the only person on the trail that late in the season. The city worker was seen by several witnesses, starting as early as 9:30 that morning. There were sightings of the city worker on the trail at 9:30, at 9:40ish, and then twice at 10:15. Following that, there'd been one at 10:25; the woman who reported that knew the time because she'd just ended a call and the time was flashing on the cell phone's screen. There were further sightings between 10:30 and 10:45, at 11:00 or so, and 11:05; the mother who reported that one was leaving to pick her daughter up from kindergarten. Finally he was seen at around noon.

Not one single account all morning of anyone *but* the same city worker.

They had to look at him again. Either he'd seen something or done something. He was absolutely the only one in the area.

No one had seen Kelly Chapman, but she'd been on just one small leg of the trail, possibly for as little as ten minutes.

But…

Clay pulled out the schematic of the path he'd been studying. All witness sightings had been plotted in red on the chart.

It all made sense except that…

He looked back at his notes.

Two witnesses had seen the city worker at 10:15 on the stretch of path they believed Kelly had skated. The city worker said he'd seen her. And both witnesses had seen the worker there at exactly the same time. Fine. The sightings were within a minute's distance from each other. One had said he was going north on the path at 10:15. The other had said he was crossing a road onto the path not far from where the first account had placed him. Which meant that one witness was off by a minute or two. Clocks right there in the local FBI office were off a minute or two from one another.

The facts all fit.

And yet…

Something was bothering him. He looked again.

One woman who'd described seeing the man at 10:15 had mentioned that he'd had a big branch under a tarp in the back of his cart. She'd recognized it as a branch she'd seen on the path when she'd gone walking the night before. It had been thick and heavy, with two other branches forming a V off the main part.

The other woman who'd seen the worker on the same

stretch of path, at supposedly the same time, had said she was glad to have the branch that had fallen just behind her house gone, but hadn't mentioned seeing anything in the back of the worker's cart.

Clay flipped sheets again, more rapidly now. Had anyone asked the second woman if there'd been a large branch in the cart, poking out under the tarp?

Yes. And she'd said not that she'd noticed. Fine, she hadn't looked. Or remembered. But wouldn't someone who testified that she was glad to have the branch removed have recognized it in the cart?

To Clay, the answer was obvious. Enough so that he assumed he was correct. If the branch that had been on the trail, bothering the woman, had been in the cart, she *would* have noticed.

She'd realized the branch was gone. Which meant the city worker had already picked it up.

She'd said the branch had been shaped like a V and the largest part of the V had been leaning against her fence. And yet…she hadn't seen it in the worker's cart.

The discrepancy was big.

Clay stood, looking down at the pages strewn across his desk.

Was he stretching the evidence too thin? So desperate to find a woman he didn't even know that he was inventing clues to make up for the legitimate ones they didn't have?

Or…

Wide-awake now, flooded with energy, Clay dropped back into his chair and sat forward.

Suppose there'd been *two* carts.

Two city workers. Dressed the same, maybe. With hats…

Fingers almost fumbling in his haste, he glanced through descriptions of the city worker—the man had worn a beige insulated jumpsuit, regulation city uniform for outdoor winter work, with glow-in-the-dark caution stripes down the sleeves, and a city-issue beige baseball cap. Some had said he had dark brown hair. Some hadn't noticed.

Flipping to Barry's notes he read that the man had dark brown hair.

But it hadn't shown enough to be noticed by everyone.

The bike trail was on the city worker's regular beat. He was the only one who serviced it—keeping debris off the path, moving fallen branches, sweeping, cleaning and mowing the sides.

A man of average size and weight, in a bulky insulated jumpsuit and black work boots, could be easily impersonated.

There'd been two carts.

Both with tarps over the backs of their carts. One with a branch on top.

And one with a captive woman beneath it?

The dogs had found Kelly Chapman's scent on the trail and then lost it. She'd been on the trail and then she hadn't been—with no way for her to have gotten off, unless she turned around. But if she'd turned around, wouldn't one of the witnesses who'd seen the city worker have seen her?

And if she *hadn't* turned around, she'd vanished into thin air. Or been dumped in a cart right there on the trail. Because when the cart drove away, her scent would have, too.

11

He wasn't coming. He hadn't thought it was safe or he would've been there.

Disappointed, not in Mac because she knew that if he'd been able to get to her without putting her in danger, he would have done so, but because she didn't know when she'd have another chance this perfect to see him, Maggie finally stood and gazed out at the darkness that had fallen around her.

Mac would find a way to get to her. He'd signal her somehow. She'd left the flower for him, as he'd told her to. He'd seen it and turned it around. Now she had to be grown-up about it and just wait.

She wasn't afraid. Wasn't going to be afraid. She'd faced a sheriff's deputy intent on raping her. She could handle waiting for Mac. And she could handle a trek through some dark woods alone at night.

Like, who would be way out there, anyway?

But she wasn't going to tell Mac about being alone in the dark. He'd be angry with her for not keeping herself safe. And frustrated because he couldn't just be there and take care of her without all this running around and hiding. He might even forbid her from visiting their spot again.

She couldn't bear that.

He'd do it, though, if he believed that being there put her in any danger. Mac always thought of her first.

Because that's what good men did for their women.

He'd been there, just as she'd known he would. He'd turned the rose she'd left for him.

Maggie turned it back the way she'd originally placed it. *I love you,* that small movement said.

"I love you." Maggie spoke aloud, her voice far too loud in the blackness. She started to shake—only because she was cold, she told herself.

But really, what kind of animals were there? Animals that kept themselves hidden by day but roamed freely at night?

Animals that were rabid or hungry. Like a fox.

They had foxes in Ohio.

Something rustled in the distance and that was when Maggie realized just how much of a chance she'd taken, staying so long. The rustling was followed by a high-pitched eerie sound. Some kind of animal. A coyote?

She'd been stupid. She couldn't afford to be stupid. She'd look like a *kid* if she was stupid.

Retrieving the cell phone Kelly had gotten for her, she held it with her ungloved hand just above the 9-1-1 speed-dial button as she walked slowly through the brush and the barren limbs. And as soon as she was far enough away from her sacred place, she moved her thumb to the most recently added speed-dial number and pushed.

"*Maggie?* Where are you? We've been frantic. Absolutely frantic…"

Guilt surged through her as Maggie heard Samantha's tension. "I'm…I just wanted to take a bike ride, like I used to when things got bad with my mom. I couldn't stay in that house all alone and I didn't know how long you guys'd be at the hospital, but I didn't want to get too far out of town so I stopped near these woods and walked, but I hid my bike so no one would steal it and so some creep didn't see it and follow me. And then…I got lost and I didn't have cell phone service until now and—"

"Maggie, it's okay, sweetie. Don't cry." Samantha reminded her of Kelly right then, and Maggie cried harder. Tears that felt like they were never going to stop. Not ever.

Because Mac hadn't come for her. He couldn't come for her. And Kelly was missing and might be dead and it was probably Maggie's fault and Mom was in jail and lying to her, and Glenna was dead and she didn't have anyone she could talk to about any of this and she'd just lied to Sam and—

"Sweetie, just stay put. I'm on my way to get you."

"You know that old red barn by the curve in the road? The one that goes to the old covered bridge that was rebuilt?"

"Yeah."

"I'm sorta near there. In the woods."

"Keep your phone on," Samantha said. "It has GPS tracking that can only be handled by the police, and I'm on my way. Don't move. Don't leave the woods. I don't want you out in the open where someone can see you. There are a lot of creeps in the world."

Maggie had kept her phone off the whole time she'd been waiting for Mac so she could say she hadn't had service. He *couldn't* call her. They'd see his number come through, and he'd be in trouble. She hadn't wanted to see someone calling and not answer, and lie about not answering. She'd already lied—and she hated lying. It made her feel dirty.

She hadn't even thought about GPS. Or the fact that Samantha was a cop and could access the emergency system.

Another rustle in the distance had her heart pounding hard all over again. She was way too cold. And couldn't see.

"What if there's a coyote?" she asked Sam, her voice barely above a whisper so she didn't alert any nearby animals—or human—to her presence.

"He'll stay away from you as long as you don't corner him." Sam's voice sounded strong and knowing, like a teacher, and Maggie believed her. "That's another reason I don't want you moving. I don't want you to accidentally corner anything."

Maggie nodded. She felt dumb. And didn't want to hang up.

"How's Kyle's grandpa?"

"He's home, resting comfortably. They'll run some tests on him later, and then we'll see."

"Is he going to be okay, though?"

"We're not sure yet, honey. He's a very old man."

"But he's still pretty healthy." He couldn't die. He just *couldn't*. Not now. Not like this—with Maggie using his death to skip out and see Mac. Besides, she really liked him.

Maybe even better than she liked Samantha. She knew for sure she liked him better than Kyle. But Kyle had been pretty nice to her today. If he hadn't gone and told all those lies about Mac, she'd probably like him a lot. He was a whole lot better than any man Mom had ever brought around.

And he loved his dog almost as much as Kelly and Maggie loved Camy. That was cool.

"I'll be there, in a minute or two, Mags," Samantha said next. And Maggie started to cry again. Mom called her Mags.

"How'd you get here so fast?" Maggie asked so she wouldn't think about Mom.

"I was out looking for you."

"Oh." When she should've been looking for Kelly, if she wasn't with Kyle and Grandpa. "I'm sorry...."

"Shhh. It's okay, Maggie," Samantha said. "The FBI doesn't have any more for me to do tonight and I'm the one who was in the wrong. I should never have left you at Kelly's house all alone. It was a bad idea. And I'm so sorry...."

Samantha's apology made Maggie feel about an inch high. She'd been glad she was alone at Kelly's. So she could try to see Mac.

And if Samantha knew that, she'd hate Maggie forever.

With a detailed longitudinal map of the bike path on the seat beside him, and a night-vision compass in his pocket, Clay drove out of Chandler at 6:30 on Saturday evening, an hour after darkness had fallen.

He always carried blankets and a survival kit in his trunk. Came from his years as a Boy Scout. His father had made sure Clay learned the meaning of the Boy Scout motto—Be Prepared.

Forge into the world, his father had said. Face challenges. Don't shy from risk. And Be Prepared.

Clay drove along the country road, the darkness penetrated only occasionally by a security light on a barn in the distance.

The temperature had dropped. It was supposed to freeze that night. And if Kelly Chapman was lying hurt somewhere out in the woods, she probably wasn't going to survive.

There'd been no word from the kidnapper after the initial ransom call. Statistically, the chances weren't good that they'd get a live exchange, anyway. Too much risk to the kidnapper to release a victim who might know something that could lead authorities right back to him.

Tonight he was only going out to take a look around. To get a feel for the exact spot where Kelly Chapman had most likely been abducted—the spot where Willie had lost her scent.

In the morning, by the predicted 7:39 a.m. sunrise, he'd have an entire team out on that bike path.

He picked up a call from JoAnne about ten minutes from the path.

"The call came."

"Where are you?"

"At the Evans farm. I was here when he called."

"And?"

"He seems to know what he's doing. The voice was obviously modified. He asked if she had the money. She told him not yet and asked for more time."

They'd discussed the plan in one of their earlier conversations.

"Could she keep him on the phone long enough to get a trace?" They'd had Kelly's line tapped.

"Nope. He told her she had until Monday morning. Otherwise, Kelly Chapman dies at noon on Monday. And he hung up. The whole thing was over in a matter of seconds."

The woman could be dead. They all knew that. At this point, it wasn't about the exchange. The more important goal was to find out who was making these calls in the hope that he'd leave a clue that would lead them directly to him.

"This guy's smart. Careful. He knew someone would be monitoring Kelly's line. Chances are he's using an untraceable phone, anyway," JoAnne said.

"I agree. But we have to hope differently. Keep a trace on Kelly's phone. And let's put one on the Evans line, as well." Assuming Samantha and Kyle agreed to that and Clay was positive they would.

"What about the girl?"

"She's back with Samantha Jones. Claimed she'd gone for a bike ride to calm down and had gotten lost."

"Which confirms that she has secrets. Which we already knew. Stay with her for a while. See if you can get anything more out of her." Other than a brief respite to sleep, JoAnne hadn't been home in twenty-four hours. And Clay fully understood that she wouldn't have it any other way.

Her older sister had been kidnapped when JoAnne was a young teenager. Investigators had eventually turned up enough evidence to know the girl had been raped, lost a lot of blood, was presumed dead, but they'd never found her body. Or her killer.

"Will do, boss," JoAnne said, which prompted him to admit he was heading out to the bike trail. But he said he was just going for a walk, to review evidence and put facts in order.

And he knew she knew he was lying.

12

Night

Maggie was laughing. Out loud, boisterously, hilariously, joyously. I laughed, too.

But no sound came.

And then there was only darkness.

The lot Kelly had parked in on Friday was barely noticeable from the long country road running through the occasional burg, but mostly through acres and acres of farmland. The four paved parking spots were adjacent to a small yard and then an old house that was small for the area. It had once been white. And it was inhabited. He could see lights in the front window and a car in the yard. On the opposite side of the lot was the bike path and then another small structure that looked like it had been a one-room church or schoolhouse in another era. This building was completely surrounded, on all four sides, by grass, as though there'd never been a need to drive up to it. While it was intact, it appeared to be abandoned. There were no curtains on the two windows. No tire tracks that he could see in the darkness. No lights or vehicles or possessions lying about the place.

The kind of place someone might stash a body. If someone wasn't all that professional, Clay thought. But they were dealing with a professional.

Only someone who had very carefully planned this could have pulled it off so flawlessly. A professional would have researched. He might not have known precisely when Kelly Chapman would go skating, but if he'd been watching her at all, he knew she'd go. And that he had to be ready to make his move when she did.

He'd probably had the four-wheel utility vehicle for a while and had made practice runs to see if anyone noticed him.

He'd probably had his plans for the body laid out, as well. And timed the attack down to the second. He'd have to have done it that way in order to get Dr. Chapman off the trail unobserved.

And what better place to snatch a busy, popular woman out from under hundreds of watching eyes, away from the formidable protection of a cop who was her best friend and a loyal small town? A deserted skate path.

Part of the problem with having routines, with having habits, was that it made you predictable. It made you vulnerable to anyone who wanted to take you by surprise.

A professional would've had the cart stowed in a place where it could be retrieved on very short notice. Someone who either had an accomplice in town, telling him when Kelly was heading out to skate or was watching her himself and followed her out to the track.

According to their best estimate, Kelly Chapman had been skating for ten minutes before she disappeared. Time enough for someone to follow her from Chandler, collect the cart and meet her on the path. Someone who knew what direction she'd taken.

The legitimate city worker had known that, of course.

Clay wasn't at all convinced that the man was as innocent as he claimed.

The kidnapper had also had access to the winter uniform of a city worker. But then, that could be purchased from many uniform companies across the country.

Pulling out his cell, Clay called Greg Gilmore. Didn't matter that he was a college boy and it was Saturday night. Greg wanted a spot on Clay's team when he graduated. The kid had to prove he deserved it.

Thirty seconds later his cell phone was back in his pocket. Greg was checking on anyone anywhere in the Midwest who'd bought a uniform matching the description of the city worker's in the past six months. Many of the businesses were closed. At the office, and with JoAnne's say-so on a three-way call to request access, Greg could get emergency numbers many independent business owners left with local police departments. It was a start.

Clay got out of the car, grabbed his winter coat from the back and put it on, then picked up the compass, map and flashlight.

The path was clean. Completely dark. The moon was out, however, a welcome companion that shed a small, shadowy glow over the recently harvested cornfields.

The kidnapper *had* to be a professional in order to pull off the abduction right under their noses, he thought again.

And the guy was probably keeping her right under their noses, as well. That was why no one had seen anything. She hadn't been taken anywhere. More likely there'd been a quick on-and-off the path. Clay would bet his career that the plan had been to dump her in a predetermined spot, someplace that could be reached with the cart without arousing suspicion, someplace no one would ever find her. Pull that off, destroy all the evidence and you had the perfect crime.

One for which you'd never have to pay.

Walking along, watching everything around him as he made his way to the place where Willie had lost Kelly Chapman's scent, Clay considered other aspects of the abduction.

Kelly's car had been moved.

Seemed like days since Clay had sat in that car, or felt a sense of the woman who'd driven it to Michigan and purchased luggage tags for herself and her new daughter.

He couldn't think about the woman now. He had to think like a kidnapper. A professional kidnapper.

A professional would've moved the car to an unrelated area to throw investigators off track—to have the lead investigator hightail his ass two states away, leaving the ground clear for Chapman to be dealt with. One way or another.

Walking all alone in a dark night that was so quiet the steps of his rubber soles on the pavement had the effect of gunshots, Clay tried to prepare himself for what he and his team might discover in the morning.

Even if Kelly Chapman was alive, the chances were pretty good that, after two days of captivity, she wouldn't be faring well. If she'd fought at all, she'd likely be hurt. And if she hadn't, she'd have been drugged. She could've been without food or drink for two days. Would probably be dehydrated. Depending on where she was, hypothermia was almost a certainty.

His pace quickened.

But he couldn't escape his thoughts. As uncomfortable as they were, he didn't *want* to escape them. Kelly's salvation might very well depend on the combination of logic and intuition that was Clay's strength as an investigator.

A professional would have a way to get back to the body without raising suspicion. The cart, stowed as before, would be that.

He called JoAnne. She was still at the Evans farm. She and Samantha and Kyle were sitting at the table having a late dinner that Kyle had fixed. It didn't sound as though she'd be leaving very soon. Maggie had already gone to bed, apparently. He could imagine that she wouldn't want to face any further questioning tonight.

He told JoAnne to arrange for someone to start looking for utility cart purchases. And to arrange a team to start searching for one in the morning. He hung up before she could ask any questions.

Walk first. Focus. And tip his hand only to a very few people. People he trusted with his own life.

JoAnne. And Barry.

Night

Black boot. Head pain.
Blinding head pain.
Please. No more.
Scrape and rub. Rub and scrape.

It took longer to reach a designated location on foot than it did on skates. Longer still if you were working with a map, a flashlight and a night compass. Clay thought about his call to JoAnne. And about their earlier conversation.

The ransom call fit his theory, too. It was being made by a professional. The disguised voice, the prevention of call tracing—anyone could've known to do that just from watching any one of the many crime shows so popular on TV these days. But an amateur couldn't easily emulate the calm of someone who has the confidence of knowing what he's doing. Confidence achieved through practice. Someone who could not only afford to be patient, but was absolutely convinced that he was safe. Someone who hadn't kidnapped Kelly Chapman for ransom, but who'd made ransom demands to throw the authorities off track, to divert them from the real crime. The real motive for the crime. The kidnapper had bought himself forty-eight hours, and now an extra twenty-four, to do whatever he was doing and then get out. Twenty-four more hours before Clay and his team knew that the ransom call was a fake.

An extra twenty-four hours to kill the woman and get the hell out of Dodge. Cover his tracks.

Or maybe just another twenty-four hours to let the trail go cold.

Night

Cold. Too cold. Death cold.

Clay stopped. Stood on the six-foot-wide black asphalt bike path and felt the cold penetrate him. He'd brought gloves in his pocket, but had left them off to more easily maneuver the map, flashlight and compass he'd been using.

He'd reached the spot where Willie had lost Kelly Chapman's scent and he closed his eyes.

Closed out the darkness around him.

She'd been skating north away from the parking lot. He faced north. The utility cart—minus the branch—had been reported traveling north, having just crossed a street. Clay had crossed a street not one hundred yards back.

The second utility cart, seen at approximately the same time, but with a branch in the back, had been just ahead of where Clay stood now. So the legitimate city worker had seen Kelly and traveled on his way. She'd skated behind him at a pretty good clip. He'd stopped to pick up a branch, and possibly clear other debris.

The second cart had come up behind Kelly. Perhaps the guy called out to her. Recognizing the city vehicle, the uniform, she would've waited. At which point the guy grabs her, restrains her and dumps her in the back of his cart. Probably knocking her out because he couldn't let her slow him down or make noise or move around when he had her in his cart. This all had to happen within two or three minutes.

Then he'd be driving off, passing the place where that branch had been at approximately 10:15 when the second woman saw the city worker.

It was a stretch. Comprising suppositions and maybes. There wasn't enough substantive evidence to take home to his cat. But the theory made sense. It was the only thing that made sense.

Standing there, imagining Kelly Chapman being abducted, possibly injured, right there where he stood, Clay was filled with a sense of foreboding. That morning he'd been in the driver's seat of the woman's car. Sitting where she'd sat yesterday morning.

Tonight he stood where she was last known to be alive.

He was getting close.

She was nearby. Dead or alive, she was nearby.

Opening his eyes, he spun around. Had he heard something?

A deer in the cornfield, maybe.

In the darkness, the quiet was penetrating. And animals roamed.

Maybe it was a raccoon. A possum.

Certainly not a woman calling out to him.

He was hearing clues in the wind now.

But if Kelly Chapman *was* close by—alive—he had to find her. Tonight.

Before her captor had any indication that someone was on to him. Clay's people were asking questions about city uniforms and city vehicles. If the kidnapper had an informant, which was a high possibility given some of the suspects, he'd know soon enough that Clay was on to him. If he didn't know already...

Clay couldn't leave her out here alone. Couldn't let the bastard come back and get her in the morning. Move her. Finish the job.

A city worker wouldn't be on the trail at night. And a professional criminal wouldn't blow his cover by being out here, either. But in the morning...

Clay had a niggling thought about the fact that he was exhausted. He wasn't up to par tonight. He was well aware of it.

The way he couldn't get the woman out of his mind was proof of that. The way he kept feeling some kind of connection to her. He was overtired. Not thinking clearly.

He wasn't leaving. Not until he found her. And if that meant he spent the night out here on a cold deserted track, guarding a hideaway he didn't even know for sure existed, then so be it.

He expected Kelly Chapman to survive the cold. She *had* to.

And he could, too.

13

He wasn't prepared to camp out, so Clay set off to cover every inch of ground on either side of the bike path, up to half a mile north and half a mile south of where Willie had lost Kelly Chapman's scent. The ground had already been covered by both volunteers and professionals. In the daylight.

He didn't kid himself that he was going to find something they'd missed. But he looked, anyway. Now that he knew about the cart, the parameters were different. There'd been no reports of utility-cart tire-track sightings, but someone might have seen them and assumed they'd been left by the city worker they'd known was there.

It was also possible the tracks had simply been overlooked. Searchers had been seeking any sign of Kelly Chapman. Any scrap of clothing or shoelace or skate bolt. Any sign of a struggle.

And it was possible that the hard December ground meant there were no tracks to see. No sign of trespass.

Clay told himself all these things and more as he walked a foot and a half out from the bike path, and then, coming back, the same distance on the opposite side. He was thinking more than searching.

There was no logical reason for him to be there. Not

really. He had to wait until morning to follow up on what he'd deduced.

In the meantime, he had to do something. And it had become very clear to him that while Kelly was out there somewhere he wasn't going to be able to go home, lie down in his bed and go to sleep.

He had to be near her. To be present in case there was any little thing at all that he could do.

To be present if she died that night?

Finishing his trek, Clay stepped out from the path another foot and a half and began the process again. Down and then back. And knew that as soon as this case was over he had to take a break.

He'd been working five years straight without a vacation. His choice. His insistence, really. Work gave him satisfaction. Energy. Adrenaline rushes. Work was his life and he wanted it that way.

But only if he did it well.

He couldn't do it well if he got personally involved.

And this woman, this Dr. Kelly Chapman, she was getting to him. More than any other victim he'd ever traced.

He had her picture taped to his dash.

That had been his first mistake.

Clay stopped. He'd heard the sound again. Maybe. It wasn't loud. In fact, it seemed indistinguishable from everything around him. Part of the landscape. Nothing he'd hear if he wasn't alone in the stillness of the night. An animal living its life in the safety of darkness, he told himself.

Still, he'd like to scare the critter up, just to be sure.

Because he had nothing better to do, Clay walked toward the sound. And then it stopped. And he returned to his journey along the side of the bike path.

* * *

So they needed another day. Didn't bother him. He was in no hurry. Everything was working out just fine.

A spider dangled from a piece of web hanging from the lightbulb.

All it took was a carefully plotted and executed strategy. He'd always been fascinated with bombs and explosions. Had made his first bomb when he was nine. A potato bomb. No one ever knew he was the one who'd blown out that car window. And he'd been careful to experiment safely after that.

Yes, time was a friend, not an enemy. Patience, planning, they were the keys to success. Time allowed the precision and care that guaranteed no mistakes. There were many kinds of bombs, many ways to make them. Over the years he'd learned many of them. And all it took was a little innocuous household shopping.

The spider dropped to the floor and started to crawl toward him. He watched with amusement as it knocked into an empty beer can and made its way around it. Getting closer to his bare foot.

He'd had a goal—to make them pay for his miserable life. To make *her* pay. The means had presented themselves.

And the bounty would be his.

Crushing the spider beneath his toes, he took another swig of beer. Belched. And crossed to the other side of the room to sit on the pot that served as a john.

Oh, yes, one more day and his goal would become reality.

"You really think David Abrams did something to Kelly?" Sitting at the kitchen table late Saturday night, Sam glanced at the FBI agent across from her. Kyle was there, too.

The three of them had switched from beer to coffee.

"I'm sure of it," Sam told the thirtyish woman who looked more svelte television reporter than cop. JoAnne's hair was a dark mahogany and hung in waves past her shoulders, curling softly around a face that was Hollywood pretty. "The man is obsessed with two things. Maggie Winston. And getting his own way."

"You're the one who's after him," JoAnne said. "Why not take you?"

"Too obvious." Leaning back in his chair, Kyle drew his finger around the tractor design on the front of his mug. "And he's not stupid. Sam killed his partner, who was also a cop. Abrams isn't going to mess with her."

"It's more than that," Sam said, grinning at the man she would never, ever take for granted. "Maggie is Abrams's key to freedom. There will never be a case without her testimony. There's just no other evidence. The man's a lawyer. A good one. Which means he knew what he had to do to guarantee he was never at risk of prosecution."

"So why have sex with a fourteen-year-old?"

"Every man has his weakness. His downfall," Kyle said, with a glance at Sam that wrapped her in a warmth she'd never have dared let herself feel a few months ago.

"The fact is," she said, "it's not exactly a secret around here that Kelly has helped many witnesses testify successfully at trial. Like the seven-year-old kid in Florida. Plus, Maggie's living with Kelly. Abrams also knows that Kelly is on to him. He knows she's doing everything she can, and will continue to do everything she can, to get Maggie to open up and see the truth. To name Abrams as the man she had sex with in the woods."

"She believes she doesn't know him."

"Right."

"But if Kelly gets Maggie to accept that Mac and Abrams are the same man, then his life is over."

"Right. The entire life he's built, the career, the family, the position of respect in the community—it all comes crashing down. His survival hinges on Maggie."

"So how can we be sure she won't try to go to him again?"

"We can't," Sam said, a sick feeling in her gut when she thought about the deal she'd made with Agent Thatcher. The danger she'd put Maggie in. The girl had been distraught when she'd come home. It had taken Sam an hour to get Maggie to stop blaming herself for everything from her mother's imprisonment to Kelly's abduction.

Sam was the cop. Not the shrink. She'd needed Kelly desperately. But she'd done the best she could.

"Which is why either Kyle or I will be with her at all times from now on. Period."

"The sting tonight was the right thing to do," JoAnne said.

She'd agreed to the plan. It hadn't worked. But that was in the past. "I'm glad it's over."

"We're going to need to try again."

"No."

"It's clear that there's something between those two. Abrams might not call her or speak to her in town, but out there, he seems to feel safe. *If,* as you say, he's taken Kelly, *if* he's the man we're after—and his one weakness is Maggie—it's quite possible that using her will be the only way we'll get him."

"Or we'll get him on Monday when we catch the creep he's hired to make the ransom demand," Sam said.

They'd already discussed the probability that the ransom demand was a cover—nothing more.

"He managed to keep himself clean before. What makes you think he hasn't done so this time?"

Sam didn't like JoAnne's intent gaze. Mostly because

she didn't like the truth behind the woman's words. For once, the truth made her feel helpless, not inspired.

"Tell me about Agent Thatcher." She might be changing the subject, but not really. Sam needed to know more about the man in charge of finding her friend. The man she'd trusted with Maggie's life.

"What's to tell? He's a good agent. Married to the job, but in this line of work that's pretty much what it takes."

"You trust him."

"Implicitly."

"I did some checking and heard he's had a run-in or two with the higher-ups."

"Clay's not a rules guy. He does whatever he has to. That's why he's one of the best at finding missing persons."

"So he's a rogue?"

"No. He just isn't afraid to risk going outside the rules if that's what's needed to bring someone home."

"Has he ever been wrong?"

"Aren't we all at some time or other?" JoAnne frowned down into her cup. "Sure, he's been wrong." She looked straight at Sam. "But no one's ever, *ever* been hurt because of a wrong decision made by Clay. No one's ever died because of what he did."

"But it must be hard to work for someone you can't count on to follow protocols."

"For me it would be harder to work for someone who did," JoAnne said. "Finding missing persons isn't about protocol. It's about getting into the nitty-gritty dirtiest parts of life. Not being afraid to question everything. Beating the bastards at their own game. *They* know *our* protocols. Hell, anyone who watches television knows them. Or a lot of them. And we all understand that knowledge is power. It's like handing them our game plan and then thinking we're going to win, anyway."

Sam wanted to disagree with what the other woman was saying, but she couldn't. Still, she wasn't feeling any better about having hauled a hysterical girl out of the dark woods less than four hours earlier. Mostly because Maggie was a big part of Kelly's life now, and Kelly would trust her to protect Maggie at all costs.

"What about Thatcher's personal life? Doesn't his wife mind that he's gone so much?"

"Clay? With a wife?" JoAnne chuckled. "Not hardly. Clay could face a gun pointing at him and not break a sweat, but ask him to even *think* about walking down the aisle and he'd be out of there and on the nearest plane to somewhere else."

"Burned, was he?" Kyle asked.

JoAnne shook her head. "No, though when you watch him tap-dance around any woman who shows the least bit of interest in him, that's exactly what you'd assume."

"Well, I'm sure he's not gay," Sam said. She had, after all, met the man who exuded sex appeal down to his toes without seeming to realize it.

"No, Clay likes women." JoAnne's tone implied that he liked them a lot.

And maybe he had liked JoAnne at one point or other?

Once the thought occurred to Sam, it hung on.

"So what's his deal?"

"I'll tell you what he tells everyone who asks that question. He says he fully believes men and women should marry if they want kids, but that he's just too aware of the control you give up over your life to ever be any good at marriage."

"He's a control freak." That she could understand.

"No, I wouldn't say that. Clay does things his own way, but he's pretty easy about letting others do the same. *Especially* when we're talking about working a case. Then he gives us all the freedom we want as long as we follow through on our assignments."

"You sound like you're very fond of him."

Smiling, JoAnne shook her head again. "As a close friend and colleague, yes. But if you're saying what I think you're saying, no way. A long time ago, maybe. But I got over Clay the first time he slept with a woman and couldn't remember her name the next morning."

"He sleeps with strangers." One step above sleeping with prostitutes, which was a sore spot with Sam.

She glanced at Kyle. A *very* sore spot. Not that Kyle would ever pay for sex. But there'd been a woman, years ago, who usually sold what she gave to Kyle for free.

"No, she was a visiting agent," JoAnne said. "Clay just couldn't remember her name."

Kyle coughed.

"Oh." Sam stood, moved over to a coffee bar Kyle had set up for her at the end of the kitchen and started measuring grounds for her espresso machine.

"You asked if I'm fond of Clay," JoAnne said after Sam had filled their cups with her brew.

"Yeah."

"I'd give up my life for him. Does that answer your question?"

Sometime after midnight Clay quit walking the half-mile stretch of ground between the parking lot and Willie's lost scent. He was going to have to sit down at least. Get some rest even if he stayed awake. He'd been going for almost forty hours with only a few hours' sleep in his car.

Grabbing the blanket out of the back of the car and shoving a bottle of water into the pocket of his coat, he made his way back to the last known place Kelly Chapman had been alive. He'd find a tree to lean against. And if he fell asleep, he'd wake up if anyone came by trying to move his missing person.

Or hurt her.

Clay was a light sleeper.

Came from growing up with a woman who needed constant attention. His mom's illness had been like a regular member of their small family since Clay was too young to remember.

But it wasn't her illness that had dragged them all down. It was the emotional neediness that accompanied her multiple sclerosis. Stress exacerbated the disease, and being alone upset Lynn Thatcher.

He heard the sound again, the one he'd noticed earlier, as he passed the now-familiar place on the trek between his car and his end point. He wasn't sure how to describe it. A kind of swishing sound? While Clay still hadn't identified the animal that was inadvertently keeping him company that night, he'd come to welcome its presence.

Veering off the path toward the woods, he started to go in search of it again, and then stopped. Each time he'd gotten close, the sound had stopped. Whatever little critter was out there didn't want him disturbing it. But regardless, it wasn't leaving whatever job it was doing.

So he continued on. He found his tree. He made his bed, such as it was, and sat down on the blanket. Wrapping the edges over his lap, he laid his head against the tree and closed his eyes.

And saw again the pretty face smiling up at him from the dash of his car. Saw those eyes. The trust. The faith.

The…naiveté? No. If anything, Kelly Chapman saw too much. Knew too much.

But she obviously believed, anyway. In some kind of innate goodness.

Maybe that was what called out to him. The hope that there really was some good left in the world.

Finding Kelly alive—

His eyes flew open.

The sound. The rhythmic swishing sound floating out into the night. Why would an animal return to a place where it had been spooked? Unless it was feasting on prey?

A dead body?

He was nuts. Clay acknowledged that as he stood, flung his blanket around his neck and headed back to where he'd veered off the path.

And this time he didn't stop.

Whether the sound stopped or not, he was going to find out what was making that noise.

No one would know he'd lost his mind. This was between him and the night.

And when he'd exhausted every avenue—then he could allow himself to rest.

14

Night

Still. Or again.
  Need to breathe. Open mouth.
  Spit…
  Blood…
  Wet…
  Wet was good.
  Please. More sleep.

Stepping carefully so that he didn't crack any twigs beneath his black leather shoes, alerting his nocturnal companion to his advance, Clay drew closer to the sound, preparing himself for the worst.

It wasn't as if a dead body unhinged him. He'd seen far too many of them.

But this one was different.

This woman…

The sound stopped again. He kept walking in the direction from which it came. And was surprised as hell when the swishing noise started up again. As though his presence hadn't been the cause of its silence at all.

Interesting.

And…there was more than one of them. There were at least two. One the swishing he'd heard before, the other a faint keening sound.

He'd seen a deer dead beside the road a couple of weeks before. There'd been a buzzard with its beak inside the animal's stomach and another gnawing on the flesh of the doe's hip.

He was probably trailing a dead dear.

Clay pressed on. He had to know.

It was his father in him, pushing him. Clay recognized the process. *Go, Clay. Find out. Know. Experience. Live.*

And come home to tell me all about it.

He could hear the words forming in his head already. "I was in the dark all alone, Dad, prepared to spend the night sitting up against a tree. It was pitch-black and I was the only human being around for at least half a mile. Just me and barren cornfields on one side and woods on the other. And wildlife. It was cold and getting colder. I was drifting off to sleep, thinking of you and Mom, and I heard this sound…."

The noise was faint, but Clay could swear he was *standing* on it—that it was coming from the ground beneath his feet.

Was it caused by the wind blowing something against a tree?

There was no wind. He scanned the leafless branches on dead-looking trees and the dips and valleys in the woods. He could see no movement at all.

Ssshhh. Ssshhh.

What the hell was it? Finding the source of that noise was a matter of pride now. Of determination. His father had taught him that the worst thing you could do in life was give up.

Giving up meant not living.

Which was why one of the most painful parts of Clay's job was being forced to stop a search without a find.

He perused the ground, searching for parts of a carcass.

Another few yards and he paused again. Listened. Turned. The noise was behind him now. Which made no sense. He would've had to step on it to get from where he'd been to where he was.

Looking down again, Clay studied the ground. Solid. Covered in masses of dead leaves that looked like they hadn't been touched since they'd fallen two months ago.

But the *ssshhhing* called him so he moved forward. One foot at a time. Foot forward. Stop. Listen. Foot forward. Stop. Listen.

And then he heard something else. A whimper.

And he froze. Waiting for the cry to come again.

He wasn't imagining things. He couldn't be.

Intent, Clay waited. He knew what he'd heard.

A few minutes later, the sound came again. A faint whimper. Not a cry for help, but more like the kind of sound someone made while asleep. Having a nightmare.

And it seemed to be coming from under his feet.

He was straddling the twigs of a large fallen log, a dead branch like hundreds of others in the wooded areas of southwestern Ohio—effects from Hurricane Ike, which had torn through the state two years before.

It was perched against some other trees, one of which was leaning toward it. If he moved that one, the other would fall.

The sound came again, and with every instinct tuned to top pitch, Clay bent down. Had Kelly ventured into the woods for some reason? Maybe to relieve herself? And a tree had fallen on her?

No, the sound was farther away than that.

His thoughts raced.

Peering beneath the tree, he heard it again. Louder.

Clay pointed his flashlight beneath the log and his heart started to pound. The leaves covering the ground under the fallen log, stretching toward the trunk of another tree, had been disturbed. Recently.

He had to move the fallen log. Looping his belt around the dead tree that held the log in place, Clay brought it down first, swinging it around to brace against a second tree. And then with very little effort, he was able to swing the rotting log over and away from the disturbed leaves.

Not sure what he was going to find, and not wanting to disturb evidence any more than necessary in case this was a crime scene, Clay brushed aside the leaves around the trunk of the tree. And hit metal.

There was no whimpering now. Just *ssshhh. Ssshhh.* A steady rhythm that pushed at his back. *Ssshhh. Ssshhh.*

Pulling off his gloves, Clay scraped against the metal, clearing away more leaves, listening for the whimper, for any sign of human life, as he tried to figure out what he had.

Less than half a minute passed before he'd uncovered a grate, similar to one that would be found over a cold-air return in any of the thousands of old homes in the area. The grates were a dime a dozen at flea markets, as well.

But although the grate was old, it hadn't been there long. From the sheen as he held the flashlight over it, he could see that the square of metal holding the grate in place was brand-new. As was the opening beneath the grate—roughly a four-by-four-foot patch of new earth.

"Hello?" Clay called urgently, silently praying for an answer as he pried at the grate.

It came away easily. Tossing it to the side, Clay lowered himself onto his belly, the flashlight in one hand as he peered down into the hole.

And suddenly his heart was pounding even harder and

he felt the familiar rush, the drive of a man about to accomplish something. Something big.

This wasn't a hole. Just beneath the newly dug earth was a room. A cavelike structure. He knew what he'd stumbled upon. Because he'd seen one before, not far from there. Back in the days of the Civil War and the Underground Railroad, some local farmers had dug similar structures to house the slaves they were bringing to freedom. From what Clay understood, they'd never been needed and had long ago been closed up.

Apparently someone had reopened one. Someone who knew where it was. Someone who'd done local research?

He had to find out who owned the land he was trespassing on, but first he had to get into that room.

Ssshhh. Ssshhh was calling out to him.

Still on his stomach Clay pushed his way inside the opening toward the noise that hadn't let him sleep. He had no preconceived thoughts now. No plans. No hopes. He just had to go.

And six feet inside the opening, he knew why.

There, lying in a heap, unconscious on the rock floor was the body of the woman he'd spent two days seeking.

And the sound? Her skates, of all things, rubbing against each other, not in any natural human movement, but as a reflex, over and over, like miniseizures as the woman slowly died.

She wasn't dead yet. And Clay wasn't going to let her die.

Moving with a precision born of need, he maneuvered himself close enough to Kelly Chapman to feel for a pulse at her neck. Her arms were out of reach, stretched behind her in a painful-looking contortion.

Her skin was cold. And clammy. But Clay was certain

he felt a faint pulse. He repositioned his fingers. Applied a bit more pressure. And found a more promising pulse.

Not only was she alive, her heart rate was steady and strong.

Okay. Victim found. Alive.

He touched her face gently to wake her. She moaned, but resisted his attempt.

"Kelly?" Clay spoke softly. He didn't want to alarm her. And he had to know if she was asleep or unconscious. If she was drugged.

He could see the swelling above and around her right temple. And, at a quick glance, what seemed to be other scrapes and bruises, as well. Her left cheek was scraped. And when he shone his light around, he noticed blood on the wall behind her.

A lot of it. Smeared on the wall.

"Kelly?" If he could get her to wake up, chances were she'd be okay.

"Mmmm?" The moan was familiar. And gave him hope.

"You need to wake up now." He was firm out of necessity. *Wake up, dammit!*

"Mmm-hmm."

"Dr. Chapman." Clay raised his voice authoritatively. Kelly Chapman's eyelids flew open. And the look of sheer terror behind them took the words from his throat.

"It's okay," he finally croaked. And then, more quietly, "I'm with the FBI. You're safe now."

She didn't believe him. Eyes desperate, she looked to either side. He pretty much filled up the space between her and the opening of the small cave.

"I'm going to get my badge," he told her before reaching behind him for the wallet in his back pocket. Pulling it out, he flipped it open to hold in front of her.

She studied his ID. And then him. She didn't say anything. Just nodded. Stared at him.

And didn't cry a single tear.

Clay had never been more moved in his life. Not ever.

Night

The man moved closer. Coming around to my other side, his back to the far end of my enclosure. He was huge.

"This is going to hurt," he said as he reached for my shoulders, jiggling my arms. I wanted to tell him they were numb, but the words were too much effort.

He put his hand in a pocket. Took out a knife. And the tension pulling at my shoulders was gone. My arms fell forward.

"Uhhh…" I couldn't help the moan. Numbness hurt. Stung. My eyes needed tears. There were none.

I couldn't move my hands. Or my arms. Didn't really want to. They hurt so badly.

He took one arm and then the other, feeling its entire length first, and then massaging it. Seconds later he laid my hands in my lap.

And I remembered that I'd wet myself. My pants were dry, or at least I thought they were. But I reeked. I knew I did.

There were no tears.

A blanket settled around me.

"Thirsty." I expected to speak. No sound.

"Of course."

I heard the lid turn on a bottle and almost threw up. And then the plastic was at my lips, hurting them, and I sucked voraciously. I got one drop of water. It stung my lips.

"Slowly now," the voice said. "One sip at a time."

I wanted to argue. Couldn't. He held the bottle to my

lips. I sucked at the first surge of liquid. Swallowed. And immediately sucked for more.

Suck. Swallow. Repeat.

Suck. Swallow. Repeat.

I couldn't stop. Didn't want to stop.

"That's enough for now. Give it time to settle or you'll get sick."

He was right.

Already I felt different. Not coherent. But alive.

"Where?"

"We're a hundred yards off the bike path. About a quarter mile from where you parked your car. In a little cave that's probably been here for almost a hundred and fifty years."

I lay there and breathed, aware that he was touching me, carefully, gingerly, his fingers moving all over my body.

And then he started to talk.

"Does this hurt?" He was holding my calf, touching my shin.

I tried to shake my head. And saw stars.

Cutting the tie around my ankles, he put one skate on his thighs and unbuckled it. Slowly he lifted the skate, easing my foot out of it.

I cried out. I didn't mean to. I held his gaze, though, as he studied my face and lowered my foot to the stone floor. Then he started in on my other foot. I watched as he examined my legs.

And looked away when he passed my groin area. He pressed gently on my lower belly.

"Does that hurt?" he asked.

"No." I'd learned my lesson. It hurt less to talk than to shake my head.

"What about here?" He slid his hands up to my ribs, beneath my arms.

"Sore," I said.

My arms were sore, too, now that feeling was coming back to them. Sore and tingling like hell—little needle-points from my fingers all the way up to my collarbone.

Bracing one hand behind my shoulder, he applied pressure with the other. And repeated the motion on my other side. "Nothing feels like it's out of place," he said.

Everything about me felt out of place. I wanted to argue with him again. But I was too glad to have him there. I stared at him instead. As long as I could keep my eyes on his face, I was okay.

"Ready for another drink?"

"Yes."

He let me have more water this time. I drank until he made me stop. And then I lay back, leaning my head against the wall. They'd done something to my head. Hurt it somehow.

The pounding had become a permanent part of me. One I'd learn to live with.

Soon.

There was no rush now. No need to move. To hurt more. Not yet. They'd found me. *He'd* found me.

"Who?"

He glanced at me with one eyebrow raised. "Who am I, you mean? My name's Clay Thatcher. I'm an agent with the FBI Missing Persons Unit."

"Know that." My throat was starting to move again. I didn't feel so much as if I was going to choke every time I tried to talk.

I still didn't even attempt to move my arms.

"Who did…this?"

"I was hoping you were going to tell me."

"Don't know." Sharp pangs shot through my midsection and up into my chest. "You…don't know?" I asked, afraid all over again.

"Calm down." The man took my hand, holding my gaze again.

Calm down? I was lying there completely limp. In body and mind. But I was scared to death.

"Right now we need to concentrate on getting some nourishment into you. After I help you out of here, we've got a distance to go in the dark to get to my car."

The last thing I wanted to do was go out into the darkness.

Or move my head.

"What if they…come…"

"We should be safe for now. I believe whoever did this to you is posing as a city worker. He'd blow his cover if he came out after dark."

I hoped he was right.

He made me drink some more, still holding the bottle for me. And a while later, a little more. He kept checking my pulse. Watching my eyes.

He could've been watching for any number of things. I'd know what they were if I thought about them. I didn't. I just lay there and let him figure it all out.

15

He had to get her out of there, but didn't want to move her. She was a healthy young woman; all those years of skating had served her well. Other than dehydration, she didn't seem to have suffered too many ill effects from her ordeal. At least not physically.

He kept a close watch, though.

And his mind raced. He'd found her. She was alive. And for all intents and purposes, she was well.

And until he knew who'd taken her—and why—she was in danger. Once he revealed that he'd found her, agents from another bureau would be called in. They'd put her in some kind of protective custody.

And they'd follow the rules.

Rules that men like Rick Thomas's enemies would know about—and shrug off—before the night was done.

Rules that thugs from Florida would scoff at.

And David Abrams? He was the one Clay worried about the most. He was the ultimate con man, saying one thing while his actions said something else.

He'd had contacts. There was no telling where he might still have insiders in place.

Clay couldn't turn her over.

Not yet. He was so close. He'd done all the preliminary

investigations. He knew the facts. The people. He was on to something. And with his victim now with him, awake and talking, he could solve this one very quickly.

With the smallest amount of danger to her.

He could keep her safest by keeping her a missing person.

So what was he considering here?

What was he going to do?

Clay didn't know. He just knew that he wasn't going to walk away from the woman sitting there staring at him with that look of trust in her eyes—that look of belief in an innate goodness.

Chandler, Ohio
Rescue Night

I knew we'd have to do something soon. And I was glad to be able to collect myself a bit, to lie there safely and drink more water, before I had to force myself to move. Or to think.

"Do you have any internal pain?"

"No."

"Were you hit in the stomach? Or the chest?"

"Don't remember being hit."

"What about…other…injuries?"

"My head."

"There's a good lump. Do you know how you got it?"

"No."

He glanced down toward my groin and I cringed again.

"You're clothed."

"Yes."

"Were you raped?"

I'd know. Wouldn't I?

"No."

Some of the tension lines around his eyes dissipated. He was really a very nice man.

And I was slowly starting to regain some of my faculties.

"I just wanted to sleep," I told him.

"I'm not surprised. Thank God you were dumped here. Underground caves in Ohio generally maintain a steady temperature of fifty-two to fifty-six degrees year-round, and with your jacket and thermal exercise clothes, you've managed to hold enough body temperature to prevent hypothermia."

"You're a cop *and* a doctor?"

"I'm a licensed paramedic, and I've had a bit of experience with health care, but no, I'm not a doctor."

A paramedic would recognize hypothermia. And vital signs and broken bones.

"I think I'm concussed."

"Your pupils are dilating normally and your pulse is steady." He paused, and I waited.

"Listen, we need to get you out of here, but I'd like a chance to speak with you first, before word gets out that you've been found. And found alive."

"Okay."

"But I need to take your blood pressure, just to be sure there isn't some immediate danger I'm unaware of. I have a cuff in my car with a survival kit. I'd like to go get it."

No! Panic, rapid and lethal, attacked my entire system. I couldn't breathe. Pain shot through my stomach.

"I know," Agent Clay Thatcher said, his voice warm and calm as he responded to something I hadn't even said. He'd climbed over my legs and was kneeling on the other side of me. He pulled a revolver out of the inside of his coat.

"I want you to take this. Hold it in your hand the whole time I'm gone." He showed me how to use it and then said, "When I return, I'll whistle." He made a noise like a whip-poor-will's. "If anyone comes through that opening without making that sound you shoot first and ask questions later."

I'd never shot a gun in my life.

But after being abducted and held captive, I knew I could.

"How long have I been here?"

He glanced at his watch. "It's about two in the morning on Sunday night. You left your office to go skating at 9:30 Friday morning."

"I've been lying here for forty hours?"

"I think so."

I had to think about that.

On his hands and knees Agent Thatcher faced what I now knew was an opening to the tiny cave that had become home to this new, victimized me. He turned back, saying, "I'll be twenty, twenty-five minutes max."

I just looked at him. It was the best I could do.

"Keep the gun ready and aimed," he said, and waited until I'd done that before he continued on his way out.

I watched him go, trying not to cry away the little bit of water I'd taken into my system as it occurred to me that the man had a lot of faith in me, a woman he'd only just met, turning his back while I was holding a gun pointed at him.

And he was planning to return while I still had the gun aimed at the entrance of the cave. If I were him, I would've been worried that a woman who'd been abducted and was still in captivity might get trigger-happy when she heard a sound at the opening of her prison.

He jogged the entire way, was in and out of his car in ten seconds flat, having grabbed the two duffels he stored in his trunk, and jogged the whole way back.

He'd found Kelly Chapman. Alive.

But there was no time for gratitude at the moment. No time to savor relief. Kelly's case was different. Had been from the start. Here was a missing adult woman with hordes of people looking for her within *hours*.

With the Bureau chief demanding immediate and focused attention.

And Clay knew, even as he acknowledged that he could very well lose his job when this was all over, that his real job had just begun.

Before he could turn over his missing person, before he could put Kelly back out in her world, he had to learn who'd abducted her in the first place.

There were agents, both at his office and at the large Cincinnati office, who'd argue that they were better at that task. They'd been trained for it. Had the experience.

But Clay had an edge they didn't—couldn't—have. He had the ability, if he was very careful, and very lucky, to keep Kelly missing until he found out who'd taken her.

The plan formed of its own accord. Details fell into place.

And by the time he'd returned to the small opening beneath the logs he'd replaced when he went to his car, he figured the only thing left to do was convince Kelly Chapman to agree to his plan.

He whistled and then, moving the log aside, slid into the riskiest venture of his life feetfirst.

Chandler, Ohio
Sunday, December 5, 2010

I was shaking from head to foot by the time Agent Thatcher came back. I'd wrapped the blanket around myself, arms aching with every move, and still couldn't get warm. A pair of feet sliding toward me had never looked so good.

"How's Maggie?" I asked before he was even fully inside the small enclosure. "My foster daughter. Do you know where she is?"

My voice was sharp. Urgent. But I'd had twenty minutes, at least, to think. And to battle the fear that would consume me if I allowed it to.

"She and your dog are out at the Evans farm with Detective Jones." Back in the enclosure, Agent Thatcher sat between me and the door, arranging the duffel bags he'd dragged in.

Detective Jones. "Maggie's with Sam?"

"Yes."

Thank God. Sam knew our situation. The dangers to Maggie. The need to watch over the girl with focused care. Sam not only knew the situation, she was part of it.

"How long has Sam had them?"

Had David had any chance to get at Maggie first?

He unzipped one of his bags. Pulled out a battery-operated lantern-style light and, flipping it on, set it on the floor, shining straight up.

I could see more of my prison now. It extended farther back than I'd realized.

I didn't want to think about what else might be back there, sharing this space with me. What might've been crawling on me.

Agent Thatcher had a blood pressure cuff in his hand. "Since Friday afternoon." My rescuer reached for my left arm, helped me out of my jacket, easing it down over the dried blood on the side of my hand and lower wrist, and pushed up the sleeves of my shirt and insulated undershirt.

I shivered again as the cold air hit my skin and I wanted to burrow back under the blanket. Agent Thatcher wrapped the cuff around my bare arm.

"Maggie's the one who reported you missing," he said,

squeezing the bulb that inflated the cuff. "When she came home from school on Friday and couldn't get hold of you, she called Samantha Jones."

The cuff was fully inflated and I sat quietly while he slowly released the pressure, studied his watch and counted. It was hard not to be impatient. I suddenly had too many questions and no answers at all.

Half an hour before, answers hadn't been important.

Funny how some water and another human presence changed the world.

"One twenty-four over eighty-two. A little high on diastolic, but that's to be expected with the stress you're under. And it's still in normal range."

I wasn't sure if he was talking to me or to himself.

The man who'd returned didn't seem to be the same one who'd left. The body was the same; the attitude was completely different. Professional. Distant.

I wasn't complaining. He'd saved my life. Now I needed to get home. To tend to Maggie and Camy and…bathe.

He pulled out some foil-wrapped packets—antibiotic wipes—and picked up my right wrist. "This is going to sting, but we need to see what you've done to yourself."

I gritted my teeth and thought about Maggie. And Camy. And waited while he cleaned my hands and wrists, applied salve, and then wrapped them both in white gauze from the tops of my palms to past my wrists, leaving my thumbs and fingers free. The raw skin throbbed, but it wasn't burning the way it had before.

His touch was warm, gentle and completely confident. Like he knew exactly what he was doing.

Like he'd done this before.

I was getting curious about him.

Agent Thatcher had opened a second bag. Pulling out a vacuum-packed foil package, he ripped into it and handed me a quarter-size disc of something that resembled dried banana. My movements were awkward, with the gauze wrapped around my hands, but I managed to hold the pieces within my fingers. "I don't want to put too much in your stomach, but we have to get some nourishment into you," he said.

I wasn't hungry. And certainly not for crunchy banana, if that's what it was. But the second the morsel touched my tongue, my mouth started to water.

It wasn't because of the taste of whatever he'd given me. That was bland at best. But when the food hit my mouth I craved more. A lot more.

I was coming back to life.

My guardian angel handed me a few pieces at a time, regulating my intake. I was embarrassed by how eagerly I gulped the food. And the water, too, when he handed me the bottle. A few days in captivity and I'd lost all my manners.

And didn't care enough to find them again.

As soon as the foil bag was resealed and stored, he faced me again. "Do you need to, uh, go to the bathroom?"

He had to know I'd already done so. More than once. I stank.

He'd given me the water bottle. I held it with both hands and said, "Not right now."

Nodding, he pulled what looked like sweats and a T-shirt out of the bag. "We need to get you changed."

"I can do that as soon as I get home," I said. And he stopped moving. His hands froze, suspended above my ankles with clothes dangling from them.

"We need to talk about that, too."

"About what?"

"You going home."

Of course I was going home. If he insisted I stop by the Emergency Room to get checked out, I'd agree, but I didn't think I needed to. And after that I was going home.

I'd just been through a harrowing ordeal. I'd been abducted and left for dead. I needed to be surrounded by familiar things. *My* things. To regain my sense of security as rapidly as possible.

I needed to talk to someone about this experience and move forward.

I needed not to dwell on it.

I needed a good night's rest in my own bed.

I needed Maggie and Camy.

I needed…

"When you're ready."

His words, interrupting my own musing, didn't immediately make sense to me. "Ready for what?"

"To talk."

"I'd rather go home first." I'd be able to talk much better after I'd showered.

"We need to talk first." His tone didn't invite argument.

And I wasn't usually an argumentative person. I was good at listening.

So I nodded.

With the clothes lying across his thighs, he sat, legs extended and perpendicular to my feet.

"I don't want anyone to know I found you."

For the first time since the man had identified himself to me, I was afraid of him.

Was *he* my captor, then? Had I been that stupid? That trusting?

My thoughts were surprisingly calm.

He watched me and I tried to remain bland. And when I said nothing, he nodded and continued.

"Forgive me for any improprieties, but I've spent the past forty hours delving into every minute and hidden corner of your life."

I hadn't thought about him knowing me. Only about

him finding me. But I knew the ropes. Knew the lengths investigators went to in their search for missing persons.

"I understand," I said. "You did what you had to in order to find me. And you did. Find me, I mean. Thank you."

His head slightly lowered, he glanced at me. "You have a lot of potential enemies."

I didn't think so. One, obviously. And I was waiting to discover who that one was.

I had an idea who it would be. And I wasn't going to be safe. But we'd get to that. After I got home and had a shower. The cops could bring me home. And stay there while I showered. They could watch over me until the kidnapper was found. I'd had cops stationed at my home several months before. I knew how it worked.

"Your abduction wasn't random," Agent Thatcher said. "And it wasn't amateur."

"What does that mean?"

"It means we believe your kidnapper was a professional. Either hired by someone else or working for himself."

Maybe I was obtuse, but... "A professional what?"

"A professional criminal."

I felt cold again. And flushed, too.

It was the word *criminal* that did it. I dealt with criminals. In my office sometimes. In various courtrooms and examining rooms and in various cities around the country.

And I was starting to understand. Sort of. I wasn't ready to go that far yet. I was ready for home. Protection. And a shower.

"No one knew I'd be going skating yesterday. They couldn't have. I didn't know myself."

"That's part of what leads us to believe this wasn't a random act. There's no way someone could've had the means to get you off that track and in here, leaving no trace, without a plan. There's a six-foot shrub in front of the opening to this cave that blocks it, looks absolutely natural and is completely mobile. That alone took ingenuity."

I thought over what I could remember about Friday morning. Courtney Whalen had canceled because she'd gone into labor. My next appointment wasn't until after lunch.

Deb was the only one who knew I'd left to go skating.

"Are you telling me my receptionist tipped off whoever did this? That she's working for them?" *For him? Deb?* I couldn't believe it.

Deb and… No. Just *no.*

"No." I thought for a second there that Agent Thatcher had heard my thanks. And then I realized he was answering the question I'd posed aloud. "She's been extremely worried about you and fully cooperative. She turned your files over to us."

I cringed at that. I couldn't help it. My files were private. Not for my sake, but for the sake of the people who trusted me to keep their secrets.

I wasn't sure finding me was worth risking the hurt and pain, the broken trust and ruined lives, that could result from making public all the intimacies that had been revealed to me over the years.

But then, police records were private, too. In their own way.

"And her phone records checked out," Agent Thatcher added. "She's neither taken nor received any calls in the past two months, on her personal or work lines, that can't easily be explained."

They hadn't accepted Deb's word at face value. They'd investigated my assistant.

And I saw, by the look on Clay Thatcher's face, that I was in serious trouble.

16

He knew the second the realization hit her. And guessed she had no idea of the hurdles they still had to find a way around. Or over. Or through.

In as few words as possible, he tried to reassure the woman who was trying so hard to be as fine as she said she was in the situation. He was worried, and he'd had forty-some hours to get her up to speed.

And it wasn't his life he was worrying about.

The potential danger would hit her far worse.

He began by telling her his theory about the abduction. About the possibility of there being two utility carts. About the city-worker cover, the plan to take her by surprise on whatever day she happened to be there.

About the obviously newly prepared holding tank. Or grave?

"Do you think he was watching me, then? In Chandler?"

She was frowning, but Clay couldn't read any clear emotions and wondered if having a poker face came with her job description or just with Kelly Chapman.

"I think so. Either that or he had some way of keeping an eye on the bike path, waiting for you to show up."

"How could he do that?"

"I'm not convinced yet that the real city worker who has the path as part of his regular beat is completely innocent here."

"I saw him…" She frowned and huddled more closely under the blanket she'd pulled up around her shoulders, hiding every part of her from the chin down. "I remember now. I was just putting on my skates when he drove by."

"On the path. In a cart."

"Right."

"Did he have anything in the back of his cart?"

Her mouth twisted, and then she shook her head. "I don't remember."

"Were you wearing safety gear?"

"Of course. I always wear a helmet and wrist and knee pads." She looked around. "They aren't here."

"No. And neither is your purse. But no credit or bank cards have been used."

He told her everything he knew about the morning of her abduction. About the sightings. He told her that her abduction had happened so quickly, so flawlessly, that not one person had seen it.

"I was on a deserted part of the path," she said, her eyes glistening. "Sam warned me about being out there all alone. But I've been skating for years and I refused to be held hostage by fear and—"

She broke off and he figured she was probably reassessing that thought.

"She's going to have a lot to say about this…."

"Not the least of which is the danger of being too predictable," Clay added, uncomfortable with the idea that this woman would thrust herself so fearlessly into danger. "But we can talk about that later."

She nodded, then looked him straight in the eye.

"If whoever did this just wanted you dead, you would be," Clay said. "He could've dumped you here, sealed up the opening and you'd have suffocated. But he didn't. He went to the trouble of putting a grate on top of the opening."

"So give me what you've got in the way of suspects."

Clay's respect for her grew. She was a fighter. "The guy you're helping to put away in Florida," he said. "They know he's responsible for twelve deaths in the past couple of years but haven't been able to pin anything on him. They've had him in a number of times for questioning. They've even charged him more than once, but nothing sticks. He walks every time."

"Until now. With my little boy's testimony he's going to be found guilty."

"And without you, there is no little boy's testimony."

"The guy—the stepfather—is in prison."

"He's also the leader of Florida's chapter of a national street gang."

"With a nod of his head he could have any number of professionals out to get me."

She was catching on. Clay decided to move on.

"Rick Thomas," he said next. And watched realization dawn. In a better world he'd be able to spare her. Not here. In this situation she had to know what they were up against.

She had to understand why he was going to ask what he was going to ask….

"I don't know that much about Rick's history, but I understand he had some powerful enemies," she said, her voice growing weaker again.

"Have some water." He waited while she did. "Thomas believes there's a possibility of a government mole in the Department of Defense. A man with everything to lose."

"And if he thinks Rick told me something…"

"They'd want you, as well as any files you have on him, destroyed."

"They broke into Erin's office…"

"For Rick's file. I know."

She leaned her head against the wall, and Clay's entire being rejected the idea of any woman suffering as she had, being forced into a state of such total helplessness.

And yet…he wanted to take care of her. *Wanted to.* Not felt obligated to. Not had to.

God, he was tired. He wasn't himself.

"But you have my files," she said.

"You have friends in the right places," Clay told her. "An investigation that would normally have taken a minimum of twelve hours to get off the ground started in less than one. We secured your files before anyone else had a chance to."

"Whoever's afraid of what Rick told me—if that's what this is all about—will be coming back to get me when they realize there's no way they can access my files. They'll want to know what I know." She paused and then slowly said, "*That's* why there's a grate and not a sealed hole. That's why I'm still alive."

"True. But as we've been discussing, there are other possibilities. For instance, our man in Florida could plan to work you over so you'll get the kid to exonerate him. That way there's no chance of another psychologist coming along to help the kid talk."

She nodded, wincing at the small movement.

"We've already cleared most of your other current clients and the people connected to them," he said. "But…"

He wished he could just let her sleep.

"There's someone else." She sat up, her mouth as firm as the tone of her voice. "A lawyer named David Abrams."

Clay nodded.

"You know about him?"

He nodded a second time.

"He has to be worried that at some point I'm going to have a breakthrough with Maggie."

"We agree. There's a strong possibility that you're Abrams's fourth victim. A businessman's wife died because of Abrams's drug scheme."

"And Glenna Reynolds." Kelly added the second victim's name.

"And there's Maggie, who—"

Kelly cut him off. "You said *we* agree."

"Samantha Jones, JoAnne Laramie, my second-in-command, and me."

"You're letting Samantha help you."

"She didn't give me much of a choice," he admitted.

Kelly sent him a weak grin, and Clay felt like grinning, too.

Chandler, Ohio
Sunday, December 5, 2010

"I saw Maggie looking at Abrams the other day," I said as a flash of memory—and stark fear—struck me. "Maggie and I were at the store. He kept his distance, but the look in his eye—it was proprietary."

"We have an agent on him."

I was eager to hear that they'd have the man in custody soon. The abduction would be worth every moment of agony I'd been through if it led to Abrams's arrest.

"And we believe he and Maggie are in contact."

"No!" I couldn't accept that. I'd watched her so carefully. "No!" I sat up, ready to get out of there. Get home. Get Maggie out of Chandler. Out of Ohio. Maybe even out of the United States. "If he touched her again…"

Oh, God, we'd made it through the whole pregnancy scare. Surely we weren't facing that again. We might not get so lucky a second time.

Maggie was fourteen years old! A child.

She deserved to be a child.

I tried to sit up.

With one hand against my shoulder, Agent Thatcher held me in place.

"It's almost three in the morning. There's nothing you can do right now," he said.

I knew that was true.

But I had to get home.

"We don't think they've had any physical contact." Thatcher's words penetrated my panicked fog. "Our agent followed Abrams to a spot in the woods yesterday morning. Detective Jones confirmed it was where Maggie had her liaison last summer. Abrams picked up a silk rose there, but returned it to the ground."

I waited. There was more. He'd looked away. And while he'd been sitting still before, now he was fingering the zipper on one of the duffels.

"We've got someone on him 24/7 and Detective Jones and her husband aren't letting Maggie out of their sight."

I sat back. Took a deep breath. Of course. Sam could keep Maggie safer than I could. She was trained to deal with things like that.

"So what aren't you telling me?"

"Maggie's been pretty upset. Missing you."

I hoped that was it. I wasn't sure. "I miss her, too. Which is why I have to get home and get cleaned up so I can see her in the morning."

"Even if you leave here, you can't be with Maggie this morning."

My senses, slow to react, reeled. *Even if you leave here?* There was that intimation again that *he* was my captor.

"Why not?" I tackled his last statement first.

"You're sitting in the middle of a cesspool of danger. Whoever took you once went to a lot of trouble to do it.

He's not going to be content just to let you go. He'll make sure he succeeds on the second try. And with his next attempt, he might not pick a time when you're alone."

I stared at him. He was saying I couldn't see Maggie until they found my kidnapper.

"What did you mean by *if* I leave here?"

"There was a ransom call."

I was almost excited at the news. "So we have a tangible lead, after all!"

"We're hoping so." Agent Thatcher's tone wasn't all that encouraging. "We believe the demand is an effort to throw us off course rather than the real reason for the kidnapping." He gave me the details of the two calls and when he explained about the caller's tone of voice and verbal cues, I could tell he knew what he was talking about even if I didn't like the message.

Odd to have a price on my head—even if it was only a diversion. I was worth two million dollars.

"And if I suddenly show up before Monday, we've tipped our hand and lost the lead before we find out who's behind the call."

"Right."

I was beginning to understand where this was going.

"So you want to take me to a safe house someplace until then?"

"Not exactly."

I frowned. And drank a little more water. I was going to need a bathroom soon.

And was trying not to think about the state I was in, sitting there with a man who'd gotten closer to me—in every sense—than any man had in years. I was relying on him. I needed him.

I understood that. And I understood why. He was my savior. It was natural that I'd feel a sense of safety and security with him. That I'd develop a sort of crush on him.

"I've put out a lot of feelers—set up a lot of investigations," he was explaining. "If I bring you in, this is no longer a missing persons case and it gets turned over. The new team might follow up on what I've started, or they might go on a tangent of their own. If that happens we lose valuable time as they get up to speed."

I was listening.

"That's one consideration. Another, far more important one is the risk that if *anyone* knows you're alive, there's a greater chance the kidnapper will find out, too. In that scenario you are immediately vulnerable to another attack. The FBI team will be following protocol, which could put you in more danger rather than ensure your safety."

"Because we're possibly looking at someone with connections." I might still be groggy, but I was pretty sure I was keeping up with him.

"Right."

"Like Abrams. He obviously has a lot of friends in town. Maybe even on the police force. I mean, besides Sewell. Who's dead."

"I'm not willing to risk finding out. Are you?" He was staring straight at me, his gaze intense.

He'd said, *If you leave here*. I was sore, tired, hungry and needed a bath. My head ached. And I was scared. My hands felt mummified. I wasn't sure what he was suggesting.

Maggie. Had *she* left that rose for Abrams?

"No." I wasn't willing to take the risk.

17

The rock surface beneath him was cutting off his circulation. Clay shifted his weight as well as he could, moving his legs—and wondered how in hell Kelly Chapman had endured two days on this surface without the ability to move more than a few inches.

"I'm reasonably certain we're safe here tonight," he said now, thinking only of the facts before him. *Focus.* That was what it took. Focus. "If, as I suspect, our man is using a city-worker cover, he's not going to blow it by being out at night. Nor is he going to risk being stopped and questioned, which he could be if he were on the trail at night. A cop driving down one of the streets the trail crosses, having seen him, would surely ask if he needed assistance."

She nodded.

"But by morning, all of that changes. There's going to be another search team out here. Our kidnapper, if he has connections and knows I'm on to his cover, that I've put out feelers for purchases of city uniforms and vehicles, could easily be among the searchers."

Her chin tightened and she bit her lower lip, but she didn't drop her gaze.

"I want to take you to my place." God, that sounded bad. *Come up and see my etchings.*

"Most of the work I do, at this stage of a case, is by phone," he said. "Coordinating, following up on leads. My agents are out in the field a good part of the day. In different circumstances I'd have other cases on my desk and be working on them, as well, but I've been assigned to you exclusively."

Eyes wide, she continued to stare at him. And say nothing.

"I've got state-of-the-art security at my place," he said, and tried to grin, but figured he'd failed miserably. "In my line of work you see how easy it can be for someone's safety to be breached."

She nodded again.

"And most importantly, I can be here in town, solving this case, and protecting you, even at night, without raising suspicion. I'll be where I'm expected to be."

"You're going to take me home with you?"

"Yes." Clay wondered why her question had instilled an aggressive need to protect rather than a sense of obligation.

"At least until Monday, when we make the ransom exchange. In the meantime, I'll have someone posted on all trail points in case the kidnapper comes back to get you before then."

"Okay." Just like that. No tears. No complaints.

Clay worked with lots of strong women. JoAnne Laramie, for example. But he'd never seen one as soft—was that the right word?—as Kelly Chapman and as self-sufficient at the same time.

He handed her the foil bag. "Eat a little more and drink what you can to get some of your energy back, and then we have to go. We need you at my place before it starts to get light."

"Where do you live?"

"Edgewood." In a nice subdivision with an acre and a

half of wooded lawns. Where she'd be trusting him with her life.

"I'm sorry it has to be this way."

"Don't be sorry, Agent Thatcher. I'm grateful. Extremely grateful. I'm just not sure why you're willing to do this for me."

The "Agent Thatcher" had to go....

Before he could say that, she went on. "I will do whatever you tell me to do until we find this guy, so I can get back to Maggie without putting her at risk. She's the one who's been through enough. The kid's fourteen years old and has endured more hardship than most adults twice her age."

She hid her fear well. But he saw it, lurking beneath the shadows in her eyes.

Was he crazy?

"I think it's a good plan," she said.

Clay studied her. And saw the eyes in the photo on his dash. What the hell was going on here?

"You're sure?"

"Positive." She nibbled on dried fruit and dehydrated beef. Swallowed. "Terrified, but positive."

"Then I have one more request."

"What?"

"Don't call me Agent Thatcher. My name's Clay."

Cave
Sunday, December 5, 2010

As Clay talked about getting me out of there, I was a lot calmer than I would've expected to be. It was like I was living in some kind of suspended reality, a place with no rules, no common understanding. I was taking each minute, each second, as it came to me.

"I know what I'm doing." I said the words out loud as I

sat there looking at the frown on Clay's face. "I don't like the situation, but I really do believe that your suggestion is the best one."

"I have to be honest with you about something." His expression was pained, his cheeks pinched. Uncomfortable.

"What?"

"I have another reason for wanting to do this."

Maybe I should've been worried. I wasn't. More of that suspended reality thing? "What is it?"

"This might be a clichéd way of putting it…but I've taken ownership of this job."

In my regular life I was used to hearing confessions— though not like a minister or priest. My job involved understanding, not judging. Or absolving.

"I don't know how you could help it in your job. You deal with life-and-death emotions every single day." It felt good to have a normal moment.

"No." He shook his head, but didn't lower his gaze. "I mean this particular case. You. I don't want to turn your care over to anyone else."

Oh. "Why?"

"Because I know I can get these guys and I don't trust anyone else to watch over you like I will."

"Are you an egotistical man?"

"Probably. But that's not what this is about."

"What is it about, then?"

"I'm not sure." He shook his head again, still looking me in the eye. "I just feel strongly that I don't want to turn this one over. I wanted you to know so that if my reasoning has any flaws, if I'm manipulating the situation so I can keep this case, you have a chance to find me out."

A man with integrity. If I wasn't already suffering from a bad case of hero worship, he'd just started one.

"Thank you," I said. "If I'd seen any flaws in your reasoning, I wouldn't have agreed to the plan."

"Okay."

"Okay." I was losing energy again. "Do you mind, though, if I change into…" I gestured to the clothes he'd pulled out of the bag. I couldn't ride in his car smelling like I did.

He held out the pants.

"Could you please turn around and move away?"

He reached into the bag and handed me a container of antibacterial wipes, then turned away, hunched down and pushed himself as close to the entrance as he could get without hitting his head.

It was fifty-six degrees in there, but Clay was sweating. He could hear fabric rustling. And squelched all visions of his victim pulling pants down those long, firm thighs. She'd be forced to go more slowly due to the bandages on her hands.

Using every ounce of mental control he had, he tried not to remember how muscled her lower limbs had felt as he'd run his hands along them earlier.

He'd been thinking only of broken bones and other injuries when he'd touched her before. What a cruel trick of human nature that his mind had stored other pieces of intimate information to taunt him now.

More rustling. She'd been wearing insulated underalls.

And one more time—barely audible. Panties.

He heard the tear of the wipe's wrapper.

Her bottom was naked over there. Behind him.

And he was a sick man for thinking about it.

He heard cloth rubbing against skin, and pictured the gauze he'd placed around those delicate, feminine hands….

First thing in the morning he'd call JoAnne. Have her come out with the others who'd be going over the bike path one more time, searching for utility-vehicle tire tracks that veered off the path....

Material rustled again. Were her legs white? Or did they have the golden sheen of year-round tan...?

"Okay, all done."

He turned too soon. Saw her rolling her track pants around a flimsy scrap of white lace and, taking the bundle, she crawled back and stashed it behind the curve in the wall. Her bottom faced him for those few seconds.

She wasn't wearing panties under those sweats....

Clay almost took himself off the case then and there.

18

Cave
Sunday, December 5, 2010

I watched Clay try to get comfortable in what had become his half of the cave during the hour or so we'd been sitting there talking. He adjusted and readjusted himself. Bent one leg, then the other.

He was a man who needed to be pacing, I decided. Whereas I dreaded actually moving. After two days of forced nonmovement, my entire body was achy and stiff.

Clay figured I should have another half hour of slow eating and drinking before we headed out.

We'd been talking about David Abrams. I told him everything I knew about the man. And then moved on to my impressions of him—admittedly biased. We repeated information we'd already discussed.

And then something struck me. A memory. Or a dream?

"I saw a boot," I said slowly, hoping I was right. And afraid that I wasn't. God, I hated this—not being in control of my own mind.

Not being certain of it.

Just the idea of not being clear-minded panicked me.

And I couldn't remember…couldn't be sure…

"Saw a boot where?" Clay's look was intense.

"I'm not positive. In here, I think. I can't remember much about Friday. I slept for a long time. I think maybe he drugged me…."

"He might've held something over your face to knock you out. You also have a large bruise on your temple," Clay reminded me—not like I could forget. My head still throbbed.

"What kind of boot did you see?"

Back to the boot. I tried to pull out the memory. Make it clear. "It's black," I said, feeling certain about that. "A work boot, maybe, with a thick rounded toe."

"What size?"

"I just saw the front of it."

"Did it have laces?"

"I just saw the toe."

"Steel-toed?" He held my gaze, and I pictured the boot.

"Yes," I said, slightly relieved to be able to answer his question. "Yes, it was one of those steel-toed boots." And then I was forcibly struck by another impression. "I think I was lying down when I saw it. It was at eye level."

Expression grim, Clay said, "Maybe that's how you got your head injury."

"How?"

"Maybe he kicked you."

God, I hoped not. Just the idea of someone kicking me, especially when I couldn't do anything about it, made me want to curl up in the fetal position.

But Clay could very well be right. I tried to remember. To know for sure what had happened to me.

"There's something else." Not about the boot, I didn't think, but…

"What?"

"I just remembered being on the track." Speaking slowly I tried to stay calm—to give my thoughts the space they needed to reveal themselves to me.

My head hurt so much. And thinking just made it worse. But I had to know. Had to help him in any way I could.

Tears choked my throat, filled my eyes. I wanted to lie down and go back to sleep.

But I made myself look at Clay. And look within myself, as well. I could do this. I was strong. Right?

"I heard a noise," I said as the memory surfaced, briefly, and then left again.

"What kind of noise?"

I stared at him. "I don't know. It was there and then… it was gone." I hated feeling so stupid. So helpless.

"Relax," Clay told me what I'd told hundreds of people throughout my career. "It'll come back to you when you're ready."

He was right. I knew that. And yet I still wanted to come up with whatever information was hidden within my brain. Come up with it as quickly as possible.

According to Clay, more than a hundred people had been up and down the eighteen-mile bike path in the past two days—although that astonished me. I hadn't heard a thing.

Because I'd been unconscious?

Or had I heard and just couldn't remember?

Those searchers hadn't heard me calling out, either, although now I wasn't even sure I had. I remembered being afraid to make a sound in case my kidnapper came back to hurt me. In case he was watching me.

"My guess is it was dark when you called out," he said. "The searches were called off at dusk."

In any case, one hundred people had been searching and they hadn't found me.

Clay had.

And there was something else I had to tell him.

Resting my head against the wall, I tried to hide. From Clay. From hard truths. And knew I couldn't hide anymore.

"There's another possibility here." Panic swamped me anew as I heard my voice say the words—as I heard the door open.

It was a more insidious panic than I'd been feeling on and off for the past two days. It climbed slowly through me and held on, destroying me from the inside out.

I recognized the feeling. And fought it.

"Did you just remember something?" Clay was staring at me and, judging by the concerned look on his face, some of what I was feeling must've been showing on mine.

"No. Except…I know of someone else who might be behind this."

"Who?"

"My father." Saying the words brought no relief. Only more of that feeling of debilitating helplessness. There were just some things I couldn't avoid. Couldn't fix. Couldn't change.

No matter how many degrees I got or how successful I became. I could help a thousand people and still not be able to help him.

"Your parents are both dead," he said slowly, enunciating each word as though he wasn't sure I'd understand them.

"My mother's dead," I told him. "My father isn't."

Some quality in my voice must have alerted him to my lucidity because Clay sat back, leaned against the wall across from me and asked, "Where is he?"

"I'm not sure. Last I knew he was someplace in Tennessee."

"Your car was found in Tennessee. In Knoxville."

Had he told me that already? I didn't remember hearing

it. And was flooded with a series of questions. "You said my purse is gone. What about my cell phone?"

"Gone, too, although no calls have been made from it. Your car had been completely cleaned out. Professionally cleaned. Vacuumed. Shampooed. Inside and out. Maggie said you had zipper pulls in the console, and a little bean-bag dog on the dash."

"That's right." Those zipper pulls had been a symbol to Maggie and me. We'd thought it an omen that we'd found a *Kelly* one and a *Maggie* one. I'd bought them and she put them on the dash. She'd said they were like a promise of more trips together in the future. We were going to collect tags from each state we visited together.

I could remember the incident as clearly as if it was happening right then.

"They were gone, too."

I teared up again. And made myself stop. I couldn't afford to be weak right now.

"Tell me about your father."

"He was my mom's dealer. And probably her pimp, too. Her pimp first. She quit hooking when she got pregnant with me." My head against the wall, I kept talking. "She tried to stop the drugs while she was pregnant, but she never totally quit using. I'm lucky I wasn't born a crack baby."

"The state let you stay with her?"

"Other than the drugs, she was a good mom. Good enough to convince child protective services that I was healthy, safe and loved. At least to their standards."

"Were you?"

"She loved me. She loved herself and drugs more. It took me a long time to figure that out."

I knew Clay was a smart man when he didn't push any further. My life growing up had nothing to do with tonight.

"Was your father in the picture?"

"On and off until I was three. Then, after that, my mother told me he was dead. I didn't find out differently until she died. He showed up at the trailer the day of her funeral."

"How old were you?"

"Twenty-four."

"And you still lived at home with her?" From one professional interrogator to another…

"No. I had my own place. I'd tried to get her to move in with me, but she wouldn't leave the trailer. I was there trying to decide what I was going to do with her stuff when he knocked on the door."

"Did you recognize him?"

"No. And I didn't believe him when he told me who he was. I assumed he was one of my mother's druggie friends trying to get something out of me. I sent him away with a threat to call the police.

"The next week, I did some checking and found out that the man named on my birth certificate was very much alive. The next time he came by, I made him give me a DNA sample. The third time, I handed over the money he asked for in return for his silence regarding my paternity."

"He's been blackmailing you."

"No. He didn't threaten to tell anyone who he was. He just wanted money. And I knew I was going to give it to him. He was my father. And although that meant nothing except a biological detail—at the same time it meant *something*. He's the only living family I have. I'm the one who made the stipulation. But if he hadn't agreed to my terms, I'd have given him the money, anyway."

"Do you think he knew that?"

"No."

I closed my eyes again, thinking back. Not because I wanted to talk about any of this, but because I had to tell Clay everything I knew in case he found a clue there. Something I'd missed myself, being too close.

"I tried to get him clean and sober. I paid for treatment centers. For personal therapy. I made weekly visits and phone calls. Nothing worked. And I finally had to realize that nothing would work for one reason and one reason only." I looked at Clay. "He doesn't want to be clean. He is what he is and he's comfortable with the life he lives."

Hard to believe, even though I knew firsthand the vagaries of the human condition.

Clay's look was intent again—and focused on me. "When was the last time you heard from him?"

"After I got back from Michigan. He stopped by the house one morning. Maggie had just left for school." And this was why I had to tell Clay about him. "I panicked." As usual. Every single time the man showed up in my life, whether by phone call or in person, I panicked. Pure and simple.

"I was afraid he'd find out about Maggie. I didn't have any clear idea of what he could do to her, or would do to her, I just didn't want him touching her life in any way. And I didn't want him in mine."

"You were starting a new family. You didn't need him."

My thoughts slowed. I heard his words, and knew I'd think about them again.

"I told him to leave, that I wasn't giving him any more money. Period. I told him that if he ever contacted me again, I'd have him arrested."

Eyes narrowed, Clay studied me until I felt like some kind of specimen. "So he has a grudge" was all he said.

"I guess so."

"But this scheme, the elaborate planning, the patience... is he capable of such a thing?"

"He has an IQ of one hundred and thirty."

My mom had barely been able to finish high school. She'd never been particularly smart. But I'd whizzed through school without even trying. I'd have gotten that ability from somewhere. So back when I'd been desperately fighting the truth about my paternity, which was staring me in the face, I'd asked him to agree to a series of tests.

The results had astounded—and sickened—me. So much potential. So much waste. And I'd gotten part of who I was from him.

"What's his name?"

I hesitated. And I thought of Maggie. Of getting home to her. "Ezekial." The word burst out of me. "Ezekial Greene."

"Ezekial?" I could see the question in Clay's raised eyebrow.

"His father was a pastor—believe it or not."

"I'll put an APB out on him first thing in the morning," Clay said.

I hoped my drug-addicted father was the kidnapper. I hoped they arrested him and got him off the street. And I didn't feel even a twinge of guilt for that sentiment.

What did that say about me?

19

Cave
Sunday, December 5, 2010

Clay knelt, grabbing the duffels' straps, shoving them toward the door. I realized our departure was imminent—and was petrified to move. To go out there, where danger waited for me. My confinement had become my safety. It was all I knew in this frightening new world.

I was outside myself looking in. Sitting in a chair in my office. I'd describe this to my clients as distancing. Taking a step back so I could better handle a situation that was threatening my emotional equilibrium.

"Can I ask a favor?"

"Of course. What do you need?"

"Just a pen and some paper. I think best when I can write." That, at least, hadn't changed.

He reached into his pocket, pulled out his notepad, ripped out the used pages, which he stuffed back in his pocket, and handed me the notebook. There was a small pen attached.

The pen looked so…normal. I was afraid to touch it.

"Something wrong?"

"I…chew on pens. I'm trying to break the habit, but…"

I was trying to find the courage to crawl out into the night and face whatever the next days would bring.

Clay shrugged and said, "You chew on it. It's yours."

Cave
Sunday, December 5, 2010

"Time to go."

I'd been waiting for the words. Dreading them. "The hardest part is getting started," I said aloud, caught in a fog of panic.

Logically, I understood what was going on. But that wasn't helping.

"Getting started?" Clay Thatcher sat there looking at me as though we had all the time in the world to embark on the Sunday stroll ahead of us.

"I'm scared." There. I'd admitted it.

"You should be."

No. No, I shouldn't be. The only thing to fear was fear itself. I knew that. I...

"Fear keeps you aware of danger. It keeps you safe."

Was he blaming me for my predicament? "Is that your way of telling me that if I'd had enough sense to be afraid of skating alone on a deserted path I wouldn't be in danger now?"

"Absolutely not! Whoever grabbed you was determined. And patient. If he hadn't had a chance to take you while you were skating he'd have found another way."

My stomach calmed a bit as I listened to him.

And then a new churning began. *He* could ease my emotional distress but I couldn't?

That was a new one.

One I didn't like.

At all.

* * *

They had to get out of there. Dawn was approaching and Clay wanted Kelly Chapman safely ensconced in his home before daylight.

"Ready?" he asked, on all fours as he faced the opening that led out into the night. She was right behind him, also on hands and knees.

"Yes." Her answer was firm. Definite. Or would have been if her voice hadn't wavered.

"Just remember what I told you." He moved forward a couple of inches and then paused. "I go out first. When I turn back for you, get yourself up to the ground as quickly as possible. Stand behind the tree trunk while I close up the cave and then we walk briskly to my car."

"Got it." Her voice was stronger. "And once we get in the car, I lie down on the floor behind the front seat until we're in your garage. I'm planning to sleep."

He moved forward a little more and then stopped. "It's okay to be afraid, you know."

"I know."

"It's okay to show that you're afraid."

She looked as though she was about to speak and then her mouth stiffened. Her entire body stiffened. "Can we go?"

He was worried about her. And she wasn't asking for his pity or compassion at all. She wasn't asking for anything from him. She was asking way too much of herself.

"You sure you're feeling okay?"

"I'm a little dizzy, headachy, but I'm fine. I'm not going to be if I have to sit here on my hands and knees much longer. My arms are shaky."

With that, Clay got his butt—and hers—out of there.

Maggie didn't sleep much. She couldn't. Life was just too awful. And every time she tried to make it better, it got worse.

She'd lied to Samantha. And Kyle, too, for that matter, but that didn't bother her quite as much as lying to Samantha.

Mac hadn't come for her yet. Hadn't sent a signal.

But he'd been there. He'd moved the flower. That was to let her know he'd gotten her call for help. He'd take care of her. He'd promised. He loved her.

And as soon as he found a way to contact her, she'd tell him her plan.

They had to leave the country. Go to one of those places she'd learned about on the internet where they allowed older men to marry younger girls.

And as soon as they were gone and Mac was safe from all the lies, she'd let Samantha know that she was afraid her mother knew who'd taken Kelly.

She'd probably burn in hell for ratting on her own mother, especially since Mom had sacrificed her whole life for Maggie.

Maggie hated that she was the kind of person who'd turn on one of her own.

It would look like she was choosing Kelly over her mom. She loved Kelly so much. But she loved Mom just as much. Just…differently.

No, she wasn't choosing between Mom and Kelly. She was choosing between right and wrong.

Bike Trail
Sunday, December 5, 2010

The night air was freezing. Clay had wrapped the blanket around me, and I held it in place with one hand while I hurried beside him to his car. Everything about me ached. Every step I took.

I didn't look to either side. I tried not to see anything at all. I focused on my goal.

The back of Clay's dark sedan. Getting there alive.

We didn't speak. And when we reached his car, he opened the front door and the back at the same time, ushering me in under his arm and into position without a word.

The car light was on for a brief second, before Clay shut it off, but that second was long enough for me to notice my picture stuck to the front dash.

The sight unnerved me.

A lot.

Two thousand utility carts of the model used by the path maintenance team had been purchased over the past six months in a fifty-mile radius of Chandler. The number increased exponentially when the search was expanded.

And those were only sales of *new* vehicles.

They were looking for the proverbial needle in a haystack.

The city itself had sold part of their working fleet of utility carts over the past year after employee cutbacks, but each of those sales had been checked out and the new, private owners had alibis.

City-worker uniforms were a standard issue sold at every farm supply store in the tri-state area.

Clay had Greg following up, searching through thousands of sales receipts, looking for any of the names on their lists, making calls. A job that could take the next month to get through.

But they might get lucky. The first or fifth or twenty-fifth call might be the one.

Seven utility carts had been reported stolen in the past month within a two-hundred-mile radius of Chandler and Brookwood. Barry looked into those. And turned up nothing.

Clay checked on the property where he'd found Kelly's

cave. It was public land. He searched maps of the area on the internet and found one that had been produced by the Fort County Historical Society. It depicted known pre-Civil War slave hideaways. Clay printed out the map and compared it to the one he'd used that night on the path. Kelly's prison was on both.

So far, no Ezekial Greene had shown up anywhere in Tennessee or Ohio. Not with the Department of Motor Vehicles in either state. Not with arrest warrants or in police databases or mortgage loan requests. Nor had he filed taxes in the past twenty years or applied for a marriage license. At least, not under the name Kelly knew.

The man existed. He'd visited Kelly as recently as the previous month. But he lived his life completely and totally under the radar.

For the record, Clay had claimed he'd gotten the man's name from a copy of Kelly's birth certificate. And he'd said that as a precaution, Barry should look for any identifiers they could find on the man. Anyone who knew him. Who could describe him. Barry had connections among some of the homeless guys downtown. Two-bit drug users. Maybe they'd know something.

The agents and volunteers who spent the morning out on the bike path had no luck. That was one negative report Clay was happy to get. He'd removed Kelly Chapman from the scene without leaving any evidence.

No one knew he had her.

She was still sleeping. She'd been ready to drop by the time they'd arrived just before five that morning. He'd ushered her into his home, an arm around her back, steadying her, and taken her straight back to the spare bedroom across the hall from his master suite. Her room wasn't much—a queen mattress on a frame. And four empty, unmatched dressers lining the walls, brought from bedrooms in his parents' home. They were probably antiques, but Clay hadn't bothered to check that out.

The room Clay had to offer Kelly bore no resemblance whatsoever to the warm, decorated and peaceful haven she had at home, but there were sheets on the bed and, through another door, she had her own bathroom.

He'd stood outside the door of that bath while she'd showered, leaving her some modesty, but ready to take charge at the first indication that she was in trouble.

She'd come out ten minutes later, dressed in the gray sweats and Boston Red Sox T-shirt he'd given her, her hair wet and sticking up. She'd apologized for being so needy and asked if he minded if she got some sleep.

He'd been dismissed.

And he hadn't heard a sound from her since.

Sometime shortly after noon, Clay made another trek down the hall to the closed door of his temporary housemate's room. When there was still no sign of life from inside, he quietly turned the knob and looked in on her. She was a small lump under his grandmother's quilt, curled up, her face to the wall.

Her hair had dried.

He swallowed and closed the door. Left a note on the kitchen counter—the table was covered with files and reports and lists—and made a quick run to a Wal-Mart about half a mile from his house.

Not wanting to be gone long, Clay got a cart and threw in toothpaste, toothbrush, hairbrush and comb. And then, as he passed by, he grabbed some feminine-looking shampoo, figuring one was pretty much like another. In the deodorant aisle, he wasn't as sure. Should he get antiperspirant and deodorant combined, like he did for himself? Or was just deodorant enough? After a second of indecision, he chose one of each.

Clothes were next. Something to get her by for a day or

two. He grabbed the first packet of women's underwear he came across, looking at them only long enough to find an *S* on the package. Kelly Chapman was a small woman.

Bras didn't come in packages. Clay stood in front of the wall with rods of hanging straps. He'd have been more comfortable facing a gun.

He couldn't do it. He turned away. And thought of the woman in his home braless.

He couldn't do that, either.

What the hell was the matter with him? He was on a *case*. A woman's life was at stake, and he was thinking about her breasts?

On a rack behind the wall were packages of sports bras. Clay guessed at her size, grabbed one and ran.

He snatched three pairs of jeans as he walked past them—three sizes in the same style—and a black fleece top, then strode back to find the tennis shoes. He added a few pairs to his cart.

He'd donate whatever didn't fit to a women's shelter.

On his way from the shoes to the checkout, Clay passed the beauty aisle.

In the picture of Kelly Chapman that he'd quickly pulled from his dash after he'd helped her into his car early that morning, she'd appeared natural—as though she wore little makeup.

But wasn't that the point of makeup? To make a woman look natural? Who knew what it took to create that effect?

He'd never lived with a woman other than his mother. And her life hadn't required artfully applied cosmetics. Or any cosmetics. She'd been too busy coping with arthritic joints—and needing his father's attention every minute of every day—to care about how she looked.

Three minutes had passed while Clay stood there staring. Impatient with himself, he got one of everything in a brand whose name he recognized. With a last-minute vision of the soda in Kelly Chapman's fridge, he grabbed some Diet Coke. Then he hurried to the checkout, paid with cash and got back home before he had to acknowledge that he'd lost his mind.

He'd just pulled in the drive when his cell rang and JoAnne's number flashed on the display.

"He called again. Still couldn't get a trace." His second-in-command cut right to the chase.

"What'd he say?" Sitting in the garage, the automatic door closing behind him, Clay had to remember to play the game from both sides—with what he actually knew and what he was supposed to know.

"That we're to put the money inside a blue backpack and leave it under the slide at the old elementary school playground in Chandler."

"When?"

"Tomorrow morning—11:45. He said that as soon as he's safely away with the money, he'll tell us where we can find Dr. Chapman. If he's detained, the bomb attached to her stomach will detonate."

It was all going to be over in less than twenty-four hours.

"Does he know he's talking to a cop?" Sam was answering Kelly's phone. She could be anybody.

"I don't think so, but he didn't seem all that concerned one way or the other. He didn't issue an order for no police."

Ordinarily that would be a problem. For once, Clay wasn't concerned about the immediate safety of his victim.

Eleven forty-five. What was particular about that time? Transportation to catch?

"He said one other thing." JoAnne's voice interrupted Clay's thoughts.

"What?"

"That there's a second bomb to ensure he makes it out of the country."

"Did he say where it is?"

"No. Only that children will die."

"And because Chapman's car turned up in Tennessee we can reasonably assume this second bomb could be planted anywhere between here and there."

"Yup."

Goddammit to hell.

20

I'd been up an hour. I'd showered again, once I found the plastic shopping bags hanging on the handle of my door, and I was feeling better in the jeans and soft black top he'd purchased for me. None of the tennis shoes fit—they were all too big—but he'd forgotten socks, too, so I'd improvised. I'd hand-washed my skate socks, and with them on, plus some toilet paper in the toes, I could keep one of the pairs of shoes on my feet.

I was happy to have a manageable task to focus on.

I'd taken the bandages off my hands so the air could heal my scraped skin, but I put on the salve Clay had given me.

My body still ached, like I'd been run over by something.

"He could be bluffing." I spoke to the man who was the only other inhabitant of my small world. He'd just told me about the latest call from the kidnapper.

We were at the table in the eating nook off his kitchen. A bay window looked out on a wooded back lot, or so he told me. He had shutters closed over them, blocking the view. The rest of the kitchen area was filled with papers. I'd even had to move some to sit down.

He'd made coffee. Served me a cup without asking. I never drank the stuff.

"We know for certain I don't have a bomb attached to my stomach," I said when Clay didn't immediately respond.

He'd made toast, too. With peanut butter. I'd eaten one piece.

No bomb. I added that to the list I'd made in the small notebook Clay had given me—eons ago, it seemed—in the cave outside town.

"If he's for real, he's likely planning to attach it to you tomorrow morning," Clay said. "Or maybe after dark tonight. If he knows about today's investigations, if he knows his cover's blown, he'll probably try to get to you tonight. You can be sure he has a back way to that spot in the woods."

I wished I hadn't eaten that toast. It felt like I had peanut butter stuck in my throat.

"So if he's for real and goes to put a bomb on me, what happens when I'm not there?"

"Any number of things can happen. If he's really after the money, he'll most likely go through with the delivery, anyway. Statistically, kidnappers often don't return their victims even after a successful ransom pay. Returned victims are evidence. Besides, he doesn't really need you at this point."

"But wouldn't he worry, if I'm gone, that you found me and that he has no leverage? If he shows up, you'll just arrest him."

"He says he's planted a second bomb. If he doesn't get safely out of the country, it goes off. And children die."

"Do you believe him?"

"I can't afford not to."

He was listening to me. But I had a feeling his mind was way ahead of mine. Which made me uncomfortable.

And scared. Okay. I was scared. Someone out there wanted me dead for some as yet unknown reason.

"Tell me what you're thinking," I finally said.

"This man sounds serious. If this is about the money, he's going to show up for his payoff whether he has you or not. Whether he knows you're in the cave or not."

"So then what?"

"We put a tracer in the money. The bills are marked. I'll have an undercover agent on him. And we hope to God we put enough pieces together to find the second bomb before it detonates. If there *is* a second bomb. But we have to assume there is."

"You think he'd still set it off?"

"Without a doubt."

"And if he's really after *me?*" I remembered Clay saying that the ransom call could just be a distraction. Hadn't he?

My mind was clear this afternoon, but my memory was still pretty foggy.

"As soon as he realizes you aren't in that cave, he's going to be looking for you. And he goes with plan B where you're concerned."

Plan B, I jotted down. Because I didn't know what else to do. *Plan B.* An innocuous statement that had no specific intent—other than to get me.

"Say the ransom call *is* just a distraction, then he won't be going back to the cave, right? He won't know I'm gone."

"Maybe not."

His look said more. "What?"

Frowning, he studied me. I withstood the perusal. And he seemed to make a decision about something.

"Whoever took you did a lot of planning. He's sharp. Aware. A guy like that doesn't just kidnap you and walk away."

"Unless it's the guy in Florida and all they need is to have me gone." I was actually hoping someone from the Florida case was behind this nightmare from which I couldn't wake up. I'd rather deal with a street gang than a national security threat. Or David Abrams.

I was hoping no one was coming back for me.

"Even if the street gang is behind this, they're going to watch their backs. Make sure you stay gone. Make sure you aren't found."

"So you do think the kidnapper's going back for me no matter what?"

"I think we have to assume he's keeping an eye on us. No one followed us last night. I'm confident no one knows you're here, but we have to assume he knows his cover is blown, because with the questions we're asking, it wouldn't be hard for him to figure out. Even without an inside source. All he'd have to do is the same thing we're doing. Check with suppliers. Ask a few people if questions have been asked." He took a gulp of coffee from a mug with an inscription that read *World's Greatest Boss.* The word *Boss* had been struck out and underneath it read *Zookeeper.*

I put his pen in my mouth. And took it out again, embarrassed. Too late. He'd seen me.

The pen was now mine.

"I don't know whether or not he's coming back for you," Clay said. "That depends on why he took you in the first place. If your abduction has anything to do with Rick Thomas, and they've now realized they won't be able to access your files, then they're going to need you."

"You've got people watching my house and office, right?" I thought he'd told me that.

"Yes."

"So they can't get to my things."

"Not without a fight and the risk of getting caught."

"If they need the information badly enough, they'll take that risk."

I was going to have to ask for a Diet Coke. I needed the caffeine.

I'd rather just go to the store and get some myself. And stop by my life on the way. Spend a while there. Like the next sixty years.

Then, if they still wanted me, I'd come back here.

"We've got three possibilities. One, this ransom call is legitimate and we'll know that when we catch the guy. Two, it's from the kidnapper and he's trying to throw us off the scent. Three, there's someone behind your disappearance with a completely different agenda. In which case, the ransom demand could be pure opportunism. For now, I have to assume that whoever wanted you gone will be watching to make sure you stay gone until he decides to free you. *If* he decides to free you."

"And that means I'm not going to be free—or safe—until you find him."

"Correct. And at this point, with a threat made against children, I have to take this ransom call seriously." He paused. "You aren't drinking your coffee. I got Diet Coke. Would you like some?"

"I'd love some," I said gratefully.

He got up to fetch me a can and a glass with ice.

I took a long drink. "What do you want me to do?" I asked.

"Stay here. Don't walk in front of any windows. Don't peek outside even from a distance. Don't attempt to contact anyone, by any means, or get on the computer, even to browse or play games. If anyone, including other FBI agents, were to get suspicious about my activities, or suspect

I've found you, and start to monitor my online activities, we don't want anything that doesn't fit my patterns."

"What about the stuff you bought this morning?" He'd picked out and paid for the underwear I had on. The frumpiest, old-lady briefs I'd ever pulled on. I'd had to roll the waistband down three inches just so they didn't come up above the waist of the jeans.

"I went through self-checkout and paid cash. And dropped off a bag of stuff in the bin at the women's shelter in Edgewood. Something I do on a fairly regular basis."

I made a note of that. On the *Clay* page I'd started.

"If someone was really looking, wouldn't he be able to tell that what you donated wasn't what you'd purchased?"

"Not without a hell of a lot of checking." He was looking for something, riffling through pages.

"How many pairs of jeans did you buy?"

He didn't glance up. "Three."

"That's how many you brought home. What'd you donate?" It didn't matter. I asked, anyway.

"A bag of stuff I already had in the car."

I watched him. And thought about that. I was more interested in his donations than in sitting there panicking over the fact that I couldn't leave. That I couldn't do anything I wanted or needed to do because if I did I could end up dead. Or Maggie could.

I thought about his donations because I needed a break from wondering who hated me so much they'd knocked me out, thrown me in a hole in the ground and left me to die.

"You randomly buy stuff and donate it?" I asked after a small silence.

"What?" Clay looked at me then. "Do I—" He broke off. "No, I buy stuff for my mother, she picks out what she wants and I donate the rest."

"Regularly."

"Yes."

He'd answered my question, but I wasn't satisfied. His answer had just produced more questions. The first of which was, *You have a mother?*

Of course, biologically, everyone had a mother. But Clay Thatcher didn't seem the type who had a mother in his life.

The starkness of his house spoke of pure bachelorhood. No female influence at all.

"I've got to make some calls, and I need to put in an appearance at the office," he said, his voice filled with the urgency I'd come to expect from him. An urgency that instilled all the fear I was trying so desperately to avoid. "You going to be okay?" he murmured.

He'd explained the security system. The dead bolts on the doors that were locked and unlocked with a key from the inside. And he'd shown me how to use the little pistol he'd produced from somewhere in the back of his house.

A smaller gun than the one he was wearing beneath the tweed jacket he'd had on when I got up. The jacket was blue this time instead of yesterday's brown.

"I'll be fine," I told him, hating the way my insides quaked at the thought of being alone again, even for a second.

"You know what to do?"

"You want me just to sit here quietly."

He took another sip of coffee as he stood. "Yes."

"I'm not good at that."

"Then get good at it."

I didn't think this was a great time to become high-maintenance.

"Contact the superintendent of Chandler schools," Clay told JoAnne as soon as he had her on the phone Sunday afternoon. She was at the office, having just come from the Evans farm. "I don't want one kid within a half-mile radius of that school in the morning."

"Okay. And Sam's checking for recent sales of materials commonly used in homemade bombs. She did a chemical search last summer and has all the resources. I couldn't stop her, Clay. She's a detective and—"

"JoAnne." He interrupted her midsentence. "It's okay." As a general rule—okay, always—Clay was territorial about their cases. No one else involved. Period. Outside help invariably got messy. And lines of command got blurred.

But nothing about this case was normal. In ways JoAnne couldn't even imagine.

"I've already put a call in to state police bomb squads in both Ohio and Tennessee," Clay told her. And the FBI would investigate, as well. Another team was being called in to assist, but Clay had been given jurisdiction.

"Any ideas about the kids?" he asked JoAnne. He had several thoughts, but wanted to hear hers.

"Obviously day cares." JoAnne named the first type of facility on his own list. "With so many of them being small private ventures, they'd be the easiest to infiltrate."

"Agreed. Because we're short on time here, we'll have to take a risk and narrow our boundaries to the Chandler-Brookwood area and Knoxville—the two places we know our kidnapper's been. I'm going to assume he didn't stop someplace in between to plant a bomb."

"What do you want me to tell them?"

"That we have a possible situation and as a precautionary measure we recommend they remain closed until after noon tomorrow. There are too many of them to run bomb checks on every facility."

"You aren't afraid of inciting panic?"

"I'm more afraid of having the deaths of children on my conscience. Are you still friendly with Gary Smithers?"

Gary was a journalist with a well-known national news channel. Not too long ago he'd been aggressively interested in JoAnne.

JoAnne's sigh should've given him at least a twinge of guilt. But it didn't. "It took me a month to get rid of him the last time you asked me that question, boss."

"I know."

And he knew she understood why he was asking, too. Because the man would do whatever she wanted—and that included spinning this particular turn in the case in a way that would prevent all-out panic.

"I'll see if he'll meet me for drinks. Now, what do you want to do about the elementary schools?"

"Let's see if there are enough local police to do a check on those. Our goal is to protect the kids, first, but we've got to find that bomb."

"If it exists."

"Right."

"What about Kelly Chapman? You think he's really got a bomb on her?"

"What do you think?"

"It's possible."

"I agree."

"Barry called half an hour ago. He found a guy who says he knows Ezekial Greene, although he hasn't seen him around in a while. He claims that the guy moved to Tennessee a while back. Barry says his source is a crackhead and could be making the whole thing up, but the Tennessee connection spooked him so he took the guy down to the office to get a sketch of Ezekial drawn up."

"Good. Get it out the second it's done."

"One other thing," JoAnne said before they rang off.

"Maggie Winston was a mass of nerves when I was there this afternoon. Sam said she hardly slept."

Clay suspected the girl knew more than she was saying, but he couldn't worry about her, or any alleged liaison with Abrams, right then. He had to deal with the immediate issue—a possible bomb detonation—first. Then he'd attempt to question the foster kid again.

"Have you heard from Mercy?" The agent he had watching David Abrams.

"Abrams took his family to church this morning, then out to breakfast afterward." She named a well-known chain restaurant. "He's been home all afternoon."

"Anything on his phone records?"

"Not that anyone's found. None of the calls from home, office or cell raise any questions or alarms."

"He could have someone working for him." He thought of Rick Thomas. Was it just the day before that he'd spoken with the ex-covert-ops agent? "Abrams wouldn't be stupid enough to make traceable calls. He'd probably use a scrambled phone to communicate with anyone working for him on a criminal matter."

Clay didn't like the idea of a quiet Sunday night and David Abrams on the loose. "Or he could be getting ready to make his move. Send someone out to keep Mercy company. I don't want to give this guy a chance to slip away from us."

"My guess is he has someone working for him," JoAnne told him. "I got an earful from Samantha and Kyle before I left last night and this Abrams guy isn't the type to get himself dirty."

No? Well, he was the type to screw little girls. And that was about as dirty as it got.

21

I wished I had my files. If I could go over them, maybe I'd find something that could help us end this terror before anyone else got hurt.

If children died because of me, I'd never forgive myself.

If a client of mine was behind the kidnapping...

In that case I should have seen the signs. Should've known.

If Maggie got hurt...

I did sit-ups. Not many. I still felt stiff and sore and didn't want to overexert myself, but after all the sleep I'd had in the past forty-eight hours, I had too much nervous energy to keep it fully contained.

And I didn't want to pace the house. It wasn't mine. I didn't belong here. And I was petrified to move. What if someone caught sight of me?

I was letting fear suffocate me. I knew it. But that didn't seem to make one iota of difference.

What if they didn't find this guy? The players in Rick Thomas's game had killed many seemingly powerful men;

they'd stolen state secrets, they'd made millions in illegal imports and exports. And I, one woman, was going to be able to escape their clutches?

What about the gang in Florida? There were a number of deaths attributed to them.

And David Abrams? A cop had died. So had a businessman who'd shot himself. A farmer who'd overdosed. So many others who'd lost their lives to the drugs he trafficked. And the innocent women the man had hurt, indirect though his actions might have been—the businessman's wife and the sixteen-year-old girl, Glenna. He'd taken the virginity of my sweet little Maggie. And I thought I could stand up to *him?* Bring him down? Was I out of my mind? Could I be his fourth female victim, just like Clay said?

I'd been so convinced that there was nothing to fear but fear itself. Maybe I'd been wrong. Maybe the true thing to fear was the *lack* of fear that led you into dangerous waters.

But I'd never allowed fear to govern me. I'd made that promise to myself when I was just a child. And I'd lived by it. I'd had to live by it.

Fear would've prevented me from believing that I could ever hold my head up in a town where everyone knew everyone's business. It would've held me back from college applications. From grad school.

It would've made me a replica of my mother.

Fear was debilitating. I'd watched it destroy my mother, who'd been so afraid to face reality that she'd hidden away in a drugged fog until it killed her.

With the thoughts tripping over themselves in my brain, I turned to the only thing I had there in Clay Thatcher's house that felt like my own. The pad and little pen he'd given me. I scanned a page of scribbles about myself.

And then the few comments I'd written about the man who'd rescued me. I flipped the page and saw the list I'd made when Clay had been relaying the latest call from the kidnapper.

Blue backpack.

Eleven forty-five.

Children!

No bomb.

I tried to relax. To open my mind. To let thoughts and impressions flow. To find a semblance of myself within the timid being I was becoming.

No bomb.

No bomb.

Blue backpack.

Eleven forty-five.

Blue backpack...

He'd specifically said blue?

My hands started to shake.

I would not fall apart. I would not become helpless. I'd rather die from fearlessness than live in fear.

Eleven forty-five.

Eleven forty-five.

Not noon. Not 11:00. Or even 11:30. No, it was 11:45. Why that time in particular?

Something occurred to me. Something crazy. Eleven forty-five. Once, years and years ago, that time had been significant, but I couldn't immediately place the reason for its familiarity. Why had I remembered?

And then I knew.

I had to speak with Clay.

But I couldn't make a phone call.

I couldn't contact anyone.

If I was going to stay alive, I couldn't exist. Or be assumed to exist.

Clay had the blue backpack in his trunk. In the morning he'd pick up the money that had been placed in a deposit box in a bank in Chandler, put it in the bag and turn it over to the team who would leave it at the school.

JoAnne, wired but dressed in plain clothes, would "just happen" to be in the neighborhood. She'd follow whoever picked up the money. And find a way to befriend him. The agent's breathtaking good looks had come in handy in a couple of previous cases, as well.

Two years ago she'd saved the lives of a couple of under-age prostitutes by coming on to their pimp. The discomfort Clay had felt on that one still lingered.

If the kidnapper showed, JoAnne would follow the man, come on to him and try to get him to tell her about the second bomb. If there actually was a second bomb. Then they could prevent what would most likely be a prepro-grammed detonation.

If that didn't work, they'd stay on him until Clay gave the order for his arrest.

Either way, by five o'clock the next evening, Clay would have the man—kidnapper, accomplice or opportunist—in custody.

And then the bastard was going to answer to him.

For the first time in maybe forever, Clay felt anticipation as he turned onto his street just before six that evening. He hadn't been gone long. An hour maybe. But that hour had dragged. He had a lot resting on his shoulders with this case, but what was driving him was Kelly Chapman's safety.

He'd made her his sole responsibility.

He had to protect her.

And he believed he could.

She was sitting where he'd left her, dressed in her jeans and black top and black tennis shoes, eyes wide as she watched him enter from the garage through the kitchen door.

"It's me," he said for the second time. He'd called out before he'd put his key in the lock.

"I know."

She looked…as though she'd seen a ghost. And beautiful, too, although he didn't think she'd opened a single one of the beauty products he'd purchased. A woman with Kelly Chapman's big blue eyes and blond hair didn't need makeup to draw attention to herself.

Not that he cared about her looks.

He was just glad to see her sitting there alive.

"My favorite color is blue" were the first words out of her mouth.

Clay brought to the table the pizza he'd picked up on the way home, setting it, and the pile of reports he'd also brought in with him, in the only available space. In front of Kelly Chapman.

The pizza was his usual order—large, thin crust, supreme. Every Sunday night. He had to maintain his routines. To appear to be living normally. The pizza usually covered two meals. Tonight it would be one.

"You want a beer?" he asked, opening the fridge, pulling out a cold one for himself and uncapping it.

"I… You don't have any wine, do you?"

"Sorry, no."

"Then, yes, I'll have a beer."

Grabbing a couple of paper towels off the roll at the sink, Clay gave her one and kept one for himself. Setting the files he'd brought in on top of the others he'd begin perusing in a few minutes, he opened the pizza box, removed a slice, took a bite.

"I went by the cave on my way home. It's exactly as we left it."

Kelly sipped from the bottle he'd set on the table as though it was something she wasn't accustomed to doing.

"I take it you aren't a beer drinker," he said as he swallowed his first bite and washed it down with a long swig.

"Nope. Just wine. Occasionally."

"There's more Diet Coke...."

"This is fine." As if to prove her point, she sipped again. More boldly.

"You do like pizza, don't you?" he asked after he was two bites up on her.

"Yes, but...did you hear what I said when you came in?"

"Your favorite color is blue."

"Right. And he said a blue backpack."

She'd been playing armchair detective while he was gone. He couldn't blame her. What else was there to do? She couldn't turn on a light. Or watch TV. Because there wasn't supposed to be anyone home.

He took another bite.

She'd been abducted. Hit on the head. Bruised. Starved and dehydrated. Her life was at stake. Of course she was trying to put pieces together.

"He had to specify the color so he'd be able to identify the bag. Blue and black are the most common colors when it comes to backpacks so the choice is an obvious one."

Kelly nodded. Picked up a slice of pizza. Took a bite. And wiped her mouth. After another sip of beer, she took a second bite. And then, with determination shining from eyes that had been calling to him since he'd first seen her photo, she said, "I was born at 11:45 in the morning."

A coincidence, he was sure.... Clay bit into his pizza, but chewed more slowly than before.

"And I went to Chandler Elementary." She named the school that was the site of tomorrow's drop-off. "My father told me once that he'd seen me there, on the playground. He'd made a delivery to my mother and for some reason he stopped by. The story was his proof that he'd been a loving father."

Pizza suspended in midair, Clay gave her his full attention.

"When he first came to see me, he had a copy of my birth certificate. I thought it was a fake at first, until I checked it against the original. Anyway, my time of birth was on it."

"And the color blue?"

"When he'd first come to me claiming paternity, I told him I wasn't his daughter. He said he knew everything about me. That my mother had kept him informed. Somewhere in the back-and-forth that ensued, I told him he didn't know me at all. That he didn't even know my favorite color."

Her smile didn't reach her eyes, but the beer bottle reached her mouth.

"He guessed red. I'd proven my point. It was blue."

Clay dropped the pizza and picked up his phone.

Ten minutes later there was a full-personnel tri-state search in progress for Ezekial Greene.

And Clay was left waiting for the phone to ring so he could go down to headquarters and do whatever it took to get the truth out of the man before anyone died.

And as he waited, he sat at his kitchen table and ate pizza with the man's daughter.

Edgewood, Ohio
Sunday, December 5, 2010

I ate because I had to. I needed to regain my strength. Emotionally as well as physically. My equilibrium was off. Rest and nourishment would take care of that and I'd be my old self.

Or so I told myself. And I wanted to believe it. Needed to believe that the woman I'd been—safe and secure and confident and happy—was still here, within me.

Change was inevitable. I knew that. But some things weren't meant to change. Some things were meant to be released. You had to let go of them.

Like my father. I'd finally let go of him the month before. Maggie's advent into my life had given me the strength to do it. I'd done it for her.

Or…what was it Clay had said in the cave? That since I had Maggie now—a new family—I no longer needed my father.

As if the man represented family to me. He didn't.

Did he?

I'd never needed him.

And now he was back?

What would my clients think when they found out I was Ezekial Greene's daughter? The offspring of a drug-dealing pimp who'd sell his own—

Well, no.

But a drug-dealing pimp with rotting teeth and nothing to show for the life he'd lived.

Except me. And that was purely by accident.

I didn't really care what my clients thought. I mean, I cared, but I didn't worry that they'd think any less of me because of my parents. Such as they were.

I just didn't want to think about Ezekial Greene at all. Or a value on my head. I was worth more than money.

"I'm assuming his picture is being broadcast on all the news stations?" I asked quietly while Clay went over sales receipts and lists of names and numerous other records I couldn't be privy to.

"Yes."

He didn't offer to turn on the television. And I didn't ask him to. He was poring over his papers, hoping to find a break in the case before morning, but we both knew that morning would come whether he had an answer or not.

"Is he being described as a person of interest in my disappearance?"

"Yes."

"So my picture will be up there with his?" I had no idea why I was doing this to myself.

Clay, who'd traded beer for coffee when I'd opted for water, looked at me. "Yes."

"I'm ashamed of him."

"He's a biological fact in your life, that's all. He had nothing to do with the person you are."

He was right, of course. "I let him get to me."

"Understandable." He'd returned his focus to his lists.

"If I'd been more honest with myself, admitted what was going on, I'd have seen this sooner. I'd have known he wouldn't just accept my blowing him off."

"Maybe."

Well, at least I didn't have to worry about the guy lying to me to spare my feelings. That was okay, though. I could handle my feelings. I decided I wasn't going to think about the past. It was gone. Done. It had nothing to do with the woman I was today.

And nothing Ezekial Greene had or hadn't done bore the slightest relevance to the child I'd been, the woman I was or the woman I would be.

I had to think about someone other than myself. Tend to someone else. That was the cure for a fall into the dark recesses of the mind.

"What about you?" I asked the only other occupant of my world—the only person to whom I could extend my need to nurture.

"Huh?" he grunted, and circled a name.

"Your mother. What's up with her?"

His pencil stopped midcircle. "Nothing's up with her."

"So why is it that you shop for her, but she rejects

enough of your gifts that you make regular contributions to a shelter? And why doesn't she come here?"

I stopped. What the hell was I doing? I knew better than to trespass into emotional territory without being invited. Or at least knew how to do it with compassion and finesse.

Tonight I appeared to be missing both.

"Why is my mother any of your business?" Clay Thatcher was staring me right in the eye.

And he wasn't a happy man.

22

By ten o'clock that night Clay's unexpected houseguest was exhausted. So was he.

He walked her back to her room, checked the place just because it made him feel better and for no other reason. Then he asked that she leave her door ajar so he could hear if there was a problem.

He didn't expect one—at all—but her kidnapper probably knew she was missing by now, and her life was in his hands. He did not take that responsibility lightly. He would keep her safe at all costs.

As soon as she was out of the bathroom and had changed into the sweats he'd given her when she'd arrived at his home that morning, he said good-night. He returned to the table, welcoming the distraction of the overwhelming piles of data. Those he could deal with. Those he was comfortable with.

But the woman in his home… He wasn't comfortable with her at all. Frankly, he had no idea what to do with her.

Had she been needy, clingy, whiny or just plain timid, he'd have known what to do. Known how to help her.

But this woman—she looked inward for everything. For strength. For answers. For truth.

She wanted the truth about things most people didn't even acknowledge. Who cared if she was ashamed of her father? Who wouldn't be? And why couldn't she just bitch about the guy, maybe cry a little, and act like the victim she was?

Watching her probe her psyche, looking for answers, was unsettling. And…strangely fascinating.

Not only that, she'd thought she was going to start probing *him*. Asking about his mother.

His mother was fine. He was fine.

And Kelly Chapman was not going to start finding something wrong with him.

Suddenly he saw lights shining in the front window. Someone was turning onto his drive.

Clay was at Kelly's bedroom door before the car had a chance to get all four wheels on his property.

She was a huddled shape in the darkness of the room. The night-light he'd provided for her was still on, but it didn't illuminate her face enough to see if she was awake.

"Kelly?"

"Yeah?" She didn't move, didn't flinch or jerk, which told him she'd known he was there. She hadn't been asleep.

"Someone's here."

She sat up and he could see the whites of her eyes.

"Don't worry," he said quickly, his hand on the doorknob. "It's one of my agents. I recognized the car. I just wanted you to know that there'll be someone in the house. I'm going to close this door and you have to be completely quiet. If you need to use the bathroom, don't flush until I tell you it's okay. And don't run the water."

He trusted JoAnne with his life. But not with Kelly's.

"You'll let me know when the coast is clear?"

"Of course."

"Thank you."

That was it. No complaints. No questions.

And as Clay shut the door he wondered if there was anything Kelly Chapman couldn't handle.

The day was coming to an end and there was much to do to prepare for tomorrow. He'd always known his ship would come in. He'd been patiently waiting. There was nothing they could do to stop the momentum. He had no concerns. Only an awareness of the need for careful movement, careful choices. They had emotion on their sides. He had none on his.

People feared death. It was their weakness. Their fear of death made them vulnerable. But death was inevitable. A process that took people to a new and better existence. He didn't fear it. Which made him an invincible opponent.

Tomorrow would come. What would be would be.

By tomorrow night, he'd be sailing away.

"You want a beer?" Clay followed JoAnne into his kitchen. She knew her way around. There'd been a time, briefly, when she'd been a regular visitor.

She got them both bottles of beer and, dropping her bag on the floor, settled into the chair Kelly Chapman had recently vacated.

Clay hoped to God Kelly's scent—the scent of the shampoo he'd bought her that morning—had left the room with her. It had been tantalizing him all evening. He didn't smell it now.

"How'd it go with Gary?"

"He's got us covered," JoAnne said. But she imparted the news with a sniff.

"That rough, huh?"

Maybe he should feel at least a little territorial—should

care that a woman who'd once been his lover was being sought after by another man. His only concern was that JoAnne be happy and safe. Beyond that, her life was her own.

As were the lives of every other woman he'd ever been involved with.

"I've got a date with him tomorrow night and if it goes beyond that, I'm turning him over to you, Clay Thatcher."

"How come? Smithers doesn't seem the type to fall for someone like me."

"I'm going to tell him that we're lovers and you're the jealous sort."

"I don't have a jealous bone in my body." He didn't care enough about any woman to be jealous of any choices she made.

"But you can't deny we were lovers," JoAnne said. "I've got proof."

Pictures she'd taken of him one night when he'd been passed out in her bed. Yeah, he knew. It was a standing thing between them. Pictures he knew she kept because their time together had been special to her. Pictures she'd never use against him. Pictures that didn't matter. He wouldn't give a damn if they were made public. He and JoAnne had been lovers. So what?

"Okay, sic him on me," he said. Not because of the pictures, but because she deserved his support. Because she was the closest thing he had to a best friend now that his father was gone.

"I've got something to show you."

He'd known she hadn't driven all the way out here to bitch about Gary Smithers.

"They found this on Maggie Winston's computer and thought we'd want to see it." JoAnne handed him a printed sheet.

He's big.

He's strong.

He goes where he pleases.

He takes what he wants.

He invades. Grabs hold.

He clutches and squeezes.

He refuses to let go.

He brings pain.

He hurts.

He kills.

He got me.

"I called Samantha Jones and had her ask Maggie about it. I thought she had the best chance of getting the girl to talk. Maggie trusts Sam."

"And?"

"Maggie says a friend of hers sent her the poem and that she didn't even know she'd kept it."

"Did Detective Jones believe her?"

"No. She said the look on Maggie's face when she was asking her about the poem was the same one she wore the night she and Kelly showed her a picture of David Abrams and Maggie denied that he was her Mac. Kelly Chapman was sure Maggie had convinced herself he wasn't. Jim says this document was created on Maggie's computer."

Jim, one of the agency's computer technicians, was right more often than he was wrong.

"Does he know when this was created?"

"Just before Kelly Chapman went missing."

Pieces were falling into place. Clay could feel them. He was beginning to see a clear picture.

"She knows more than she's telling us about Kelly's disappearance. That's why she called so soon, to notify the authorities. She says, 'He kills.' She knew what was going to happen. And 'He got me.' The man has enough power over her that she couldn't stop him. Couldn't tell him no.

On some level, she knows what he's doing is wrong. But can't stop it."

"Sam said Kelly's theory was that Maggie had been so badly hurt that she couldn't see David Abrams and her Mac as the same man. That her psyche couldn't handle the betrayal of her most sacred gifts—her heart and her virginity. She's in a suspended state of reality. If David is behind this attempt to get rid of Kelly, and Maggie knows, she'd be powerless to stop him. She's his slave, chained by her intense emotional need. Yet she cares about Kelly."

"Which is why, when Maggie was given the opportunity, she went to meet Abrams last night. But why she was so distraught when Sam came to get her?"

"Well, for one thing, he didn't show up," JoAnne said. "So we have a distraught girl. And a missing counselor-turned-foster-mom."

"We have a fiend with no conscience." Clay often thought aloud with JoAnne. "And his one weakness is a teenage girl."

"You think the only way to get him is through the girl."

"The only way to get a man like Abrams is to find his weakness and exploit it." Clay liked his version better. It was about weaknesses, not about a teenage girl. His version was less…tragic sounding.

"You want to set up a second sting."

"I want to get the bastard tomorrow morning so we can all go home." So Kelly Chapman could go home.

So she could get out of *his* home. Out of his head. And his life.

And tend to the foster child who so desperately needed her.

"You are home." JoAnne's dry reply wasn't lost on him.

"If we don't get him tomorrow morning, we'll set up

another sting. The man already has the girl. She'll go to him with or without our supervision. A sting is the only way I can see to save her. At least we pick the time and place, we control the outcome. And we get him."

"What if it turns out Abrams *isn't* behind Chapman's disappearance? Then this won't be our concern."

Righting wrongs was always Clay's concern. And if it turned out that Abrams wasn't part of his case... He'd cross that bridge when he came to it.

Edgewood, Ohio
Sunday, December 5, 2010

I waited until Clay Thatcher's lover was gone, but only just. I listened as the car drove away and was down the hall before he'd settled back into his seat at the table. Still in the slacks and blue cotton dress shirt he'd had on all day—with his jacket over the back of his chair—the man looked good. Commanding.

He'd saved my life.

And I was so angry I hardly recognized myself.

"Another sting?" I barely managed to keep my voice at a decent level. I wanted to scream at him. To throw something. To stomp my foot and slap his face.

"How could you?" I stood there in his sweats and T-shirt, my bare feet freezing on the ceramic tile floor, and faced down a federal agent almost twice my weight.

Why was he just standing there staring at me? Why didn't he say anything?

"She said a second sting. She said Maggie was with Abrams last night. Last night! While you were telling me that Maggie was safe with Sam, you let her go meet that *bastard?*" I couldn't stand it.

But I couldn't do a damned thing about it. I was trapped.

Helpless. Because if I took a step out that front door, I could be dead.

If I went to Maggie, she could be dead, too.

"I trusted you." My voice had dropped. My whole spirit was sagging, along with my shoulders. Because I'd lost. And I knew it.

I wanted to cry. To shed all the anguish that came with loving a child who was so misguided. Who was so starved for affection that she'd fallen prey to a pedophile.

Oh, God, Maggie. You don't need him. Don't you know how much I love you?

Of course Maggie didn't know how much I loved her. She gave Mac something in return for his supposed affection; she believed she had nothing to give me. I understood, in logical terms, what was going on.

But I had no idea what to do with the emotions attacking me. They were brutal. And they were winning.

I had to step back. To take the space to choose my response rather than react.

"Your trust is not misplaced."

Just hearing his voice pissed me off all over again.

"How could you?" I asked instead, more quietly but still with every ounce of accusation I'd hurled at him previously.

He stood there, hands in his pockets, easily deflecting my blows. The man was a rock. Not a human being. Did he feel nothing? About anything?

I remembered my picture on his dash.

And the gentleness with which he'd looked after me in the cave.

I remembered his honesty when I'd agreed to his plan—his admission that he could be acting out of an elevated opinion of his own abilities.

His fellow agent—his ex-lover—had come to him. The tone of her voice told of a long-standing friendship and affection. They'd seemed to understand each other's thoughts. She'd said something about their being lovers....

A person had to possess a certain amount of sensitivity to be part of such a relationship.

My legs were shaky. Probably more because of the emotions tormenting me than any physical consequence of my days in the cave. I sat. "I need answers." A beer bottle with only a few sips missing sat in front of me.

Dropping down to the table by the second beer bottle, one that was three-quarters empty, Clay looked directly at me.

"Time was running out. We had to find you. It's clear to everyone who's spoken to her that Maggie knows more than she's saying about what's going on here. We set up a sting to get Maggie to lead us to Abrams."

Every time he spoke, I got mad all over again. I just...

"'We...' Who was involved in this...sting?" I asked before I'd finished thinking about what I should say. "Where was Sam when you were all using Maggie to do your jobs for you?" Not one of my better efforts.

I'd cringe about it later, I was sure. For now, I simply didn't care. Maggie Winston was a child who'd been through far more than she could handle already. And these people...these caregivers, these keepers of the peace, had thrown her to the wolf.

I just couldn't bear the thought of that man with his hands anywhere near that child again. The idea of it made me physically sick.

"Sam was in on it."

Shock, betrayal, squeezed the air out of my lungs.

"But before you start hating your friend, hear me out," Clay said. "Everyone knows the precarious state of Maggie's emotional health."

That was the first thing he'd said that didn't make me want to spit angry words.

"But you were even more right than you realized in your assessment of Abrams's power over her. Sam is convinced that Maggie intuitively knows something about your disappearance. Something that contradicts her version of reality. The knowledge is eating the kid alive. She's not sleeping. She's not eating. She's getting hysterical. After one of the agents saw Abrams in the woods yesterday, it became obvious that he's continuing to feed the hold he has on her. We figured it was only a matter of time before she slipped away from us and went to him. So…we let it happen. Kyle took her to your place. Sam called, with a supposed emergency with Kyle's grandfather. He left, telling Maggie to wait there for him. He wasn't gone five minutes before she was on her bike and headed out to the woods. We had agents on the streets, in the woods, even in a tree above their meeting spot. There was not one second that she was out of sight of trained professionals. The idea was that as soon as Abrams showed, Sam had him. All she needs is evidence of them together to prove the association, to be able to get charges pressed against him and put him away. That's why she agreed to the plan.

"Our part in it was to get Abrams to confess what he'd done with you. Or to get Maggie to do it after he was arrested."

I wasn't placated. I would never have agreed to the plan. But I was able to keep my mouth shut long enough to think about what he was saying.

"Until my agent saw Abrams in the woods, Sam truly believed the man wouldn't risk his life, risk everything he'd built, for a meeting with Maggie. After we told her Abrams had been to their clearing in the woods, she knew that—for Maggie's sake—she had to do whatever it took to get the man. We'd much rather have her go to him while we're watching, than sneak in a rendezvous behind our backs when there's nothing we can do to help her. Or stop him."

"What happened when she saw him?" I had to know. Even if the answer destroyed me.

"He didn't show."

"So Sam was right. Maggie's not worth the risk to him."

I wasn't as surprised as I could've been when Clay shook his head. "He's not going to give up on her," my rescuer said. "He can't. His going there is proof of that. But he's being careful. Very, very careful. Which concerns me most of all. The man's calculating. He has plans. He doesn't make mistakes."

"He's biding his time," I said, understanding what he was telling me. Maggie was in danger. Terrible danger. And what could I do except sit here? "He's going to get her, but in his own time and his own way."

Clay Thatcher leaned forward, his forearms on his knees, and took one of my hands in both of his. He met my gaze with a look so steady and serious I was captivated.

"He is not going to get her," he said. "I give you my word on that."

I wanted to believe him.

23

More than three hundred tips came in on the Ezekial Greene hotline. Most of them led nowhere. Clay had Barry and JoAnne following up on the ones that could be legitimate while he followed up with the state and FBI bomb squads.

All elementary schools included in the original search were clean. He expanded the search. And added day cares in the Knoxville and Chandler areas. A couple of discount stores in the Dayton area had turned up on Clay's radar. They'd sold all the materials needed for various types of homemade bombs during the time frame in question—and Clay went with members from each of the squads to speak with store managers and owners, to view tapes of purchases where available, hoping that if they hadn't found the bombs before the 11:45 drop-off, they'd at least know what kind of bomb they were dealing with. *If* they were dealing with one… But they couldn't take the chance. They'd have protocols in place to disarm the bombs and limit damage.

He focused on facts and piecing together puzzles. He did not think about the woman he'd left still asleep in the bed across the hall from his room. He'd set the security alarm and resecured the dead bolt lock just after six that morning.

He couldn't call her. Couldn't text message or email her. He couldn't have any contact with her outside his home. He had to trust that she'd do as he'd instructed and, if something went wrong, that she'd use the gun he'd given her.

A man matching Ezekial Greene's description had purchased enough quantities of propane and alarm clocks to assemble at least three self-detonating explosives. They knew about plan A. He obviously had a plan B, as well. Which didn't surprise Clay at all. Fit the man's profile.

He showed the manager of the department store the composite drawing they had of Greene. A drawing Kelly had already confirmed as a depiction of her father. The manager, in turn, showed Clay and the agent and officer with him the video of the man who'd made the purchase.

He had a printed photo of the man in his jacket pocket as he made his way back to Edgewood just before ten o'clock Monday morning. They had an hour and forty-five minutes to find Kelly Chapman's father.

Or to find the bombs he'd made.

Fifty men and women were in the field, combing the neighborhoods and areas in and around the purchase store. They were showing Greene's picture to public transit drivers, and an emergency newsflash was being broadcast on all local programs.

Schools and day cares within a fifty-mile radius were being evacuated, just in case Greene planned to have the bomb delivered somehow rather than planting it.

And Clay was heading home to a source no one knew he had.

Edgewood, Ohio
Monday, December 6, 2010

I'd spent much of the morning in the bathroom off my bedroom. It was actually rather pretty. Whoever had owned the home before (since Clay Thatcher would never have done this) had hung wallpaper with little pink roses, complemented by a mauve chair rail.

The cupboards were white, the counter marbleized porcelain, and most of all I loved the garden tub. It was completely stark now—except for the dust that congealed when it got wet—but I pictured it with a vase of flowers in one corner, a basket with some pretty bottles of bubble bath and a loofah in another, a rose collage on the wall.

A separate shower stall—which was what I'd used the day before—stood at the other end of the bathroom.

With some plush rugs on the ceramic tile floor, a light pink silk shower curtain and some thick mauve towels hanging on the rack, the room would be lovely.

That morning it was perfect for me because it had no windows. I could pace and move about and not worry about attracting attention from anyone who might be out there. Anyone who might notice movement in the home of a single man who was supposed to be away at work.

Who knew if Clay Thatcher had nosy neighbors?

Or kind neighbors who watched out for him?

I cleaned the tub. And using the flowery-smelling shampoo my host had purchased for me, a purchase I was going to repay as soon as I had access to my own funds, I prepared a bubble bath.

I'd made a brief trip to the kitchen earlier, ducking when I passed the windows, to help myself to some granola bars and Diet Coke. I'd gone over my notes. I needed to skate.

And every time I looked at the pair of wheels I'd worn for forty-eight hours, I couldn't breathe. I had to get back on those skates as soon as I possibly could.

I was not going to let this fiend, whoever he was, rob me of one of my most joyous pastimes.

Now that I was feeling physically better, I checked my body over more thoroughly as I stripped for the bath. The swelling on my temple had gone down, and with my hair covering that bruise, I didn't look quite so battered. The scrape on my cheek had been superficial and was barely discernible. Or so I told myself. My hands were scabbing over and didn't sting at all except when I got them wet. But I had a lot of bruises. Some larger than others. A peculiar one just under my right armpit, on my side. It looked like fingerprints.

Where the guy had lifted me? I checked my other side, but didn't find a matching set.

I'd heard a sound on the bike path that morning. Behind me. The memory was briefly there, and then gone again.

But I was certain the sound had come from behind me. I just wasn't sure what it was. Or where, exactly, I was at the time. On my skates?

I tried so hard to remember.

But I couldn't.

The bath would've been much better in the evening, with soft music and a glass of wine. And my own tub.

It would have been better, too, if sitting in the tub hadn't brought back memories of sitting on a hard surface for hours and hours. That feeling drove me from my bath before I'd even turned off the water filling the tub.

I'd hurriedly soaped and sponged myself. I was clean. And wasn't that what baths were for?

My hands were shaking too much to use any of the makeup Clay had provided. I didn't use a lot of the stuff, anyway, but a little eyeliner would've been nice. And some foundation to cover the bruising. Sunscreen.

Because I might just be free today. Within hours.

I couldn't wait to feel the sun on my face. Even if it was cold December sun. One thing was for certain: I was never, ever going to take the weather for granted again. Rain. Sun. Snow. I wanted them all. Wanted to feel them all. See them all.

By the time I was dressed, I was feeling somewhat okay again. As though I could manage. I was going to be fine. I knew that. I'd get through this. And I'd move on and life would be good.

I'd make it good.

Because I'd learned a long time ago that I could.

I had to focus on the future. And when I got home, I'd focus on the present.

I could start by getting back up on my skates. Clay had a two-car garage. His car was gone. Which meant there was a two-bay space for me. The only windows were small, up at the roofline, which let in light but didn't make the inside of the garage visible.

Skating was part of my mental health regime. It was how I dealt with stress. Kept myself healthy and fit. I was not going to be victimized even further by allowing someone to make me fear what I most loved.

I would skate. Period.

I would be healthy.

I repeated the mantra as I grabbed my skates from the floor of the room I'd been assigned. I didn't look directly at them, but I picked them up. Their weight felt familiar in my hands. The padded rim at the ankle, the loops I crooked my finger in to transport the skates, all were normal.

Walking slowly for some reason I didn't dwell on, I made my way to the garage, careful to open the door quietly. Clay had more than an acre of land. The sound of a door opening and closing was unlikely to travel. But being extra careful wasn't a bad thing right now.

I hadn't changed back into the sweats, though I never skated in jeans. It wasn't like I was going to get a workout in the garage. I was just going to put the skates on. Move around in them. Let my feet get comfortable with them again. I was going to feel the ground glide beneath me, a feeling I knew well. One that denoted wellness to me.

Wellness and strength. Ability. Freedom.

Heaviness engulfed me as I sat down on the garage floor and took the first skate in my hands. I'd put on my socks to go with the two big tennis shoes. All that was left to do was slide my foot inside the waiting boot.

I tried. And couldn't breathe. Which was ridiculous. There was absolutely nothing the matter with me physically.

I tried again. The skate was heavy. I let it drop. And picked it back up. My toes cramped, and I wiggled them. I couldn't catch my breath. What if I was having a heart attack?

I was *not* having a heart attack.

I shoved my foot into the skate. My throat got tight, as if I was going to cry. I swallowed past the lump that formed there and picked up skate number two.

By the time I got my foot into the skate I was crying.

Fine. If I had to cry, I'd cry. Tears weren't going to stop me from doing this. I would not let someone else take my life from me. I would not.

I stood.

I would not let anyone take my life from me.

I rolled a couple of inches. And lost my balance. I didn't fall down, but I lurched and righted myself. Because I was a good skater. I had instincts. I'd save myself. I knew how. I could count on myself.

Couldn't I? I'd show me. Pushing off gently with one foot, I glided a couple of yards, turning before I hit the wall, then pushed with my other foot. One foot and then the other. That was all it took.

I was sobbing. Huge racking sobs that were interfering with my balance. But I would not stop. And I would not fall.

I would not—

I heard a car in the drive.

And dove for the door into the house. I had to get in that door. Get to safety. Clawing at the door handle, my hand slipped. Missed. I bumped my wrist, my feet were sliding out from under me. I grasped the knob. Turned, shoving with all my might, and crying so hard I could barely see.

The door gave. I fell inside, curling up into a little ball against the kitchen cupboard as I heard the door close behind me.

Clay's eye was trained on the eating nook at the far end of his kitchen as he came through the door from the garage. There was no reason for him to expect to see Kelly Chapman sitting at the table, except that, other than when she was sleeping, that was the only place in his house he'd seen her.

In his mind, that chair had become almost synonymous with her. Which explained the immediate shard of panic that went through him when he saw the vacant chair.

He strode forward and…tripped. Clay just caught himself, avoiding a face-plant on the hard ceramic floor, but noticed, in the process, that he'd stumbled over an in-line skate.

A second later, realized that the skate was attached to his reluctant housemate.

"I'm so sorry." Kelly's eyes were wide, her voice steady as she pulled her foot back. She'd been sitting upright, leaning against the cupboard, as though she hadn't heard the automatic garage door that should've alerted her to his presence. Or heard the car door or his key in the lock.

Kneeling down, he took in her body at a glance. Nothing was twisted or out of place. There was no blood that he could see. And then he looked at her face. "It's like falling off a horse," she said with a tremulous grin. "You have to get right back up on the darn thing or be afraid of it for life."

She'd been trying on her skates. And she'd been crying.

"How'd it go?" he asked, settling on the floor beside her because he wasn't sure what else to do. This woman was like none other he'd ever known. She didn't give up. She didn't give herself any slack, either.

He was beginning to feel like a slacker.

Her shrug said it all. "Okay, for a first try. My facilities were limited." She excused what was obviously more of a failed attempt than a successful one. "A garage floor and a bike bath provide vastly different opportunities."

"So what really happened?"

She looked right at him. "I heard your car, and I remembered what that noise was, the noise I told you about, and panicked." Her eyes teared up.

"What was the sound?"

"A motor, coming up behind me. He was on a cart, just like you said. I turned to look and saw him zip up beside me. I thought he was going to drive on by. He was off the cart before I knew what was happening. He tripped me. My helmet hit the pavement—and that's the last thing I remember."

"He. You saw him, then."

"No." Her expression pained, she shook her head. "I saw the hat. The brim was low. He was wearing a jumpsuit and gloves."

"What about his face? His chin? Was he black or white?"

"I only caught a glimpse. He wasn't dark-skinned, I know that. His face was shadowed, though, so I'm not sure...."

"Was it Ezekial?"

"I don't know, Clay. I should. I'm so sorry for not being more help, but I just don't know."

"It *could* have been, then?"

"Yeah. It could've been."

"Is this him? Is this Ezekial?" Clay pulled the photo from the store's surveillance video out of his pocket. He hated to stress her any more at the moment, but he had no choice.

She took a quick glance, then turned her head away. "Yeah. That's dear old dad."

"He bought explosives, Kelly. Enough to make three pretty good-size bombs. He bought them in Trotville." Clay named the chain store in the town next to Brookwood, another Dayton suburb. "Paid cash for them. He's not fooling around here. We've cleared out all schools and day cares in the area, but I need you to think. If you had to predict what he'd do next, what would it be? Something involving kids. I need every memory you've got. No matter how insignificant. Anything you come up with, anything you can tell me…it could mean the difference between saving lives and losing them. There's only an hour and a half left before he starts his rampage. His possible rampage."

Her eyes widened, as though some possibility had occurred to her, but she didn't say a word.

"Please, Kelly. I know this is hard, but you're all I've got."

She closed her eyes. Her skates slid away from her body until her legs were extended straight out onto the floor. She crossed her arms over her stomach and Clay knew he'd lost.

Unless the men and women out on the streets turned up a miracle, some innocent children could very well be breathing their last.

The woman had picked one hell of a time to fall apart.

24

A hand reached down inside me, twisting and pulling. Ripping. Dragging out the deepest, most painful parts of me. It laid them there. Letting the light shine on them. Letting everyone see.

But there was no one there. No one besides Clay.

And the children whose laughter could be quieted forever, if not for me.

My eyes closed and I forced myself to let the memories pushing at me come forward. If I hadn't already been crying, been feeling so low and vulnerable, maybe they wouldn't have been able to surface. Maybe I could've kept them hidden. I couldn't breathe. Was suffocating. And pieces fell into place. In that moment I knew exactly what my father was doing. "I don't know where, but there's a place. In Dayton."

Dayton, the failing metropolis between Cincinnati and Columbus, best known for being a crossroads, where two major interstates, 70 and 75, crossed. Or was it best known for Wright-Patterson Air Force Base and the Wright brothers? Or maybe for the six General Motors plants that had shut down in the past decade.

It was the nearest major city to Chandler, Brookwood and Trotville. And Edgewood. Clay's office was there and—

"Kelly? What place, sweetie? What are you talking about?"

Mom had called me *sweetie*. I'd liked that. And…

"It might not even exist anymore," I said. The words were forming in my mind. I had to get them out without hearing them. Without thinking about them.

I had to face the fact that—

"When I was three, my father tried to sell me." I was talking about a little girl who'd lived long ago. The story didn't affect me now. "Funny, huh, since he's doing it again? All the money I've given him and it's never enough."

I was crying. And getting off topic. This wasn't about now.

"He tried to sell you…where?"

"There's a place in Dayton. I don't know where it was. I've tried to find it many times over the years. I even re-ported it to the Dayton police when I was in college, but I never heard anything back about it."

I'd never followed up. I hadn't wanted to know.

"I suspect they ran a legitimate adoption business—but they had a sideline. They let people who didn't want their kids bring them there and they match the kids with couples who want to adopt them. I think. That's the way my mother explained it when I asked her about it years later."

I had to continue. He was running out of time. Little kids might be running out of time. I thought about them. And about the other little kids I'd seen in the room that day. "My father took me there. I remember being there. I remember being put in a room with other little kids. I re-member other adults. Someone, another kid, had peed their pants. It stank. A lady in charge took hold of my arm and wouldn't let it go. I was crying for my mom. I wanted my dad to take me back to my mom, but the lady's fingers were pinching my skin and I couldn't get out of the room."

Under my closed eyelids, the scene played out perfectly and I had to escape. Daylight was bright. Made my eyes water. And showed me Clay's tense features only inches from my own.

He didn't touch me. Didn't crowd me. But he was there.

"My father had taken me from my mother. She'd refused to turn any more tricks for him because of me. He needed drug money, so…he came up with another approach," I said. "I was saved that day. My mother showed up at the last minute and I never saw my father again—until Mom died. He must've lost a lot of money, at the adoption place that day because the fit I threw gave my mom time to get there…. My father is very methodical. Every single thing he does is for a reason. It's all calculated. When he chooses his food, there's always a reason for the choice. The blue backpack. The time of the meeting. The school. There were reasons, and they all had to do with me. If he's going to set off a bomb in a place where there are children, it'll be at that place, if it still exists." I started to cry. It all made sense now. I hated myself, but I cried, anyway. "I'm so sorry, Clay. I'm sorry I didn't remember this sooner. It's like I've always known, but I just wouldn't think about it and—"

"You didn't need the information until now. You're doing great, Kelly." His steady, warm voice reached me.

He sounded genuinely impressed.

"Can you recall who you spoke with on the Dayton police force? What office you contacted?"

Now that I'd opened that door, the details were there. More than I'd realized. More than I wanted.

"Detective Scott Needmore. I remember because it's like that road in Dayton, Needmore Road. There was a bar on that road called Need One More. I used to drive by there…."

Clay was already on his phone.

I was forgotten.

And I was thankful for that.

After several phone calls and some file-pulling, Clay connected with retired detective Scott Needmore at 10:45 Monday morning.

He was living with his wife in Florida and was out on the golf course, but he took Clay's call.

"I remember the case like it was yesterday," Needmore said after Clay identified himself as a special agent with the FBI. Clay had men searching all the files Needmore had worked on during the year Kelly remembered contacting him, but it was taking too long. "It was one of those that stick with you until the day you die," the retired police detective was saying.

The case didn't end well, Clay translated.

"I spent six months following dead-end leads, mostly on my own time, because all I had to go on was the memory of a girl from when she was three years old and questionable testimony from her wasted mother."

Yeah, that was the case.

"I'm working on a possible homicide, Detective," Clay said. "Where was this agency? And does it still exist?"

"As far as I know it still exists," Needmore said. "That was the bitch of it. I eventually track down the place. They'd moved to a different neighborhood. But I can't shut it down. It's a legitimate adoption agency in South Dayton. It has a lot of high-society clients." The man gave him the name and even remembered the second address.

Clay was out the door before he'd disconnected the call.

Not until several seconds later, while he waited for the speed-dial connection to his office, did he realize he hadn't so much as told Kelly Chapman goodbye.

The Happy Day Adoption Agency was housed in a sprawling building in a part of town that was once glamorous and now was not. Although the building itself, and the grounds on which it stood, were still immaculate, the neighboring land was garbage-strewn, with boarded-up buildings that hinted at better times.

Many years ago.

By the time Clay arrived, the place was taped off and surrounded by emergency vehicles with flashers going. Cursing at how far away he had to park, he locked his car and ran between fire engines and ambulances, police cars, a canine unit and a couple of bomb squad trucks, all haphazardly stopped on the street and in the yard of the statuesque old building.

Worried-looking men and women, obviously personnel from the adoption agency, stood in huddles of two or three outside the black wrought-iron gate at the entrance.

"All the children are out." Marcus Williams, an agent who'd worked for Clay until his transfer six months before, hurried over to Clay.

He nodded. Thank God they'd made it in time. And they didn't need him. He'd had to be sure.

"The dog found something, a propane tank buried beneath the window of the playroom. There's a timer attached and they don't know what's inside. Bomb squad's got it now."

Clay couldn't wait. He had thirty minutes to get to Chandler before the money drop. He'd already turned the bag over to the female agent who was posing as Samantha Jones. He'd drawn the line at allowing the detective to make the drop herself. He'd only won her agreement when he'd reminded her that Kelly needed her with Maggie.

JoAnne and Barry and the rest of the team were in place.

With the bubble out on his dark-colored sedan, Clay squealed his tires, backing up to return to Chandler. He'd just put his car in Drive and was pushing the pedal to the floor when the explosion happened.

Maggie saw it all on the news. The picture of the man they were saying was Kelly's father. His teeth were rotten and his shirt didn't fit over his gut, which was hairy and gross.

He looked dirty, too, like the guy her mom used to bring home sometimes who stank. Looked about as nice as that guy had been, too. He'd hit Mom. And Maggie'd called the cops.

And then gotten in trouble for it because they could've taken her away from Mom.

But that had been years ago. When she was just a kid and didn't know how to handle stuff like that.

She saw all the emergency vehicles surrounding the fancy-looking building downtown. They said it was an adoption agency.

She saw the explosion, too.

"I'll be damned." Sam was sitting next to Maggie on the couch in the living room. Grandpa was in his chair. He'd been sleeping pretty much all the time since Maggie got home Saturday night and found out Grandpa was home from the hospital already.

She figured they'd sent him home to die. They'd done that with Jeanine, too. Jeanine had been Maggie's best friend until she'd died of leukemia right before they'd started ninth grade.

"Oh, my God." Sam stood, hands covering her mouth.

She walked around the room, staring at the television the whole time.

They hadn't told Maggie what was going on. Well, they had, but not really, just stuff they thought would satisfy her. No one got that she was grown up now. Anyway, she'd figured it all out.

"That bomb was meant for Kelly, right?" she asked. Obviously, they'd gotten Kelly out of there. With all those cop cars and ambulances and fire trucks, they would've cleared the whole street by now.

Kelly was going to be safe. The plan had failed.

Thank God.

"No." Shaking her head, Sam turned up the television.

"A bomb planted, police believe, by the father of Kelly Chapman, a person of interest in Ms. Chapman's disappearance, detonated this morning in the five-hundred block of Old Sycamore Street in South Dayton. We're here outside the Happy Day Adoption Agency now, and while initial reports said the building had been cleared and there were no injuries, it now appears that there's been at least one fatality. A member of the Ohio state bomb squad who was working to disarm the bomb apparently did not survive the blast...."

"Oh, God!" Sam wailed, and Maggie got scared. Really scared.

"Sam?" She felt like she was going to throw up. Seriously.

"Yeah?"

"Is that guy going to kill Kelly?" She'd thought no one even knew Kelly had a dad except for her. How had Mom found out?

And what about Mac? He knew everything about everybody. Why hadn't he told her if Mom knew that?

"Of course not, Maggie," Sam said. "Not as long as they give him the money he's asked for."

It wasn't just about money. Maggie was sure of that. She was surprised Sam hadn't figured that out by now.

Or maybe she had and she was just giving Maggie a dumb kid answer.

"Are they giving it to him?" she asked, wondering if she was going to die soon. God would punish her for being such a rotten person.

"Yes, they are." Sam turned off the television. "They've got it all under control, Maggie, I promise you. The best agents in the state are working on this. By tonight Kelly will be safe at home. You'll see."

Right. So why did Sam look like she'd just eaten something bad?

"Do they know where she is?"

"Not yet. But the guy doesn't get to leave with his money until Kelly is safe with the police."

Creeps like Kelly's father didn't do what they were *allowed* to do. They did what they *wanted* to do.

Maggie needed Mac to hurry up and get in touch with her somehow. To kidnap her and take her away from all this so she could do what *she* wanted to do, too.

She'd tell the police about Mom wanting to get rid of Kelly, but she had to do it without getting Mac in trouble.

Scared to death that they were going to kill Kelly before she had a chance to save her, Maggie made a dash for the bathroom.

And threw up all over the hallway floor.

The other two bombs were apprehended along with their suspect at 11:56 Monday morning. Ezekial Greene had grabbed the blue backpack. He strolled through the playground and out to the street, whistling. Clay heard and saw everything from his vantage point in the disguised delivery vehicle outfitted with recording equipment.

And then Ezekial, the pimp, made the mistake of looking at the beautiful woman walking down the sidewalk across from him. She smiled at him. He smiled back. And she paused.

"Got any money, big boy?"

"Maybe. You got anything I want?"

"Oh, I'm sure of that," the woman said, running her hand up her side, letting her fingers linger on the edge of her breast. Her skintight black jeans, the formfitting white fake-fur coat and her long dark curls were exquisite. Nope, a pimp couldn't be blamed for giving in to his weakness, Clay thought cynically.

And it was that weakness that got 'em every time.

"You got somewhere we can go?" JoAnne Laramie asked while Clay listened from the van. She was wired, and he could hear every word as clearly as if he'd been standing beside her.

"I got a place," Ezekial said, moving closer to JoAnne. "It's only temporary, mind you, just until I check into my room at the Regency tonight." The man had crossed the street and approached JoAnne. He eyed her breasts. And then reached for her crotch. "If you're real good to Daddy, you can come home with him tonight. And maybe never have to go out looking for work again."

"Mmm." JoAnne ran her tongue over her lips, and Clay marveled at her acting ability. The woman had missed her calling.

No, that wasn't true. She was the best damned agent he'd ever known.

"I'll be that good, Daddy, I promise," she drawled. "But first you gotta do me one little itty-bitty favor."

"What's that, princess?" Ezekial ran a finger over JoAnne's breast.

Get your hands off me, you creep. Clay read his agent's

mind at the same time that he heard, "I got a little problem and need a man to take care of it."

"I'm your man, baby, what's your problem?"

"I got a boyfriend who's rough, you know? I try to get away from him and he hunts me down. Shares me with his buddies, too, and keeps all the cash himself." She rubbed a knee against the man's fly.

"You know where this dude is?"

"Mmm-hmm. He's sleeping it off over at his place by the fairground."

"How's about an itty-bitty little explosion to fix your itty-bitty problem?"

"Explosion?" JoAnne pulled back, sounding shocked. "Wait a minute. I don't want no trouble. I'm not goin' to jail! I just thought maybe you could, you know, beat him up."

"Don't worry, baby, this explosion ain't gonna hurt you," Ezekial said. The disgusting excuse for a human being practically slavered as he looked Joanne up and down. "Today's payday. And Daddy got paid double. Your dude got a gas grill?"

"Yeah. Beside the house."

"Well, I got a itty-bitty propane tank that just might accidentally-on-purpose explode."

And it was done.

For once, something went like clockwork.

JoAnne made the arrest. And if she happened to apply the handcuffs tightly enough to dig into the pimp's skin, Clay didn't care to notice.

With the tape they'd just made, combined with the rest of the evidence they'd collected, they had enough on Greene to put him away forever.

Now it was time for Clay to go to work.

One way or another, he was going to get the man to tell him the rest of his sordid tale. Ezekial Greene might have fathered Kelly Chapman, biologically speaking, but he was no father.

He had no right to anything in her life.

Clay was going to make sure the man knew that before the day was over.

25

I was going crazy sitting there. Hours had passed since Clay had walked out, still talking on the phone. Many hours. It was after five. Getting dark. I couldn't turn on any lights until he came home.

I didn't dare turn on the television either.

Not only would I be in danger if the kidnapper knew where I was, but Clay had put his job on the line for me. I owed him my cooperation.

I had no idea what was going on and not knowing upset my emotional equilibrium. It was making me paranoid. Afraid to move. Clay had left hours ago. Looking for an adoption agency that could be a figment of my imagination for all I knew.

Looking for the man who'd sired me and then tried to sell me. Twice.

The time for the ransom drop had long since passed.

And...nothing.

I'd tried to sleep. I'd taken another bath. I'd jotted notes to myself about things I wanted to do when I got home. Made lists. I'd thought about Maggie and Camy, and taking us all on vacation. I'd walked through Clay's house, noticing how little there was of any beauty or peace. Based on that and on what I'd observed, I analyzed him. I recognized that there were a lot of gaps in what I knew about him.

When all else failed, I had a beer.

Something must have gone wrong. That much was obvious. If I was a free woman, Clay would've called to tell me. His home phone hadn't rung. Not that I would've answered if it had.

What if Clay had been hurt? No one knew I was there. No one would know to contact me. I could be there waiting for days before someone came here to deal with Clay's estate.

What was I thinking? Of course he was okay! He was working. And couldn't contact me.

Still, something must've gone wrong or I'd be free by now.

Maybe my father hadn't been the kidnapper, after all.

At 5:30 I took the notepad Clay had given me to the table and, pen in hand, concentrated on my current and recent clients. I went through them one at a time. Made notes on everything I could remember about each of them.

The woman from Denver who had Munchausen's; I'd testified against her to save her husband from wrongful conviction. Melanie Bonaby—who'd come to me when she discovered her husband was unfaithful to her. I'd helped her through the divorce, but she'd let the bitterness consume her. She'd become obsessed and begun stalking and threatening his new wife. She'd eventually lost her children as a result and had expected Kelly to help her again…. Jane Hamilton and Marla Todd. They were two of the three victims of a bigamous, abusive man. I'd been able to be of some benefit to Jane and had attended her wedding the previous summer. Erin and Rick, of course. There were others. Plenty of them. I kept writing.

I would figure this out—and have a list for Clay when he got home. Someone wanted me gone. We'd find out who. And deal with him.

One step at a time. That was all it took. One step at a time.

And what about Maggie? Sam hadn't let her go to school, had she? Abrams could get to her there. Maggie could slip away.

We weren't just fighting Abrams. We were fighting Maggie, too. Fighting her desperate need to be loved. Her delusions about romance.

When it got too dark to write, I moved from the kitchen into the windowless bathroom attached to my bedroom. There were shutters on the kitchen window, but slits of light would show through. Piling towels on the bathroom floor to cushion myself, I settled down and continued to write. When I filled one page, I'd start another. And another. Writing on the back as well as the front.

My hand ached as it sped across the tiny pages. I was racing against my thoughts—trying to keep up with them. I jotted down client information, but other things that came to mind, as well. I wrote about Maggie. My mom. About myself. And about Clay Thatcher.

I wrote until I heard the garage door into the kitchen slam shut.

Was Clay home? Straining to hear through two closed doors, I couldn't make out a single distinguishing sound. No footsteps. No keys.

No calling of my name.

Wouldn't Clay have called out to me?

I sat there, trapped in a windowless room, with no idea who was there.

What if it *wasn't* Clay?

What if he'd told someone about me?

Did the kidnapper get Clay's keys? And his address

from his driver's license? Had Clay given me up for some reason?

Had someone picked the lock on the kitchen door?

Shaking, clutching the gun Clay had left for me, I curled into a corner of the room, into the smallest shape I could make, facing the door. And waited for him to come to me.

"Once more, Mr. Greene." Alone in the interrogation room, Clay stared down the man slouched across from him. "Tell me what you did with your daughter."

They'd been at this a long time. Too long. Hours. But he'd go as long as it took to get a confession.

"I gave the bitch my genes, that's what I did." Hairy knuckles rested lightly against the partially exposed belly pressed up against the table, which separated Clay from his suspect. "She is what she is because of me."

Clay had heard the asshole's version of truth ad nauseam.

"You think she got her smarts from the dumb bitch who raised her?"

"Her mother, you mean," Clay said. "The woman you got pregnant."

Greene had accountability issues. Everything in the world was someone else's fault.

And the man thought *he'd* given Kelly her intelligence?

He'd given his daughter her eyes, though. Clay wanted to puke every time he looked over and saw the vivid blue eyes—unlike Kelly's these were filled with…emptiness.

"Listen, Greene, your opinions don't mean a damn thing to me." The hell with JoAnne and anyone else who was watching this from the other side of the glass. He was done with this guy. "I don't care who you are or what rights you think you have. You're in my world now, and in my world, you're a murderer. You got that?" Clay leaned in, his voice hard. "A man died in that explosion at the adoption agency today. A cop. From where I'm sitting your life isn't worth shit. The only thing you've got going for you at this point is the possibility that you can point us to Kelly Chapman. You tell us where she is and that'll count for something."

In his next life, maybe.

Clay needed the confession. He needed to know Kelly was safe. And then he was turning this bastard over to a D.A. who'd already said he was going for the death penalty.

"You don't get it, do ya?" Greene's rotten-toothed grin was sickening. "Prison ain't so bad. I been there. I know. The beds are better 'n sleeping on the floor, and the food ain't so bad, either. Best part is the price is right."

"And what about the death chamber?" Clay wanted to squeeze the air out of the man's throat. But he sat back. He wasn't going to let the slime get to him. He was going to get to the slime. One way or another. "You got some good memories of that, too?" he asked.

"Appeal, man. I've got my right to appeal. By the time my number comes up, I'll be old and gray and ready to go. And in the meantime?" Ezekial Greene scooted back from the table, grabbed his crotch. "You know what they do to cop killers in prison, man? They revere them. I'm going to be king of the castle. I'll get what I want from whoever I want when I want. You be sure and tell that to my little girl when you find her. You tell her that her daddy's king of the world. You tell her that others will get some, but she got the best of him." He squeezed his fly one more time. "She *is* me," he said.

Clay was over the table before he had a single thought, his hands going for the throat.

It was Greene's laughter that did it. Clay had to shut the

man up. He had to rid the world of that sound. Remove any possibility of its ever reaching Kelly Chapman's ears.

But although he'd leaned across the table, he didn't touch Greene. Didn't make contact at all. He wasn't giving the fuckwad any chance for a way out.

JoAnne was in the room before Clay had a chance to warn the bastard what was coming to him if he didn't tell Clay what he wanted to know. Barry was right behind her.

"Clay? There's a phone call for you," she said as Barry slid into the seat Clay had just vacated.

"I'll be back," he warned with a long look at the smug fiend breathing air that was wasted on him.

"What was that about?" JoAnne didn't wait until they were in Clay's office before she started in.

"Who's on the phone?" he asked, but he knew.

"No one."

"I wasn't going to touch him."

"Then what was it about?" Standing outside the door, with the viewing window in plain sight, JoAnne glanced at the prisoner and then at Clay. "I've never seen you lose control before. What's going on?"

"He killed a cop."

"I've seen you interrogate a sex offender who raped and murdered an eight-year-old girl. You never left your seat."

"That guy confessed."

"Maybe Greene *didn't* kidnap Kelly Chapman."

He did it. He *had* to have done it. He'd murdered a cop and been prepared to murder young children. All without conscience. He'd killed a man and then been ready to fuck JoAnne.

"Maybe it happened just like he said." JoAnne's quiet voice infiltrated the self-talk Clay couldn't escape. "He heard about Kelly's disappearance on the news and, as he put it, thought his ship had come in. He'd just been waiting for his moment and that was it."

One of the problems with this theory was that it meant Kelly Chapman's kidnapper was still at large. Out there. Somewhere.

"Greg got a confirmation from local police in Tennessee. The landlord was out of town and just got back. He checked out, and so does Greene's alibi for Friday morning."

Goddammit to hell.

He'd lost an entire fucking day.

And Kelly was home alone. Virtually unprotected.

Edgewood, Ohio
Monday, December 6, 2010

Someone was in the house.

And it wasn't Clay.

Clay would've come to find me immediately.

Shivering, from too much time spent on the cold floor, or so I told myself, I huddled. And listened. And wished I'd decided to spend the day under the bed.

My skates were inside the bedroom door. They wouldn't be visible if the intruder just looked in. They'd be completely visible—and a dead giveaway—if he came into the bedroom.

There was nothing else of mine there. I'd considered every move I'd made over and over during the half hour I'd been sitting there, waiting for something to happen.

I held the gun up, pointed at the door, but my arms were getting shaky, my trigger finger stiff.

The bed was made. My clothes had been disposed of. The extra clothes Clay had purchased were in his car, ready for his next trip to the shelter in town. I'd washed the dishes I'd used that morning. I'd left no sign of Clay having had a visitor.

So did that mean whoever was there was waiting for him? Prepared to kill him the minute he walked in the door?

I had to warn him.

But how? Without exposing myself? And bringing more danger on Clay. And me. And maybe even Maggie.

Clay might have confided in someone today. Abrams was well connected; he could've sent someone to Clay's house. To take us both out.

I tried to take a deep breath. And couldn't. My chest was too tight.

What should I do?

I had to hide.

Had to trust Clay.

Had to stay quiet. Not make a sound.

Something fell on the floor somewhere in the house. On the tile, not the carpet. Whoever was out there was either in the kitchen or the eating area.

Slowly, silently, I lay down flat on my back, sliding over until my head was at the door. With the pistol at my chin, pointing under the crack, I peered under the bathroom door toward the bedroom. I was pretty sure the bedroom door was still closed. And it looked like there were no lights on anywhere.

Either he'd already checked out the house, or he'd known Clay wouldn't be here.

Was I right? Was someone out there, sitting in the dark, waiting for Clay?

Someone sent by David Abrams?

What should I do? What *could* I do? I was a psychologist. I should be able to outthink this guy.

But we weren't dealing with amateurs here. And there's such a thing as a psychopath. It referred to people who had no conscience, who lacked empathy and compassion. It meant that any interaction I had with this guy, any attempt to influence or persuade him, might not have any effect.

Something else moved—a chair, maybe. And then nothing. I had no idea what was going on. What I wasn't hearing.

I didn't want to accept the inevitability of attack. Of cruelty. Of death.

Just then Marc Snyder appeared in my mind. The young soldier had recently returned from Iraq. I'd chased him down the street more than once when he'd come for an appointment and had left because I hadn't been at the door to greet him.

Marc required much of me.

Because he'd been through so much. He'd seen a young boy lying on the street with his stomach ripped to shreds, bleeding profusely and screaming for his mother. He'd watched while an insurgent raped a woman. Heard her screams, too.

He'd been unable to let go of what had happened and move on to what could—should—come next in his life. The memories were tearing him apart. Eating him alive.

Why had Marc Snyder just occurred to me?

Because he was tortured by his own mind, and I was beginning to feel that way, too?

Because he felt helpless? Unable to make his life right?

Or because he was my kidnapper?

Did he need me gone because I was the only one pushing him to face his demons? The only one who really believed he could get beyond PTSD and have a full and meaningful life?

Was he the person waiting to kill Clay? For saving me?

But how would he know I was in Clay's house? He

wasn't David Abrams. He didn't have seemingly unlimited connections.

Rick Thomas. What if it was someone who was after him? Or the gang leader in Florida? How could I possibly win against either of them?

The thoughts ran crazily through my brain. Some I dismissed. Others lingered.

One remained steadfast.

If I didn't figure out what to do, and do it soon, Clay and I could both die.

26

Clay knew the second he opened the door into the kitchen that someone was in his house. Someone besides Kelly Chapman.

There was a smell. A density. And silence.

Keeping the door between him and the inside of the house, he paused, pulled his gun, tripped the trigger and then, weapon leading the way, he slowly pushed into the room. Ready to shoot first, to take out whoever dared to invade his home.

Beyond taking down the interloper, he had one thought.

Get to Kelly.

If she'd been hurt…

No one charged him as he came into the room. No one lunged or shot or even moved.

Eyes adjusting quickly to the light, Clay immediately noticed the lump on the floor. A body. A female body.

"Freeze. I've got a gun and I will use it."

The voice was off to his left. Clay couldn't see who spoke, but he recognized the voice. He was flooded with a relief that almost made him weak. For that brief second, his gun felt heavy. His arms felt heavy.

"Kelly, it's me, Clay," he said firmly. "Stay against the wall and don't move."

"Someone's here, Clay." Her voice had lowered. "I…"

Clay flipped on the light.

And groaned when he identified the body lying limply on the floor.

"Oh, my God! A woman! Who is she?" Kelly wasn't flat against the wall as he'd told her to be. She'd rushed over and was leaning down, placing two fingers along the neck of their trespasser, obviously feeling for a pulse.

"She's alive, Clay. Call an ambulance."

"We don't need an ambulance."

"But…"

"She's not dying, Kelly, she's asleep."

"In the middle of the kitchen floor?"

Those vivid blue eyes stared up at him. Her panic and fear gave Clay a glimpse into the day she'd spent.

Spent in vain. He had nothing for her.

No name. No arrest. No freedom or even safety.

"She's breathing, isn't she?" he asked.

"Yes."

"Normally."

"Well, yes."

"Her color's okay."

"Yes."

"She hyperventilated. Had a panic attack. And then took a tranquilizer."

Frowning, Kelly looked at him as though he'd lost his mind. He wished he had. He wished he'd conjured up this recurring nightmare in his life.

"You know her."

"Yes."

"Who is she?"

"My mother."

* * *

Clay didn't waste time hating many things. He hated asking Kelly to hide again while he dealt with his mother.

Kelly needed answers. She needed space and peace. She didn't need to be treated like a fugitive.

But instead of tending to his invited guest, he had to deal with a woman who couldn't ever find the strength to help herself.

"I don't trust her not to say anything," he said to Kelly as he walked her back to the bedroom. "I'm going to call my aunt—my mother lives with her. She'll come and get her. And then we'll talk."

"I've waited all day, Clay. A little while longer isn't going to make any difference." Kelly's calmness unnerved him almost as much as his mother's hysteria would when he woke her up. "It looks like she needs you far more than I do."

Maybe. Clay wasn't sure anymore.

But looking at the frail body of his mother lying on his cold kitchen floor didn't bring feelings of compassion and concern as much as resentment.

He detested that about himself.

But all of this was old news.

Really old news.

"I'll be as fast as I can," he said.

"She's your mother, Clay."

He figured his tone of voice had led to that comment. He nodded, rather than responding further. Some truths weren't worth the time it took to tell them.

It took Clay ten minutes to rouse Lynn Thatcher. He'd placed her on the couch and was sitting beside her, holding her hand, when her eyes fluttered open.

"Aunt Bessie's on her way," he said, hoping to cut the

worst of the episode off at the pass. Bessie, his mother's younger sister, was a widow who doted on Clay's mom.

She was also very active in her church and left his mom alone a lot, something Clay and his father had never done. The times they'd left her, they'd always paid someone to care for her until their return.

Lynn raised a hand to his face, caressing him gently. There'd been a time, long ago, when that caress had been a comfort to him. Now he didn't trust it to mean anything.

"Oh, Clay, I'm so sorry, honey."

"It's okay, Mom. You have a key to my house because I gave it to you."

She was his mother.

"I needed you, Clay. I just needed to be near you."

"I know."

"You're angry with me."

"No, I'm not." He wasn't. He was angry with himself.

Angry because he'd spent the past couple of days with a woman whose voice was already in his brain, challenging him to face what was inside of him instead of just accepting it and moving on.

He wasn't about to let Kelly Chapman get to him. To question his beliefs and decisions. He needed his mother to be stronger than she was. He didn't need a shrink.

"Can I stay here with you tonight?"

"You know you can't, Mom. I have to work in the morning. I'm on a case. And Aunt Bessie takes much better care of you than I could."

"You take fine care of me."

He'd learned from the best. And had been at it his entire life.

"So does Bessie."

"Yes, she does. I'm very lucky to have the two of you."

Her voice was getting stronger and Clay breathed a little easier. The panic had passed.

"How'd you get here?" he asked Lynn. She was still pretty, still slim, her limbs slightly twisted by the disease that sometimes rendered her incapable of caring for herself.

The rest of the time it scared the shit out of her.

"Took a cab."

"Where's your walker?"

"At Bessie's. I didn't want to have to lift it in and out of the cab."

"The driver would've done that for you."

"I didn't want to ask. I was stronger today. It was only a few steps from Bessie's door to the curb and a few more to get in here."

"I found you on the kitchen floor."

"I tripped when I bumped into the leg of the chair. I fell."

And couldn't get up. Panicked. And swallowed one of the pills she kept in a little porcelain vial on a chain around her neck.

Clay's father had bought the vial for her, to alleviate her worries that she'd have a panic attack and not be able to help herself. He'd made a big deal out of the fact that the vial was pretty enough to be jewelry.

"You should've called my cell and told me you wanted to visit, Mom. You shouldn't have come out here alone. You know that."

Being trapped in her body was hard for Lynn Thatcher. Clay understood that. Sympathized with it.

The last tears he'd shed had been for his mother. With his mother.

After his father died and she'd been so physically helpless, believing she couldn't survive without him.

That had been a long time ago.

"You just would've told me you were busy," his mother said now.

She was right.

"And you would've told me if you really needed me and I would've come," he answered. Because he always did, if she insisted. Just as his father had.

Usually, as long as she wasn't alone, Clay could soothe his mother's fears with a phone conversation.

And when that didn't work, he went to see her.

Her lower lip started to tremble, and Clay's insides cramped. "I love you, Mom."

"I love you, too, son."

Maggie hadn't been able to eat much dinner. She'd tried. Samantha and Kyle were, like, all over her, fussing around her as if she was a sick kid or about to croak on them or something.

If everything hadn't gotten so messed up, she'd probably have started to like Kyle. She already loved Rad, Kyle's six-month-old colt. She'd always wanted her own horse. And Zodiac was great for a big dog. The farm would be all right, too, if she wasn't trapped there.

It wouldn't be long now before stuff just fell apart. If they didn't find Kelly—and it wasn't looking hopeful, was it?—Maggie knew she wasn't going to be able to survive on her own.

Where was Mac? Why wasn't he doing something?

He'd promised. If she really needed him, he'd be there. He'd said so.

Her stomach was hurting again.

The TV was on and Kyle and Sam were watching some show about a guy who went around the world eating weird foods. Maggie didn't think they were really paying attention. They were just sitting there staring. Waiting.

People were still out looking for Kelly. Flyers had been printed up and posted all over. The FBI was getting tons of calls. Samantha was monitoring a lot of it by phone and still going over records and paperwork and stuff. If not for Maggie, Samantha would be out there, too, searching for Kelly. Maggie knew that.

She wished she could do something. She was about to freak out.

She wished she was back home with Mom in the trailer with the hole in the floor. Back then, all she'd had to worry about was Mom going off on her for putting highlights in her hair. That, and staying away from that creep, Deputy Sewell, and trying to pretend Mom wasn't having sex with him.

The phone rang. The one that had Kelly's line forwarded to it. Maggie tensed.

Please, God, let Kelly be okay.

She glanced at Samantha. So did Kyle. Samantha picked up the phone.

"Hello?

"Hello?

"Hello-o?"

Shrugging, Samantha put down the phone. "No one's there."

That was creepy. And Maggie wondered what else was going to happen. If someone else was going to get hurt. Like Samantha and Kyle. Because they had Maggie.

The phone rang again.

"Hello?" Samantha sounded weird, like she knew the hang-up meant something bad.

"Hello?"

She hung up again.

And then something clicked in Maggie's brain and she knew. It was a sign from Mac. Just like that other time when there were hang-ups at Kelly's and she'd seen Mac the next day around the corner from school and he'd looked her straight in the eye and smiled. Mac was telling her he knew where she was staying.

Or maybe he didn't realize that Kelly's line was ringing at Sam's now. Maybe he was just letting her know he was thinking about her. That he was working on a plan for them. He was telling her to be strong. To hold on. He'd contact her when it was safe to do so. She had to wait, but it was so hard. She had to tell him her plan. And then she had to leave town with him.

The whole thing made her feel jittery and queasy. But she had to suck it up. She wasn't a kid anymore. And she couldn't stay in this town. She was Mom's kid. And now, because of her, Kelly was gone.

Mac *had* to contact her soon. She'd tell him her plan, and they'd go away.

She couldn't take another day like this one.

Edgewood, Ohio
Monday, December 6, 2010

Clay came to get me as soon as his mother was gone. He'd picked up Chinese for dinner and retrieved the cartons from the workbench in the garage outside the kitchen door, dumped the rice and chicken in separate bowls and put them in the microwave.

I uncapped a couple of beers. I didn't need to ask him what was going on to know that I was going to want one.

"I'm assuming you didn't get him," I said when he seemed prepared to busy himself with silverware and plates in total silence.

I wanted to talk to him about his mother, but Ezekial Greene was the reason I was there, in his kitchen, hiding out.

"We got him." His voice was grim.

And I stood there. Waiting. If they got him, then why wasn't I going home?

"He didn't kidnap you, Kelly."

I wasn't hungry anymore.

"Maybe he did. Maybe he's lying. You can't believe a thing he says, Clay…."

He turned to face her. "His alibi checked out."

"So he's free."

"No."

I was surprised—and confused—when Clay shook his head. My father didn't kidnap me. I supposed, in one sense, that was good news—but then why wasn't *he* free?

And we were back to square one.

"He's dead?" I asked the next obvious question.

"No. He's in custody. He didn't kidnap you, but he *was* behind the ransom calls. He'd heard about your disappearance on the news and saw his 'ship coming in,' in his own words."

I wished I could say that didn't sound like dear old dad. But it did. He'd had a price on my head my entire life. He'd never wanted me, never wanted to be a father, but I'd always been a form of insurance to him.

Well, maybe now I could be done paying his premiums.

"What's he charged with?" Inciting panic?

Clay arranged the plates on the table. He sat. But he was more interested in the bottle of beer I'd opened for him than in the steaming rice and spicy chicken.

"You were right about the adoption agency."

The answer seemed strangely disconnected from my question.

"The bomb wasn't a bluff."

I got hot all over. I knew what was coming. And didn't want to hear it. Didn't want to know.

"They got the kids and staff out. The bomb squad was there, working to disarm the bomb, but it detonated. A member of the squad was killed. A thirty-five-year-old father of three."

No. An innocent man dead. A father—a real father—gone. Because of my own father's selfish greed. I had to find that injured family. Do anything I could to help them.

If they'd let me. For as long as they'd let me.

I wasn't just the daughter of a couple of druggies anymore. Or a pimp and his hooker. I was now the daughter of a murderer.

"The D.A.'s already said he's going for the death penalty."

Ezekial Greene on death row? I felt no compassion for the man at all.

But still needed to cry.

27

They made it through dinner, such as it was. Kelly ate. Clay wouldn't discuss anything further until she did. They both knew the score. Her kidnapper was still unknown. And at large.

She needed her strength. And he needed his.

After the plates were cleared away, he sat down with her at the table. His home workspace. Because the only connection Kelly Chapman had to his life was through his job.

She was a job.

"I made another run out to the bike path this morning and then again on the way home." He started with what he thought would be the least threatening piece of information he had for her. "Doesn't look like anyone's been there. The branches are just as we left them. It's been three days. Most people can't survive more than four days without water."

"So whoever took me was planning to leave me there to die?"

"It appears that way."

"Then as long as I stay dead, I'm safe."

"Potentially."

"I could go away. Start a new life…"

"You wouldn't be able to take your name, your credentials, your degree, your money…."

"I'd have to leave Maggie."

"And if David Abrams is behind this, you'd be leaving her in his hands."

Judging by the resolute and steely look on her face, that option was not acceptable to Kelly Chapman.

"But if the guy's left me for dead, he could be long gone by now. You say there've been no hits in your search for the cart or the city worker's uniform. So how do we find him?"

"That's what we have to figure out. What I have to figure out. I've got to lure this guy to us *somehow*."

"By letting him know I'm alive?"

Clay ignored the question.

"I had a call from Washington." Her life was at stake. He couldn't protect her from the truth. "I can't disclose a lot about the conversation and, frankly, don't know all that much, but we still can't rule out the possibility that your kidnapping was connected to your interview with Rick Thomas."

Her only visible reaction to his announcement was thinned lips. And while Clay admired her composure, her strength, he was also bothered by it. Because he didn't know how to handle that kind of reaction. Why didn't she just fall apart as his mother would have done? *That* he would've expected.

"There was an explosion at Rick's home. A problem with the furnace. Rick and Erin and Rick's brother, Steve, all perished."

When her mouth fell open and tears filled her eyes, Clay did something he'd never done before.

He betrayed his security clearance.

"I heard that a new family settled someplace. A man, a woman and a mentally handicapped adult. The woman will have law school credentials and will need to pass the bar exam but she'll be able to practice again."

Kelly's tremulous smile, her silent nod, meant enough to Clay to put him in danger.

He cleared his throat. Took a sip of the beer that was growing warm. He pulled his files toward him. The explosion had been carefully rigged by government agents. Rick Thomas and Erin qualified for the witness protection program. Rick could get a new identity. A missing Kelly Chapman could not.

And if Clay came forward with the information that he'd found her, she'd become part of the system. Subject to protocols. And out of his hands.

"Agents in Washington are following up on all leads in the Thomas case," he said.

"But with Thomas gone, I wouldn't be of much use to either his enemies or our government, would I? Any testimony I have would be hearsay."

"Unless you're alive and can somehow identify your kidnapper. Which seems unlikely. Or unless Rick gave you something that could prove his theory. He didn't, did he?"

Her whispered "No" was his answer.

"My team and I are continuing to look at what we have here," he continued. "There've been hundreds of calls on the help line and the FBI has offered reward money for information."

The notebook he'd given Kelly slid into his line of vision. As did her slender fingers. He couldn't see the scabs that had formed on the backs of her wrists and on her palms, but he knew they were there.

"I made notes on some of my cases," she said. She'd also ripped out quite a few pages. The tablet she'd just presented to him was much slimmer than when he'd first given it to her.

What was on those missing pages? He wanted to know. Didn't like not knowing.

"I'm concerned about Marc Snyder." Kelly flipped a couple of the pages in front of him. The returned soldier's name was at the top of the sheet. He read her notes on the young man. Kelly's handwriting was like her—quick, darting, confident. But not neat. After three days of investigating her, he recognized the scrawl.

And as he read her theories about the reasons Snyder might have for kidnapping her, he could've become convinced he was their man. There was only one problem.

"We've been watching Snyder since your disappearance. You're spot-on about his resenting how hard you're pushing him. He's not upset that you're missing, but we don't think he's guilty of anything more than resenting you. He claims he was working out at the Y when you disappeared. His mother verifies that he left the house in his workout clothes and carrying his gym bag at the appropriate time."

"Doesn't mean he went to the Y."

"His membership badge was scanned ten minutes after he left his home."

"Does anyone know how long he was there?"

"Not for sure. The place was busy and Marc keeps to himself. A couple of people remember seeing him there Friday morning. One, a trainer, didn't remember exactly when. The other, a woman about Marc's age, said she saw him there about an hour after you went skating."

"So he could've gone to the Y and left. Maybe even gone back." Possible. But chances were slim. JoAnne and Barry had both spoken with Snyder and both were certain that he had nothing to do with the kidnapping.

And if Snyder *had* been at the gym, how had he known Kelly would go skating? Unless he was on the take and working for someone else…

Like Abrams?

"We searched his home. And his car. There was no sign of any kidnapping. No key to a utility cart. No city-worker uniform. Not even a smudge of dirt or a twig from a tree in his car. And the vehicle hadn't been cleaned. Apparently, Marc's a heavy smoker."

"What about black boots?" Kelly asked. "I saw the toe of a black boot."

"He does have boots like that. They're with forensics now." Clay studied her. "Let me ask you this. If Snyder *had* taken you, do you think he's stable enough to calmly profess his innocence again and again? Or would there be some crack in his armor? Some hint of desperation? A change in his story?"

"Marc…when he starts to feel trapped, he bolts."

"He's not bolting. In fact, he's cooperating fully."

"Then if he did take me, he feels justified in the action and there's no guilt associated with it. Remember, Clay, this young man was trained to kill."

Clay glanced down. He'd just read something….

"You say that he wasn't able to accept the inevitable."

"When it came to injustice. To innocent people being hurt."

"And he wouldn't see you as innocent?"

"Right. I believe that in his mind, I'm part of the war."

Clay still didn't think Snyder was their man, but… "I'll have Barry continue to keep an eye on him."

"Tell me about your mother."

They'd been going over Kelly's notebook. Discussing each of her clients, the notes she'd made, her impressions.

"Leave my mother out of this."

Her eyes narrowed and he could feel her assessing him. He didn't need assessing. There was nothing wrong with him. And to prove it, he muttered, "She has multiple sclerosis."

She nodded. Said nothing. What, now she was humoring him?

"She was diagnosed when I was two."

"That must have been hard."

"I don't need a shrink."

"Are we done here?" She stood.

"Where are you going?" He was being an idiot. And blamed…himself.

"To my room," she said, not taking her notebook.

"Look." Clay didn't stand. He didn't even meet her gaze. He flipped his pen against the edge of the table. "I'm sorry, okay? Please sit down."

He was relieved when she did as he asked. And yet, he didn't like feeling that way. What the hell was the matter with him?

"My mom," he started, stopped and began again. "I… How much do you know about MS?"

"I know it's chronic, but generally patients live normal life spans. There's a large range of symptoms, ranging from blurred vision to certain types of paralysis, depending on the part of the central nervous system it attacks. Those symptoms can be continuous or go into remission between occurrences. They're often exacerbated by stress, fever or exposure to sunlight."

She knew a lot. "Depression is also a side effect."

"It is with a lot of crippling and chronic diseases."

"Have you ever treated someone with a chronic disease?" Lynn had seen her share of counselors over the years. Mostly to no long-standing effect.

"Of course."

"Then you know about the paranoia."

She nodded. "It can be debilitating to the patient—and to the patient's family." .

"From the moment Mom was diagnosed, she was afraid to be alone. Afraid she'd have a spell and wouldn't be able to take care of herself. Personally, I think she's terrified of dying alone."

"A lot of people are. Most of us are able to manage our fears. Some people aren't."

"My mom's one of them. From what I hear, she used to be quite independent, but once she got sick, everything changed. It's like she lost confidence in herself. She clung to my father. He was her sole source of security. As long as he was around, she did pretty well—so mostly he stayed around."

"Which enabled her fear."

"My father loved her. He was concerned. Frankly, I think he wanted to be with her as much as she wanted him there." Though he'd never actually framed that thought until right then.

"It's like that sometimes. Especially with spouses who are close. What happens to one happens to the other."

Clay considered that. "As I got older, she seemed to feel safe with me, too."

"She would. You're her son. And your father's son."

"She lives with my aunt now, her younger sister. That's the arrangement they both wanted after my father died. My aunt's a widow, as well. And dotes on Mom. But Mom still has moments…."

"Depression isn't necessarily just a side effect of the MS," Kelly said. "It can be a separate condition. The disease affects the parts of the brain that control emotional equilibrium. Just like she could have a flare-up that temporarily numbs her legs, she could have one that sends her into depression."

He'd heard it all before, of course. So why, tonight, did the facts sound different?

"I can't desert her," Clay said. "Which is why I gave

her a key to my place. I want her to know I'm always here if she needs me."

And otherwise he had his freedom. Unlike his father, who'd lost most of his life when Lynn had gotten sick. Lost it to the point of living out the rest of his years vicariously through his son.

"You're good to her."

Right. He resented the hell out of his only living parent for having a disease—not that she could help it. No, he resented her for not being stronger in dealing with the situation. For being so damned needy...

"Your mother trusts you. She comes to you because you're there for her."

What else could he do? Lynn was his mother. He loved her.

"Has she ever seen a counselor?"

"Yes."

"Have you?"

He didn't need one.

"I was just wondering...you know...because, based on what you've told me and what I've observed, I thought you might have problems with commitment."

"I don't have...problems."

"I couldn't help overhearing the other night when your agent...JoAnne, I think you said...was here. Obviously the two of you had something together at some point."

"Yeah, it didn't work out. I sure don't need a shrink for that."

"Of course not. But...you're what—thirty-five or so?"

"Thirty-seven." Not that it was any of her damned business.

So why was he allowing this? Why wasn't he shutting her up? Like he did any other woman who dared to get too close to parts of him he reserved for himself.

"Thirty-seven and you've never been married, correct?"

Had he told her that?

"Yeah."

"I can tell you've been here awhile," she said, waving her arm around the room. "The paint's faded around the key hook you've got there by the door. And around your microwave, too. But there are no feminine touches in here. No *personal* touches. None. Except the wallpaper in the en suite next to my room."

"We thought Mom was going to live here. That was going to be her room. She chose the paper. I had it hung."

"There are no mementos of life here. No pictures. No hints of interests or hobbies or vacations."

"My job takes most of my time."

"Most people need relationships, too. Unless they're running from something."

"I'm not most people." And they were going to leave this conversation at that.

"I just want to help if I can, Clay. You saved my life." Kelly Chapman's voice had changed, softened, getting his attention.

"Don't make me wish I hadn't," he said half to himself, but loudly enough for her to hear.

"I'll let it go, but if you ever want to talk…"

Marc Snyder was right about one thing—the woman pushed too hard.

"You want to hear what I have to say?" he asked, fueled by the unwelcome emotions she'd churned up in the two days she'd been in his life. Three, if you counted the day he'd spent with her picture on his dash.

"Yes."

"I have a kidnapper—most likely a professional—out there someplace, plotting God knows what. I can't even tell what I'm up against. I could be fighting a threat to national defense, a street gang, an unbalanced American soldier or a powerful and highly connected pedophile. And after three days I'm no closer to finding him or proving who it is. I've risked my career by bringing you here and possibly your life as well if I don't manage, on my own, to keep you safe until we get this guy. I almost strangled a prisoner tonight to force him to talk to me. I'm tired. I'm frustrated. And right now all I can think about is what you'd feel like naked in my bed."

There. That would shut her up.

And he could get back to work.

28

Edgewood, Ohio
Tuesday, December 7, 2010

I'd been up, showered and dressed since six. I'd watched the shadows on the wall of my room as the darkness of night gave way to daylight.

I'd written on the backs of the pages I'd ripped from my notebook, careful not to get salve from my hands on them.

The sheet with the name *Clay Thatcher* on top went untouched.

I had no clear plan for the rest of the day. No idea when I'd emerge from this room. I'd excused myself and gone there after Clay's outburst the night before.

Nor was I going to let him know that I'd spent a good part of the night hearing his words. Over and over. *Naked in my bed.*

Naked in my bed.

I listened for him to go to bed in his room across the hall from me. If he had, he'd done it quietly enough that I hadn't noticed.

Naked in my bed.

The comment had been completely inappropriate. And

that was exactly why he'd whipped it in my direction. I understood that much.

I wasn't afraid of him. If he had any intention of acting with impropriety he certainly wouldn't have announced it.

And…I just wasn't afraid of him.

I couldn't say the same for myself.

Naked in my bed.

Naked in my bed.

Every single time the words repeated themselves in my brain I got turned on.

Clay's cell phone rang.

He answered. He seemed to be in the kitchen. I couldn't make out the words, but there was no mistaking the urgency in his voice.

I left my room.

"That was the prosecutor in Florida," Clay said with a glance at Kelly as she entered the eating area.

Dressed in the same clothes as the day before, she was as unforgettable as she'd been the first time he'd seen her picture. The bruise at her temple didn't look so bad anymore, but he'd never forget it either.

"Miguel Miller just took a plea."

"Why would he do that *now?* With me missing, the prosecution doesn't have a great case against him." She sounded normal. Like any other time they'd talked in the past couple of days. She was meeting his eyes.

Good.

"Exactly. If he knew you were missing he wouldn't have taken a plea bargain. So it looks like we can cross him off our list of possible suspects."

"What if someone kidnapped me for him, but he doesn't know about it yet?"

"That's possible, but not likely. The underground information network is pretty sophisticated. And Saturday was visiting day."

Kelly helped herself to a bottle of water and a granola bar and sat at the table where he'd spent much of the night.

The rest of it he'd passed on the couch. He'd gone to his room across the hall from hers only long enough to shower and pull on a pair of black slacks, a white shirt and a black-and-white tweed jacket with his black dress boots.

"I also had a call from the Bureau in Washington about an hour ago," he continued. "They arrested an aide to the secretary of defense last night. They've connected him to a plan to kill Rick Thomas, but it doesn't look as though you were anywhere on their radar. They haven't determined yet who else is involved, so it's still possible that they have something to do with your disappearance, but it's not as likely."

"So that leaves Snyder."

"Or David Abrams."

She didn't reply to that.

"Or someone else we've missed," Clay added. He'd spent the night combing through his files—and her notes.

"Someone who wants me dead. We know now that this isn't about money."

"I spoke with JoAnne first thing this morning," Clay said. "We're both fairly certain that Abrams is our man, Kelly. Everything about him fits. He has the most to lose. A wife, kids, a career, his standing in the community. His entire life is over if his relationship with Maggie is exposed. And you're the key to that exposure. We're focusing our investigation on him—finding a way to get him to make a mistake if we can't come up with anything that leads him directly to you."

"Use me as bait, Clay. If he needs me gone, learning that I'm not will force him into action. It's the only way."

"If we make your rescue public, if Abrams knows you're alive, he's going to start getting desperate. He could go after Maggie."

"Go after her how?"

Clay shrugged. He'd been over and over this during the night. With no one else aware that Kelly was alive, this was an aspect of the case he had to handle alone. To rely only on himself to see every angle. "If he thinks she'll buckle, that she'll turn him in, he could kill her."

Kelly's gasp hit him hard. Made him feel like he was failing her.

"Could also be that if he's really in love with her like she thinks, he'll try to run off with her."

"David Abrams is in love with David Abrams," Kelly said, her voice hard. Unyielding. "There's no way he'd leave his perfect life—his wife and kids—to live on the run with a fourteen-year-old girl."

But Clay wasn't sure she was right.

"Think about this," he began slowly. "The man is allegedly the mastermind behind a methamphetamine superlab that grossed maybe a million dollars—the majority of the money being slipped into the city budget via so-called donations—and he manages to keep his hands clean. His one mistake was Maggie Winston. She's his weakness. If we're going to get him, it has to be through her."

"You aren't using Maggie as bait!"

"Would you rather she be left out there exposed to Abrams's next plan? Whatever that might be?"

"Can't she be put in some kind of protective custody until this is over? She could be taken somewhere, out of state, even out of the country, just until we get Abrams?"

He'd thought of that. "But how are we going to get him?" he asked, aware that the question was a rhetorical one. "If Sam had been able to do that, she'd already have done it. Once Maggie's gone, you aren't of any value to him, so using you as bait wouldn't work. I also don't believe he'd let Maggie go. He'd hunt her down. His only safe recourse is to keep her close, to keep her devoted to him."

Kelly frowned. "What you're saying is you think she's safest right here, with him convinced that he's still got her in his control."

"Don't you?"

"I don't know. Maybe."

"I understand that you don't want to consider this, but it's possible that Abrams believes himself in love with Maggie. Why else would he have risked so much to be with her?"

"Because he's a pedophile."

"Then why not go after any of the other girls who were delivering for them?"

"Maggie was the only one he was personally exposed to." But Kelly's response had a hint of desperation about it. Maybe Maggie was her weakness, too. Her blind spot.

"Pedophiles aren't generally exclusive in their needs," he said. "I'm assuming there wasn't any other evidence against Abrams, no suspicious activity with children, no child pornography found on his computers or Samantha would have arrested him."

"She didn't have enough to get a warrant to look at his computers, but I know that in the past couple of months she's been monitoring his IP addresses—not legally or officially—and there's been nothing."

"I'm telling you, the man has a thing for Maggie."

"It's sick! Disgusting. She's a *child*."

"If he wasn't in love with her, if he was just protecting himself, why kidnap you? Why not simply arrange for something to happen to Maggie? With his connections that shouldn't be too hard."

She didn't answer.

"He's not going to hurt Maggie because he has feelings for her," Clay said. "And he's egotistical enough to believe that her feelings for him will keep her loyal. It's a win-win for him. You're gone and he still gets Maggie. The only way that changes is if he thinks there's a chance Maggie might turn him in."

The pinched look was back on her face.

"We know he's still holding on to her. He went to their place in the woods. And so did she, at least twice. Once to drop off the rose and then again on Saturday when we left her alone. He moved the rose to let her know he was there, that he loved her. There's still something going on there. He risked spending time at their spot. And there's another element of this we haven't considered. Maybe Abrams didn't just want you gone to protect himself from eventual exposure. Maybe he wanted you out of the way so he could have Maggie."

"He knows Sam is watching him like a hawk."

"But he also knows that Maggie loves you. You were competition for her affection and loyalty."

"You think he's that far gone?"

"Don't you? With the risks he's taken? By all accounts David Abrams is a highly intelligent man. A winner. A guy like that isn't just going to throw away his perfect life. Maggie has a hold on him as surely as he's got a hold on her."

The silence was painful. An unpalatable, unacceptable truth was painful.

"It's really him, isn't it? He's the one behind this?" For the first time since he'd known her, Kelly Chapman sounded needy. "I've been telling myself that someone wanted *me* dead. I've worked on a lot of cases. There are a lot of people who could be upset with me—and any number of them could become unhinged enough to do something desperate. I've been telling myself this is only about me. That Maggie would be fine."

Tears spilled from her eyes. "I'd rather be facing a street gang that's after me than have David Abrams go after Maggie. He's insidious. He always gets what he wants. And I don't want Maggie hurt again. I promised her I'd protect her."

He'd promised Kelly he'd protect her, too.

"I'd give up my life for Maggie, but from what you're saying, with David Abrams, giving up my life only makes his quest easier."

"We have to use her, Kelly. We have to come up with a way to use Maggie to get to Abrams and end this."

He didn't like it. Didn't like putting the kid in any more danger.

Didn't like using her as bait.

But he didn't have any better ideas.

And he couldn't hide Kelly Chapman in his home forever.

Edgewood, Ohio
Tuesday, December 7, 2010

Was I actually willing to use Maggie, exposing her to possible danger? Could doing that actually be safer for her than not doing it?

There had to be another way. We *had* to find another way.

Clay's cell rang again as I sat there frantically trying to figure out an alternative and still trying to think of someone else who might be responsible for my kidnapping.

I'd been trapped for four days. A prisoner. This *had* to end….

"You're sure?" Clay's gaze was intense as he spoke on the phone and looked at me.

"Thanks. I'll get back to you."

"That was Samantha," he said as he disconnected the call.

My stomach dropped. "Is Maggie okay?"

"Sam's worried about her. Maggie's not just missing you, and worried, she's nervous. She asked Sam this morning how long a person can survive without water."

"How would she know I was without water?"

"Unless she knows where you were being kept."

Maggie knew what had happened to me and was just leaving me there to die? I couldn't believe that.

And yet I could. The girl had been through too much. Lost too much. And she was being given impossible choices. Turn in the person you believe to be your soul mate, the one person who'll love you forever—or leave the counselor and foster mom you'd only known a few months to her fate.

"That's not why Sam called, though," Clay was saying. "There were a couple of hang-ups on your line last night. They came from a pay phone in town." He named the location of one of the few remaining pay phones in Chandler. "Video from the parking lot of the store shows David Abrams leaving the area just minutes after the call was made. There were no fingerprints on the phone. There's no way to prove that Abrams made the calls, but Samantha doesn't think it was a coincidence. And frankly, neither do I."

Oh, God, what was I supposed to do?

"Samantha said that Maggie was upset by the first call, but seemed a bit calmer after the second. Almost as though it was some kind of message to her."

"There were a couple of hang-ups, one right after the

other, at home, too…" I remembered aloud, feeling a sense of horror. I hadn't thought anything of it at the time, but…

"It could be a signal to her to meet David at their spot in the woods."

I knew what was coming next. No! Just no. I shook my head.

"We have to do this, Kelly. We'll watch her every second. He won't get his hands on her, but we have to let him hang himself. These past months without her, playing this game, worrying that you were having an influence on her…they've obviously taken their toll. He's getting desperate. Otherwise, why take you?"

"Desperate people do desperate things." Not exactly a profound analysis of the situation, but I knew how true it was.

"Well, yes…"

"I need to talk to her. Let me see her, Clay. Let me show her I'm alive and that I'll be here for her. Sam said she was nervous and struggling, more than just because of missing me. What I know is that Maggie's a good kid. Really good. Bone-deep good. If she knows anything about my disappearance, then she's in true crisis mode right now. I'm terrified that if she doesn't connect with Abrams or me, she might commit suicide…" I was blubbering, I knew that, I could hear myself. But I couldn't stop. "If she sees that I'm okay, that nothing happened to me, that'll free her from at least part of the nightmare. Free her enough to see what Abrams did to me, but also to her—she'll see the price he expected her to pay to be with him. And if I'm there to offer her security, if I'm there as proof that I'm not going to leave her…she just might be able to tell us the truth. This could be the moment we've been waiting for."

"Or she could tell Abrams that you're alive which, given

the man's probable state of mind, could lead him to silence you—and Maggie—forever."

"She won't have a chance to tell him. We'll keep her under guard until he's arrested."

"And if she won't talk? You going to guard her until she's eighteen? Keep her in hiding? Because as soon as your kidnapper knows you're alive, your days are numbered."

He was pissing me off.

"You've had her for several months already," Clay went on. "And you've been unable to break the bond between her and Abrams. If she feels at all responsible for your disappearance, even if it's just through knowing something and hiding that information, she's also going to feel an even greater bond with Abrams. Because if that's the case, they committed a crime together. They have to protect each other."

I didn't want to listen to logic. Or common sense. I was listening with my heart. Fighting for something that was bigger than I was.

Fighting for someone who belonged to me. Needed me.

All these years—my entire life, really—I'd managed to do just fine on my own. I was happy helping other people. And now, suddenly, I had a family.

I had a life of my own.

And it scared me.

Because I wanted it.

I hadn't even known how much I wanted it, until right now, when I was on the verge of losing it.

Clay's words about my father, about my not needing him now that I had Maggie, came back to me again.

Was he right? This agent who lived his life so alone. Had he seen something about me that I hadn't seen about myself? Had he seen how badly I needed a life, a family of my own? So badly that I'd cling to a criminal father just to belong?

Had he also realized that until I was forced to, I didn't dare expose the ugliness that was so much a part of me?

The truth of my parentage.

And my own lack of a sense of value because of it.

Did he know that, deep inside, I'd never felt as if I was enough?

Well, no, that wasn't true. Of course I was enough. I'd made a good life for myself. I was proud of what I'd accomplished.

Looking at myself from the outside, through the eyes of a man who'd found out more about me in four days than anyone had known in my entire life, I was horrified at what he might see.

He might think that…

Now was *not* the time to fall apart!

Or to suddenly have a life-changing revelation. Or an onslaught of fear.

And now, with my back to the wall, was exactly the time.

29

Clay had left the room. Giving me time to digest every-thing he was asking of me, I supposed.

Or maybe he just had to use the bathroom.

I didn't appreciate his absence. Being alone was excru-ciating.

He obviously didn't think Maggie would choose me over Abrams in a showdown.

He thought my kidnapping gave Abrams more power over Maggie—that it created a stronger bond between them.

I was ready for him as soon as he reappeared.

"We don't know for sure the kidnapper wasn't someone after Rick Thomas," I reminded him as he sat back down, but even I realized that scenario was probably far-fetched at this stage.

Maggie was connected to my disappearance. I could see that. She knew *something*. Abrams, too. His visit to the woods the day after I was taken couldn't be a coincidence.

Nor were the hang-up phone calls.

"What are you proposing?"

"That we stand back and see what happens."

That was it? His grand plan?

"Everyone's on edge right now. Someone's going to lose it. Soon. Either Abrams or Maggie, or both. I suggest Samantha tell Maggie that since so much time has passed, they should start preparing for the fact that you might not be coming back. That investigators have followed all the leads and haven't turned up anything substantial and we have to cut back on our investigation. There are other cases that we have to work on. And that she'll likely be put in foster care."

"No! That's cruel. We can't—"

"Would you rather she made the decision herself—the wrong decision—while no one's watching? All we're doing is pushing her into action sooner. Because, mark my words, she'll be going into action at some point. The way I see it, Maggie will either be prompted by Abrams, or by us, on his timeline or ours. If he has her under his control, which appears obvious, she's his puppet and will act as and when he dictates."

He leaned forward, pinning me with a look I didn't like but couldn't avoid. It forced me to acknowledge the truth. "She's going into foster care, anyway, if we don't find your kidnapper and get him off the street. The state won't leave her with Sam indefinitely."

She'd already been awarded to me. But my custodial rights weren't permanent yet. And if being with me posed any kind of threat to her, Clay was right. She'd be placed in foster care.

Where her new caregivers might or might not put any stock in our theories regarding Abrams.

And that was what he wanted, wasn't it? To continue living a family life with his wife and kids, and keeping Maggie on the side?

"There was a story in the news last week," I said out loud. "It was about a churchgoing guy with six kids and a wife. His kids adored him. His coworkers thought he was a conscientious employee and his neighbors thought he was a great guy. He'd just been arrested for conducting a four-year relationship with a girl who's now sixteen. They found pictures of her and him. He'd first touched her inappropriately when she was twelve."

"In a few years that could be Abrams," Clay said. "And Maggie."

"Over my dead body."

I meant that literally.

Once again Kelly Chapman's visible struggle, the way she seemed to torture herself with a quest for personal integrity, was excruciating to watch. And yet, Clay couldn't look away, either.

He had a sudden vision of her photo on his dash. Of those eyes that spoke to him.

And, for a second, felt a twinge of fear. What if he was leading her wrong?

He couldn't think of anything worse.

But he had a job to do.

"If I have your okay, I'd like to make the calls to get the plan in motion," he said, gathering up his files, which he'd left open during the long night.

She was tapping a pen against the table. The same pen she'd had in her mouth several times that morning. "I'm a missing person. You don't need my okay."

Clay stilled. Reached for her hand. And held on until he had her full attention.

"I need your okay."

She stared at him. And then nodded.

Clay picked up his phone.

* * *

"They can't do that." Maggie turned to Sam and didn't look at Kyle at all. He was like a judge or something. He just watched and you could never tell what he saw. Or what he knew.

Besides, he'd cleaned up her puke in the hall.

She was afraid she might throw up again even though breakfast had been two hours ago. "She'll *die* if they don't keep looking," she told Samantha. "It's illegal just to let someone die. It has to be."

"They've done all they can, sweetie. They have other cases to work on, other crimes to solve."

"But that Agent Thatcher guy, I thought he only looked for missing people."

Maggie had been out at the barn with Rad. She'd cleaned out his stall like Kyle had shown her. Mostly she was trying to be where Mac could get to her, waiting for Mac to contact her in case he knew where she was. Trying not to think about Kelly. Trying not to miss her so much. And then Kyle had told her Sam needed her in the house.

So here they all were, sitting at the kitchen table and it was horrible. Worse than anything she'd imagined.

"You're right, that's all he does, but Kelly isn't the only person missing in Ohio. There's a woman who didn't come home from a date over the weekend. And two girls who've been missing from a downtown Dayton neighborhood for over three weeks."

"Three *weeks?*" And no one had found them yet? They must've run away. And downtown...everyone knew that was a rough area.

But Kelly, she was...

"The reality is that many people who go missing are never found," Samantha said, and Maggie really didn't like her at all right then. "Agent Thatcher told me he has files full of unsolved cases. Some of them are more than twenty years old. They keep looking, keep hoping, but a lot of times you never know what happened."

But they had to solve this one. They had to.

"They're calling off the search," Samantha said. "Tomorrow someone from the state will be coming to talk to you about foster care. It'll take a few days for all the paperwork to be done. They'll be really careful about finding a place for you to live where you'll be happy, though probably not here in Chandler. You'll stay here until it's all arranged. But don't worry—I'm not just going to send you off and forget about you. Kelly loved you and she's the closest thing to a best friend I ever had. She'd want me to keep in touch with you, to watch out for you. And I want to do that, anyway."

Shut up. Would she please just shut up? Maggie closed her eyes, blocking the truth—and the tears she couldn't hold back. They slid out from between her eyelids no matter how tightly she closed them.

And rubbed Camy. The poodle was always in Maggie's lap. Anytime she was sitting down.

It used to be Kelly's lap that Camy considered her own personal sanctuary.

"I'm so sorry, sweetie," Samantha said.

Maggie looked at her then—because seeing Samantha was better than the darkness of not looking.

"And I was thinking," Kyle added. "Rad needs someone to look after him. Someone light enough to get up on his back without hurting him. I'd like him to be yours, and for you to come out here and take care of him. I'll teach you."

He was serious. Watching her, Kyle just kept on talking, offering her the best dream in the world at the same time her whole life was ending. "We'll arrange transportation from wherever you are, but if you want the job, it's yours. I'd pay you, of course." He named a sum that was twice what she'd made when she had her paper route last summer and was babysitting, too. More, even, than her friend Glenna had made as a full-time nanny during the summer. "That way you'll have some independence." Kyle wasn't done talking yet. "But I have to know you want the job, and that you'll be responsible with him. I can't have you start and then just quit because you're tired of him."

"I wouldn't do that," Maggie said. "I'm not a quitter."

Or a loser like her mom.

She couldn't take his job. Because Mac had to get them out of here. He'd be in trouble if they caught him with her. Because of her age. But she was his woman. Really and truly. She had to be with him. That meant if he had to leave, so did she.

She really wanted the job. It was better than a dream.

But she was an adult now. Mac's lover. She had other things to do with her life. She had to love Mac. Take care of him.

And someday, when she was out of college, to have his babies.

They'd raise them in a house with a lot of rooms and a big yard. And…they'd have a barn and buy a horse for their kids. Maybe Rad. Or another of Kyle's horses…

Maggie was crying. She didn't know what to do. "We have to keep looking for her, Sam," she said. She had to tell them about Mom. And she had to get to Mac. Now. She had to get out of town with him so he could be safe from their lies. And then she'd tell them about Mom so they didn't give up on Kelly.

If they gave up on Kelly, Maggie couldn't live with herself.

"Can't you do something? Start your own investigation?"

"Not officially," Sam said. "This is out of my jurisdiction."

Maggie had thought Sam could do anything. She'd

killed Sewell with one bullet when he'd been shooting at her. She'd brought down a whole drug ring when no one else even believed there was one.

She'd saved Maggie's life.

And she couldn't help Kelly.

Maggie couldn't wait for Mac to get in touch with her. They were going to give up on Kelly. And ship Maggie to a foster home and maybe he'd never find her again.

"Can I go back out to the barn?" she asked, wiping tears off her face. "I just want to be with Rad for a little while."

Samantha looked at Kyle, who nodded.

And Maggie knew this was her only chance.

Edgewood, Ohio
Tuesday, December 7, 2010

Clay had a multiway phone conference call set up at the kitchen table. He was using a landline with a speakerphone and it was killing me just to sit there and quietly listen.

An FBI team, my friends and other officers were all in place, all with jobs to do, to save my life and Maggie's, too. Clay was running the show. Everyone reported to him. He gave the orders and asked the questions. The entire operation rested on his shoulders.

And I...I just sat there.

While the young woman I'd taken into my home, into my heart, the young woman I'd dared to love, was on the run.

"She's on the road out by where the fire was." I recognized Kyle's voice. Keeping a safe distance, he'd followed Maggie on horseback, riding Lillie, after Maggie had taken off crossing his land on foot. The girl didn't have anything with her that they knew of. Not her phone. Or her purse. "A car went by and she stuck out her thumb."

"She's hitchhiking." That was Sam, her voice grim.

I missed Sam. My lips started to tremble and I would've given a lot right then to be sitting in her kitchen with a cup of her specially brewed coffee in front of me. I'd even drink it.

So what if I hated the stuff? Taste didn't matter. People did. Friends did.

"Sandra, move," Clay said. "Pick her up."

Sandra, an agent Kelly knew nothing about. JoAnne was out there, too, but apparently she'd been at Samantha's the other night. Maggie would recognize her.

Silence on the line. Clay didn't look at me. He had a map spread out on the table, with dots representing the various people under his command.

It was like a board game.

One in which winning meant everything.

30

"Thank you so much." Maggie took one look at the woman dressed in jeans and a sweater and a dark blue insulated hoodie and slid into the car, closing the door behind her.

The woman smiled. Her hands were nice, like Kelly's. Soft-looking. Not all rough and chapped with broken nails like Mom's. "Where you headed?"

"Into town. I had a fight with my boyfriend and made him drop me off. He wanted to…you know. I never should've come out into the country with him." The story Glenna had told her about the quarterback she'd broken up with over the summer just came out of Maggie without her really even thinking about it.

Did that make her like Mom? Mom was the best liar Maggie had ever heard. And she did it all the time. It was how she got things to work out the way she wanted them to.

Maggie hated the idea of being like her mother.

Could she go to prison for not telling on Mom?

What if Kelly died?

Shivering, Maggie zipped up the winter ski jacket Kelly had bought her a couple of weeks before. She'd worried about wearing it out to the barn, worried the light blue would get dirty with the horses, but it had been cold out there.

And then, when she'd had to leave, she'd been glad to have it.

"Do you want to call your mom?" the woman asked, and Maggie hoped she wasn't going to insist on talking.

She'd run out of lies miles before they got to town.

"No, she's not home."

"Would you like me to call the police? Did the boy do anything to you? Touch you in ways he shouldn't have?"

"No!" Whoa. She'd screwed up on that one. "It was nothing like that. He just asked me if I wanted to, you know, kiss. He's sixteen and has his own car and I... We've gone out a few times, but I didn't want to kiss him. And then I just didn't want to be in the car with him. That's all."

"You're sure?"

"Positive."

The woman nodded and Maggie started to breathe more regularly again. Once she got to town, everything would be fine.

Thankfully the woman didn't say anything for the rest of the ten-minute ride into town. Until the first houses and businesses on Main Street appeared and then she asked, "Anyplace in particular you need to be dropped? I can take you home."

"No, downtown's fine."

"What's your name?"

"Sarah Prince." She said the first thing that came into her head. She didn't know any Princes in town. No one this woman might be acquainted with and want to talk to her about.

"Well, Sarah, if you're sure I can't do any more to help you..." The woman pulled up to the curb outside the court-house, which was directly across the street from the office building where Mac had told her she could find him if there was ever an immediate life-and-death emergency. She could only use it as a last resort. She was supposed to go to the women's bathroom at the end of the hall and talk into the duct in the ceiling. His office was right above that duct, he'd explained, and he'd hear her.

His office. Hard to imagine Mac in an office. It felt weird because he'd never talked to her about his job or what he did there… She understood, though, that he'd only been protecting her with his silence.

"I'm sure," Maggie said, shaking now as she opened the door. She stumbled against the curb and then righted herself. "Thank you," she said to the woman.

"You're welcome. Listen, my name's Sandra—"

Maggie didn't hear the rest because she'd already swung the door shut.

Edgewood, Ohio
Tuesday, December 7, 2010

"Barry, Leo, get in place," Clay spoke softly, writing on the pages he'd set up in front of him as he looked between them and his map.

Barry and Leo were inside Abrams's office building. They hadn't known that was where Maggie would go. Sam had called in favors and there were teams at Abrams's home, his office, at their spot in the woods, at the department store in town and on standby, too, waiting to be dispatched wherever Maggie might go.

But they'd confirmed that Abrams was in his office.

I got up. Paced behind Clay. My hands were trembling. My stomach was queasy. I needed to do something.

I needed to be there. To help Maggie.

To stand between her and the creep who'd stolen her innocence, who'd changed the girl's life forever. Who'd taken advantage of a young girl's vulnerability and gained control of her mind. Her heart.

"She went into the women's restroom at the end of the hall," a male voice reported softly. "It looked like she knew exactly where it was."

"You think she'd been told where to go?" Clay asked.

"Yeah. She didn't look around, didn't talk to anyone, just went straight back."

Clay studied another map. A diagram of Abrams's office building. I waited. And chewed on my lip until I tasted blood.

Please, God, let Maggie be okay. Please.

I wasn't one who prayed a lot. But this wasn't for me.

And there was nothing else I could do.

"There's a cold-air return that leads from that bathroom to Abrams's office," Clay said, and my heart froze.

"Barry, get upstairs. Now."

"On my way…"

"Just a minute." Another male voice came over the line. "He's coming down."

"She called to him," Clay said. He might only be guessing, but I believed him. "They had this prearranged."

Just as Clay had thought. David Abrams wasn't leaving Maggie alone. He couldn't. She was his weakness.

Waiting for him to reach my little girl was making me sick.

He'd answered on her first call. And Maggie started to cry. He told her to hang on and he'd be down. He told her to unlock the bathroom door, which she'd locked when she hurried inside. So she did. And she waited.

And as soon as the doorknob turned, she threw herself at the man she hadn't been able to touch since he'd made love to her four months before.

"I was so afraid," she said, her arms around his middle

as she hid her face in his sweater and bawled like a baby. She just couldn't help it. The sobs hurt her ribs so much she could hardly breathe. She'd been so scared. And so alone. And…

Mac's hands were all over her, rubbing her back, in her hair, on her backside, pushing her up against him. He'd missed her as much as she'd missed him.

She was his now. All his. He'd take care of her. She was safe.

Looking up at him, she saw that he had tears in his eyes, too.…

"Dear, sweet Maggie. Little love, you can't be here. The hall was empty, no one saw me come in, but we can't stay here. Not together."

"We have to go, Mac. We have to get away from this town. It's not safe anymore."

"Hey, wait a minute, little one. We can't just pick up and leave. Where would we go? How would we live? And most importantly, how would you get to school?"

"I don't care about school, Mac. I care about *you*. About us. They want me to believe you have a whole other life. They told me lies just like you said they would. They said you're this other guy. But I told them you're mine. My Mac." She looked up at him. "You are, aren't you?"

"Of course I am, my sweet Maggie." He hugged her tight. "You're my life. But you have to finish school. We can't go like this. On the run. Hiding from the law. I'm not going to have you living like a hunted animal."

"I don't care about that, Mac." Maggie started to feel desperate again. Scared to death. She couldn't stay here. Not once she told them about Mom. And Kelly. They were going to ship her off. To a foster home. Or to prison. She raised her arms, bringing his head down to her lips, kissing him with her mouth open like he'd taught her to do. Touching her tongue to his.

And when he growled, deep in his throat like he had when he'd been inside her, she knew she'd be okay.

She was special.

Mac was going to take care of her.

And if that made her her mother's daughter, she couldn't do anything about it.

Edgewood, Ohio
Tuesday, December 7, 2010

"Go."

My entire body was paralyzed as Clay gave the order. I stopped breathing. I couldn't move.

I heard a door crash in.

"What the hell…" David Abrams's voice.

"Mac?" And Maggie's.

"David Abrams, you're under arrest—"

"No!" Maggie's scream penetrated my heart and it was a sound I knew I was never, ever going to forget. Not in a hundred lifetimes.

"No-o-o-o!" Maggie's terrified, heartbroken cry tore through the air, masking all the other noise.

"Come on, sweetie, let's get you out of here…." My gaze flew to Clay and he mouthed the word *JoAnne*.

"No! I'm not going with you. I'm going with him! I'm not leaving him! Ma-a-c!"

I wasn't sure what happened during the commotion that followed. I just knew I had to get to her.

Grabbing the keys off the hook, I was in the garage with the car door open, before Clay caught up with me.

"I'm driving," he said, snatching the keys out of my hand.

It was a good thing he didn't try to stop me from going.

* * *

David Abrams was being taken to a jail in Dayton.

Until he'd had a chance to interrogate Abrams regarding Kelly's kidnapping, Clay had jurisdiction over the prisoner. After that they could cut his balls off for all Clay cared.

JoAnne was bringing Maggie to FBI headquarters. Which was where Clay was taking Kelly.

Abrams could rot in a cell for as many hours as it took Clay to get to him.

He'd arranged to hold the press at bay. As of yet, no one knew he had Kelly, but they'd know soon.

"They were in and out so quickly, no one has any idea that Abrams's arrest had anything to do with your disappearance," Clay told Kelly as they drove. "Until we get a confession out of Abrams or Maggie, I want to keep your whereabouts under wraps."

"What about Samantha?"

"She's meeting JoAnne at my office. My plan is to take you in the back way and into a room downstairs. I'll tell Samantha and JoAnne that I found you and bring them to you. I'll be letting the other law enforcement officials involved know, as well. We're keeping you from the press until we're absolutely certain that Abrams is our man."

"And Maggie? I have to talk to Maggie."

"We have to talk to her first, Kelly. We need her to think you're still gone—at least long enough to try once more to get the truth out of her. I want this one wrapped up clean. No loose ends. No more surprises. We're pretty convinced Abrams is behind your kidnapping, but we also know he didn't do the job himself. We need to find out who did. And get him in custody."

"And then you'll bring Maggie to me?"

"Yes, I promise you, before this night is over, you'll be back with Maggie."

Edgewood, Ohio
Tuesday, December 7, 2010

I watched the bare trees go by, feeling as though I was from another planet. In another world. It had only been four days since I'd seen daylight. It felt like years.

I wasn't the same woman I'd been when I'd walked out of my office to go skating the previous Friday morning. I'd left her far behind and knew I'd probably never see her again.

I wasn't all that familiar with Edgewood so didn't recognize much as we drove out to the freeway. Fast-food places were all the same. And gas stations. Some of the older homes reminded me of homes in Chandler.

And none of it seemed real to me.

"You said you have to question Maggie. She's not going to be in trouble, is she?"

"I have no interest in charging Maggie with anything."

Which didn't really answer my question. He was all business now. Had been since this morning. I didn't like this man as much as the one I'd been living with for the past couple of days.

"She's a minor, Clay. You can't question her without her guardian present. Or another adult."

"Sam's responsible for her right now. She'll be there."

I could fight that. I could present myself at any time. I knew that. And he knew it, too. I was going along with this because I thought he was right.

But just because I believed we were doing the right thing didn't mean I felt good about what we were doing.

"Whatever Abrams did, Maggie had no part in it."

"She knew more than she was telling us. I have to find out what that is."

I couldn't let it go. I was worried. "And if you find out

that she knew about the entire plan? If she knew where I was and who took me, then what? Is she an accomplice to kidnapping?"

He looked at me and I had a glimpse of the man I'd trusted with my life. And Maggie's life, too.

"I have no intention of making that child suffer any more than she already has. Besides," he added, his gaze back on the road, "what would be the point? With you as an expert witness, no jury in the world would hold her accountable, considering the circumstances. She's in a fragile emotional state and simply following the dictates of a man who's brainwashed her."

"She's a pawn in a sick man's game," I said. "A victim, more than I am."

"Agreed."

I wasn't comfortable or satisfied with the plan for the upcoming hours. I needed to help. But again, I had to sit and wait.

"Hey." Clay reached over and grabbed my fingers, avoiding the scrapes on my hand with his grasp. He let go as soon as I looked at him. "I'm not going to hurt her, Kelly, I promise. I know how much Maggie's suffered. I care about that."

I believed him.

But I was still worried.

31

Conscious of Kelly's wishes, Clay went in immediate search of Maggie the second he had her foster mother safely locked in a holding room. He'd managed to get Kelly into the building without anyone seeing her. He'd had her put on a cap and a coat he kept in the trunk so no surveillance cameras would give her away. And he turned off the camera in the room where he'd left her.

At that point he'd acknowledged, at least to himself, that Kelly Chapman was more than a job to him.

His "more than a job" was almost done. And he couldn't be happier about that. He needed a night at home, alone with a case of beer and sports on the TV. Make that two nights.

Maggie was on a couch in the family waiting area closest to Clay's office. Samantha sat on one side of her, JoAnne on the other.

Her look as Clay approached was encouraging, since fear outweighed belligerence.

"Mac didn't do anything," she said. "You're making a big mistake."

"You ladies want to come to my office?" Clay asked.

He led the way and then stood back as JoAnne took one armchair and motioned Maggie and Samantha onto the couch. He'd chosen the gray upholstery because it didn't require much—hardly any cleaning, no decor or even any attention.

Unlike his job, which usually required too much. Of everything.

"Maggie, did they offer you a drink?"

"Yeah."

Clay took the other armchair. He sat back. And then forward, elbows on his knees.

"Okay, first," he said, his focus totally on Maggie, "you and I need to get something straight here." He wasn't being mean, but he wasn't going to coddle her, either. He couldn't. Not if he was going to get to this kid.

And he *had* to get to her. He couldn't give her back to Kelly until he did. He couldn't save her from herself until he did.

"We're going to be completely honest with each other," he continued. "That means I'm going to tell you exactly what's going on, and you're going to tell me the whole truth about whatever you know. Understood?"

Looking him straight in the eye, Maggie nodded. Which surprised the hell out of Clay.

"Good," he said, not breaking eye contact, not even for a second. He had her. He had to keep her.

He just had to figure out how.

"You seem mature for your age," he said, going with instinct when logic drew a blank.

Maggie didn't say anything.

"Mature enough to realize that Mac lied to you."

"I love Mac and he loves me."

"His name is David, Maggie. You know that now. You were standing there when he produced his identification for the arresting officer. JoAnne told me you heard him confirm his name. David Abrams is an attorney in Chandler. And he has a wife and kids."

He took Maggie's silence as a near miracle. Dared he hope they were getting through to the young woman? Or had today's episode handed them David Abrams on a platter but shut Maggie further inside herself?

Knowing that Kelly Chapman would be far better at reading Maggie's emotional state, Clay went on. He could call in the department shrink, and would if he had to. But he'd rather leave her to Kelly, or someone of Kelly's choosing. "You said David didn't do anything. That we're making a big mistake."

"You are."

"You sound sure about that."

"I am."

Clay could feel the eyes of the other two women on him, but he tuned them out until it was just he and Maggie sitting there. "How can you be so sure?"

"Because I was there. Mac didn't even touch me. I reached up and kissed him, that's all. He didn't do anything."

She'd glanced away.

"I'm not talking about you and David, Maggie. My jurisdiction is the missing persons case. We think David Abrams had Kelly kidnapped."

Maggie's shock couldn't be faked. Her eyes flew wide-open and her head snapped forward. "No way! Why would he do that?"

"Because he knew that you cared about Kelly. And you were living with her. Eventually Kelly would win your loyalty and you'd tell her what you and Mac did in the woods that Saturday."

"Kelly already knows all about that."

"But you wouldn't tell her that Mac was David Abrams."

"Mac is Mac."

"And he's also David Abrams."

She shook her head and tears filled her eyes. Clay had a tough time sitting there watching the child's heart break. And he knew he couldn't give her a chance to re-erect her walls. "You know something about Kelly's disappearance, don't you?"

Maggie nodded. Clay was aware of the slight movement from both officers of the law sitting there with him. He was coming in for the final landing.

"I need you tell me what you know, Maggie."

"I was going to, as soon as Mac and I got away. I just didn't want Mac to get into trouble because people don't believe he loves me."

"David probably does love you, Maggie," Clay said, even as Kelly's voice in his head told him to shut up. "But he's a married man with a wife and kids who love him."

Maggie's silence made him uncomfortable. He had to be careful not to push her too far.

"He made promises to his wife. Can you imagine how hurt she's going to feel when she finds out what he did with you?"

Tears were falling down her cheeks.

"You feel older, Maggie, I understand that. But David is older. And you're only fourteen. It's against the law for anyone to have sex with you."

"My friends all do it."

"It's statutory rape."

"No one does anything about it."

"They do when the other party is an adult. David Abrams is a lawyer. More than that, he's a father. He has daughters of his own not that much younger than you. One of them is nine."

More silence. And more tears. He'd never felt like such an unfeeling lout.

"He knew he was breaking the law, Maggie. He knew what he was doing with you was wrong. And he knew he was involving you in something illegal, but he did it, anyway."

Shoulders hunched, the girl didn't say a word.

"I need you to tell me about Kelly's kidnapping."

"Mac didn't do it. My mother did."

Life was over.

Maggie didn't see much reason not to tell them everything and just let whatever they did to her happen. She couldn't fight them. Couldn't fight any of them. She'd never been able to.

Not Chuck Sewell or her mother or people who treated her like trash because of where she lived and because of whose kid she was. She hadn't been able to help Glenna, to keep her from getting killed.

She'd ruined her mother's life by being born, which forced her to quit high school. It was Maggie's fault Kelly was gone.

And now they wanted her to believe Mac was married. And that she, Maggie, had hurt his wife. He'd just told her again that he was *her* Mac. Only hers.

She'd thought she and Mac were like a fairy tale. A dream come true. Had she been crazy or what?

"Your mother's in jail, Maggie. She couldn't kidnap Kelly."

Agent Thatcher's voice had changed, like he was talking to a little kid. Or an adult who'd lost her mind.

Maggie wished she'd lost hers. If she could just forget…

"She knows someone," Maggie said. "She told me she was going to take care of Kelly. That she'd be out of jail soon and then we'd be together again."

"Is that what you want?"

Maggie finally glanced at Sam, who hadn't said a word. She could take the woman's hatred. She deserved it.

Sam reached over and took Maggie's hand. Kind of like Kelly had done the night Sam and Kyle had come to tell Kelly lies about Mac.

If… *Were* they lies?

Maggie started to cry again. And then to sob. Worse than when she was with Mac a couple of hours ago. Her chest hurt and her body hurt. But most of all, her heart. All she'd ever wanted was to love and be loved. That was all.

How had she messed up so badly?

Samantha Jones walked on one side of Clay as he took her and JoAnne to what they thought was a private conference with him. After Maggie's breakdown, he'd called in the staff psychologist, who was trying to get her to eat something.

And to talk more, if she could.

Clay hoped to have her back with Kelly by the end of the day. He had these next minutes to get through and then he was leaving to take a stab at David Abrams. Barry had phoned and said the man had lawyered up and didn't say a thing.

Clay was going to talk to the guy, anyway. The lawyer's lawyer could be present. Clay didn't give a rat's ass who was in the room.

"What do you think of Lori Winston being behind the kidnapping?" he asked.

"She specifically requested Kelly as Maggie's legal guardian," Samantha said. "That's partially why the initial paperwork came through so quickly."

That, and because Kelly was…Kelly, Clay figured.

"But what Maggie says about her mom turning on Kelly, changing her mind and deciding that Kelly orchestrated this whole situation to steal Maggie away, sounds feasible," JoAnne said.

"Lori's a professional victim," Samantha said. "I know—I conducted the initial interrogation. Even when she confessed, she had someone else to blame for every single thing she did."

"I guess if she sees her kid wearing nice clothes and doing well without her, she has to blame someone besides herself," Clay said, going with the theory.

"Only problem is, the woman has no money and no real connections," Samantha told him. "I don't see how she could possibly have arranged for a hit on Kelly, no matter how badly she might have wanted one."

"But she's in jail," JoAnne said. "She's with the people who know the people who'd be willing to take money to ensure that Kelly Chapman never sees the light of day again."

"Abrams went to Lori," Clay surmised. "He got her all riled up. Told her how Maggie's loyalties were switching, and that Kelly was stealing her daughter. He probably swore up and down that he really loves Maggie. That he was going to do right by both of them. He reminded her of his power. And he promised to help her get out of jail…."

Samantha shook her head. "I don't know. The whole reason Lori Winston confessed was because she couldn't bear the thought of Maggie and Abrams together. She didn't mind selling her daughter into the drug trade, but she couldn't bear the thought of Maggie ending up like she did—another teenage pregnancy statistic."

"Right, but Abrams has money. Position. He could give Maggie everything. And if he promised to do that—*and* get Lori out of prison so she could watch over Maggie…" JoAnne started down the stairs first.

"And all she had to do was ask around inside to find someone who knew someone who'd be willing to kidnap a popular psychologist and dump her body for a wad of cash," Clay finished for her. He was sure David Abrams had used Lori Winston to find someone who'd take care of Kelly. The pieces were falling into place. Now all Clay needed was a confession.

They were downstairs, the only people in the seldom-used hallway that at one time had housed an FBI fraud unit, which was moved to Cincinnati when Dayton's big businesses started moving out of state. Clay stopped outside a locked door at the end of the hallway.

"I…" He glanced at JoAnne. Lying to her hadn't been easy. And she wasn't going to forgive him easily, either.

"What's going on, Clay?" she asked, while Samantha Jones looked curiously from one to the other.

"I have something to show you two," he said, knowing he sounded lame as he opened the door.

Clay barely had the door closed behind them, muffling Sam's scream as the detective saw the room's lone occupant.

"Kelly!" Rounding the table, Sam knocked over a chair as she reached Kelly, who'd just stood. "Oh, my God! Kel!" Kelly's body was engulfed in a crushing hug as tough girl detective Samantha Jones started to cry. "I can't believe it. You're alive! I thought we'd lost you and I never told you that you're the best friend I've ever had. I never thanked you…."

Clay looked away. And his eyes met the hurt gaze of the woman who used to be *his* best friend.

32

I felt like the Queen of Sheba and a poor imprisoned maid at the same time. I was rich beyond measure and poorer than dirt as I sat in the FBI holding room with Sam and talked about everything that had happened.

All those years Sam and I had danced around each other, friends without really admitting how deeply we actually cared about each other. To see us right then, you'd have thought we'd been bosom buddies our whole life.

For the first time I told Sam about my dad. She knew, anyway. I didn't have to say anything, but as we sat alone in that room, while Clay went to interrogate David Abrams and JoAnne alternated between checking on Maggie and handling details of the case from Clay's office, I was completely honest. With Sam. And with myself.

I got weepy again, but there it was. "My whole life I've tried so hard to be enough and I never felt like I was…"

"God, Kel, you're the most 'enough' person I've ever known! I wish I could've told you that."

"I guess I didn't give you—or anyone—a chance to do

that." I'd changed more than I'd thought. And had no idea where I went from here.

"You've come clean now—and there's no going back."

A shard of fear shot through me. And a new sense of knowing, too.

"I hope you remember that when I come knocking at your door."

"I'm going to be watching you, Kelly. If you don't knock, I will."

They'd both been through so much in the past year. A time of momentous change for both of them.

JoAnne poked her head into the office. "Clay just called. Abrams will neither confirm nor deny his involvement with drugs, with Maggie or with Kelly's abduction. You probably know he's lawyered up."

And I stood. I couldn't let him walk again. Not when he'd already trampled all over me. And my loved ones.

"Clay needs to know what you want to do with him." JoAnne was looking at Sam.

"Book him," my friend said immediately. "The Fort County D.A. is going to press charges against him for rape and child endangerment, plus gross sexual exploitation of a minor. And that's just for starters." I sat back down. I didn't have to do everything myself anymore.

That lesson would take a while to sink in.

Clay was in his office after leaving the jail where Abrams was being temporarily held, awaiting transport back to Fort County. It would be an interesting time for the lawyer, bunking in with some of the scum he'd sent down.

Might teach him a thing or two about humility. Compassion. Maybe even about sex abuse.

He could only hope.

What the man had done was heinous, and Clay wasn't going to lose any sleep for thinking so.

He might lose sleep over his next move, however. The fact that he knew it didn't stop him from making a couple of phone calls and putting his plan into action.

Maggie Winston was on the cusp. She loved Mac. She had to love him, considering that she'd given him her virginity. And her love, her trust, her loyalty. She'd given him absolutely everything pure and innocent that she had.

And she'd almost caught a glimpse of the man he really was. Clay had the chance to help her with that. To set her on the road to freedom. And then he'd bring her back to Kelly, ready for love and healing and all the tender compassion Kelly Chapman wanted to bestow upon her.

He waited the half hour before Abrams's wife and children arrived in his office. He didn't go to see Maggie. Or Kelly. He hadn't let Samantha Jones know he was in the building.

He sat at his desk and did paperwork. Started the report that would close this case.

And possibly lose him his job. Because he was telling the truth.

To himself. And about himself. About everything.

He'd learned by example.

From a woman he wasn't going to forget as long as he lived.

And when he got the call from security and then, a few minutes later, met the elevator bearing a very pregnant Susan Abrams and three of her children, the oldest beside her, the youngest on her hip and another little one holding her hand, he knew he wasn't ever going to forget the next few minutes, either.

He'd told Susan the truth. She already knew about her husband's arrest; she knew why she was there. Maggie was in a different waiting room. One with toys and a couple of couches and a television set. She didn't know it yet, but he was going to be taking her to Kelly soon. As soon as he'd introduced her to some very important people.

"Maggie?"

She'd been looking out the window and turned when he called her name.

"There's someone here I want you to meet," he said, hoping he wasn't going to hate himself for what he was about to do. Susan Abrams deserved to meet the girl so she could believe, accept and eventually move on.

And Maggie had to see the truth if she was ever going to be free to live and love.

"This is Susan Abrams," Clay said, knowing full well the girl would make the connection. "And these are three of her four children."

"Hi." Susan, wearing a concerned look, still managed to smile. She glanced at Clay.

"Hi," David Abrams's nine-year-old daughter said.

Maggie just stared, horror-struck. She didn't return the greetings. She just stared. Eyes wide, mouth open. And then she bent over and started to sob again, attended by the FBI staff psychologist.

Clay hoped to God he hadn't sold his soul for a conviction.

He hoped it again twenty minutes later as he ushered Susan Abrams out of his office and back to her kids, leaving them with Sandra in the waiting room closest to Clay's office.

The expression on Susan Abrams's face was similar to the one on Maggie's. Similar, but not quite. The woman was strong.

And while still in complete shock over the day's events, Susan was already beginning to accept what had happened. She wanted to help in any way she could. Her brother's death the past summer, the rumors she'd heard—and the things that David had told her—had been bothering her.

She'd known something wasn't adding up.

And she'd just agreed to testify against the man who would soon be her ex-husband.

FBI Headquarters
Tuesday, December 7, 2010

I was sitting alone with Sam, still debriefing the first thirty-one years of our lives, interspersed with monologues about the past four days, when her cell phone rang.

"It's Clay," she said, reading the screen.

I had no idea what was being said, but Sam wasn't happy. She did, however, agree to whatever Clay was asking of her.

My stomach knotted up all over again.

It had to be dark outside by now. Past the dinner hour. I had no sense of time. Or place, either, beyond this room that had become my new home. My new prison.

"Clay's bringing Maggie down." Sam's expression didn't convey the gloriousness of the news.

"She doesn't know you're here," Sam said.

"Then you need to go out there and wait for them. You need to prepare her, Sam."

Sam shook her head. "Maggie's on the verge of turning on Abrams," Sam said. "We have to do this, Kel. We have to get her away from that man. We have to bring her back to us."

I was a new me. I had to trust someone besides myself. I had to accept help.

"This is what Clay wants?" I asked.

I didn't really understand Sam's odd expression, but I noticed it. "Yes," she said with more curiosity than conviction.

"He thinks that if she suddenly sees you alive, Maggie's going to be putty in your hands. And if you talk to her now, she'll tell you everything. But only you. He wants me to leave."

I nodded.

Finally, something I could do.

Maggie didn't want to go to another room. She just wanted to lie down and be left alone. But when Agent Thatcher showed up in the second room they'd taken her to, she went with him. At least it got her away from that psychologist woman who thought she knew everything about Maggie.

Who thought she understood.

She didn't know anything.

Besides, there were no words that could help Maggie. No magic that could save her now. She'd just ratted out her mom. She was no longer sure she trusted the man she loved. And Kelly was gone because of her. Probably dead because Maggie hadn't had the smarts to tell Samantha about Mom and her plan right away.

She wanted to die, too.

"Here we are," Agent Thatcher said, not touching Maggie but staying beside her as they came to a door at the end of the hall.

"Why are we here?" Maggie asked, not that she really cared. "Is this where I get taken into foster care?"

It was better that way. Going home with Sam, being at the farm, would be too hard because she knew she'd have to leave.

But she still wished she could. For one more night.

"No," Clay said. He looked like he was going to tell her something, but then he didn't.

He smiled, though. And Maggie figured he was really

a pretty nice guy. In spite of all the crap he'd done to her. At least he'd been nice about it.

It wasn't his fault she'd ruined her life. *She'd* screwed up. A lot.

"You don't like me, do you?" she asked when he just stood there looking at her. She didn't want to go in that room. Didn't want to be shipped off.

"I don't really know you," the man said. "But from what I've seen so far, yes, I like you."

Hmm. He didn't seem to be lying to her.

"I'm scared, Agent Thatcher," she admitted. "Please tell me what they're going to do to me."

She hated begging. But he was the only person she knew who might be able to help her.

"Don't be scared, Maggie." His voice was soft. "Trust us, okay?"

Maggie had no idea what that meant. But she wanted to do what he asked. She really, really wanted to do what he asked.

Before she could say anything, he'd opened the door.

He was handing her over. Just like that. Maggie didn't blame him. She deserved whatever happened to her. Still...

She entered the room because he held the door for her, but she couldn't look at the person sitting at the table. Not even when that person stood. She couldn't face anyone else right now.

Everyone knew what she'd done.

She heard the door close behind her. And turned to see that Agent Thatcher had gone without saying another word. He'd just left her there.

"Maggie?"

It was a woman who sounded so much like Kelly that Maggie started to cry, even though it was embarrassing.

"Sweetie?"

She looked up then. And couldn't believe her eyes. Kelly was there. Standing in a shirt she'd never seen before and jeans that didn't fit. She looked different, but she looked the same. She had a bruise on her face, but her eyes were Kelly's. And her hair. She held out her arms and all Maggie could see were the scabs on the sides of her hands.

They'd hurt Kelly.

Her back against the wall, Maggie slid down to the floor, still sobbing.

33

My baby was in trouble.

No, not my baby. Lori Winston's baby. Who was in my care.

The distinction didn't matter much. Or even register. All I knew was that Maggie needed me.

I was around the table and on the floor with her before I could figure out what was going on.

"Maggie? Sweetie?" I pulled the girl into my arms. I held her, half on my lap and half on the floor. I rocked her. I stroked her hair over and over. I could hardly believe I was with her again.

She cried. But she didn't grab hold of me. I held her.

"Maggie? It's okay, love, just get it out."

The more I talked to her, the more I seemed to be upsetting her. And eventually, I understood.

"Maggie." I sat her up against the wall. "Look at me."

She didn't. She just hunched over and cried.

"Maggie," I said more firmly, "I want you to look at me right now."

Slowly she raised her head. And, more slowly, her eyes focused on mine.

"I'm here," I said, holding her gaze with mine. "I'm alive. I'm okay. And I'm here. For you."

I didn't mean to cry, but when I saw those sweet brown eyes well up with tears again, I started to cry, too. "It's not your fault, sweetie," I told her. But even as I said the words I knew it was going to take a while before Maggie accepted them.

We had a rough road ahead of us, my new daughter and I. But I knew something else, too. I was enough for Maggie.

And she was enough for me.

Clay insisted on taking Maggie and Kelly home. He didn't like the fact that he had no confession out of Abrams and that Lori Winston wasn't talking. They knew Abrams was the mastermind responsible for Kelly's disappearance, just as they knew he'd stolen Maggie Winston's innocence. But he still hadn't figured out who Abrams had hired to kidnap Kelly.

She refused to listen.

"I can't take any more, Clay," she said as she sat on the floor of the holding room, Maggie cuddled against her, sound asleep. "I need to be home, in my own bed."

"Then I'm staying there," he said. He wasn't budging on that one. "At least until tomorrow. After Abrams has been charged. And after I've had a chance to interview Lori Winston myself. I'll sleep in my car, but I'm not leaving you there unprotected."

"You've been in my home, Clay. You know there's plenty of space," she said. "You have something against my third bedroom?"

Nothing. Except that he didn't belong there—and had no business finding the prospect enticing.

"What? Your home's good enough for me, but mine's not good enough for you?"

What was it with this woman? "I don't want to be in your home as an FBI agent." She tore honesty out of him. And he hated it.

Kelly's grin disarmed him completely. "Yeah, we've kind of become friends these past few days, haven't we?" she said, looking like the ultimate Madonna with the exhausted and traumatized girl asleep at her breast.

When he said nothing, because he had no idea how to respond to her, she said, "Face it, Clay, we've grown up together."

Maybe. What he knew was that she was making him grow.

Chandler, Ohio
Tuesday, December 7, 2010

It felt so good to be home.

And it felt weird, too.

Maggie wasn't leaving my side. But she wasn't talking much, either.

Camy jumped from my lap to Maggie's as we sat on the couch in the living room. I'd offered to turn on the TV. No one was interested.

Clay had been on his phone in the kitchen for much of the hour we'd been home. We'd stopped by his place briefly on the way to Chandler. He'd run in for an overnight bag. I'd stayed in the car.

And looked the other way when he'd brought my skates out with him.

I had to have a session with them. I knew that. In another day or two.

We'd stopped by the Evans farm, too, to pick up Camy and Maggie's stuff. I'd cried again when Camy greeted me.

Guess all these years I hadn't been as independent as I'd thought.

"Did he hit you?" Maggie's voice was soft. I hated the look in her eyes. The fear and guilt…

"I don't know," I told her honestly, but didn't add Clay's theory that I'd been kicked. "I slept most of the first day. Passed out, I think. I don't remember much."

"Did he…hurt you?"

"I can't remember."

"But…were your clothes on?"

And I understood. Maggie wanted to know if David Abrams had done to me what he'd done to her.

"Yes, they were," I told her. "David didn't kidnap me, sweetie. He hired someone to do it. Just like he hired other people to run his drug ring."

Maggie had told me everything she knew regarding the meth lab. It was strictly hearsay, but it was enough to finally be able to charge David Abrams with drug trafficking. And to get the warrants Sam needed to find out what else he might've been involved in. Sam had questioned all the other kids. She knew about the ones Maggie had mentioned.

She'd also admitted that her Mac and David Abrams were the same man. Meeting Susan Abrams had been the catalyst, nudging Maggie from fantasy to reality. She seemed to recognize that Susan and her children had been betrayed far more than she had.

I hoped to follow up with the family if they wanted me to. And with the family of the deceased bomb-squad officer.

My biggest job was going to be teaching Maggie about faith. And about a love that was healthy.

I had a feeling I was going to be learning right along with her.

"So you weren't raped?"

The girl was sitting upright on the couch. A foot away. I pulled her closer, until her head was resting on my shoulder. The rumble of Clay's voice in the other room completed the strange scene.

"No."

"What happened to your hands?"

"They were tied behind my back. I rubbed the rope against the rocks to fray it. My hands got scraped in the process." I wasn't going to lie to Maggie. She'd been lied to enough.

But I could give her the easy version. I had to. No matter what she thought, or what anyone else thought, I knew that Maggie Winston was still a child.

One who deserved protection.

The media had the full story now, minus Maggie's involvement with Abrams. It was inevitable once I came out of hiding. For Maggie's sake and my own, I was avoiding TV and every other form of news.

Clay peeked around the corner, his gaze taking in Maggie and me, and the room, too.

"He's nice," Maggie whispered.

"Yeah."

"You spent three whole days with him?"

"Yep."

"He took care of you."

"Yeah." I had no idea where this was going, but I was going to answer all her questions.

As long as she had questions to ask.

"You like him," she said.

"Of course I like him. As you said, he's nice."

"But you *more* than like him."

"Do I?"

Maggie sat up and her grin was worth any discomfort I was feeling at her chosen topic. "Yeah," she said matter-of-factly. "It's obvious, Kelly. You're different when he's around."

I didn't want to know what she meant. But if it made Maggie feel good to think I liked Clay, I was okay with that.

"It's just…I have something else I have to tell you."

Clay came around the corner. "There's no beer in the fridge," he said. He held up a bottle of Riesling.

"I don't…"

"Like beer," he finished. "I saw a market on the corner," he said. "If it's okay with you, I'd like to pick up a six-pack."

It was fine with me and I told him so. Clay had been looking like he needed a beer ever since we'd pulled into my drive.

We'd stopped for hamburgers on the way home from Dayton. Still, I wouldn't mind having a glass of wine later. After Maggie was in bed.

I wouldn't mind having it while he drank a beer.

I'd known him for just a few days, but they'd been an intense few days. And he'd been my only contact with the world.

I missed him as soon as he'd left.

"What else did you want to tell me?" I asked Maggie.

"It's just…I did something. I thought it was good, but now, with Clay, well, I think I screwed up again."

We'd fix it. Whatever it was, we'd fix it. We were going forward from here. The bad stuff was over.

"What'd you do?" I asked, ready to take it on. To make it better.

"I wanted you to, you know, have a chance to be in love. I thought if you had someone, maybe you'd understand…"

Maggie broke off and I tried to read between the lines.

"It seems so stupid now. I mean, you knew all along. I was the one who didn't get it."

I waited. The rest of the story would come.

"I just thought, if you were in love, you'd understand about Mac and me and not be so angry at me for…for loving him. For *thinking* I loved him," she added in a low voice.

"I was never angry with you, Maggie. I was worried sick about you."

She nodded. I could feel the movement against my shoulder. And I realized it would take time for Maggie to fully understand, to assimilate, what had happened.

But that was okay. We had all the time we needed.

Something rattled against the back of the house and Camy barked. A winter storm blowing in. A branch against the window.

"This guy wrote to you," Maggie continued as soon as Camy settled back in my lap. "He was a relative of one of your clients."

"What guy?" I didn't see any letter.

"Just this guy. He wrote to you. He said you interested him. That he admired the way people respond to you. That's what he said. I guess you helped one of his relatives in a court case. Anyway, he seemed to really like you so I wrote back to him."

"You did."

"Yeah, pretending I was you."

"He wrote to me at home?"

A client's relative would have written to my office address. Wouldn't he? Particularly if it was an expert-witness case, which it would've been if court were involved. Maybe this guy got my home address from the internet.

"Yeah. But when I wrote back, I didn't just *think* I knew what you'd say," Maggie said. "I asked how you felt about stuff. Like when I asked what a girl should say to a guy if she liked him, but she wasn't sure if he liked her or not."

I remembered the conversation. I'd been hoping Maggie had met a boy at school. A boy her own age, who might distract her from David Abrams.

"Well, I'd ask you questions and put your answers in the letters I wrote to him. I typed them on your computer and then I deleted them," she said.

Boy. This was unexpected.

"How long have you been writing to him?"

"A few months."

Okay. I had a male pen pal who thought I liked him.

Camy barked again. Standing, ears perked, she looked toward the kitchen. Clay was probably back.

"We're going to have to write to him, both of us together and tell him the truth."

"I'll do it," Maggie said. "I made the mess, I can clean it up."

I thought I might let her. Because she needed to be able to control something in her life. "Okay, but I want to read the letter first," I told her.

She nodded again. "He seems like a nice guy," she said. "Or I wouldn't have written back to him. He's a college professor. I think he wrote to you from work 'cause he had a strange address."

"Really. What does he teach?"

"English. He was really glad you helped Jane. But his last letter was kind of weird. He said Marla knew he was writing to you and that she was upset but he said not to worry about her. It sounded like you knew her so I played along. I think she's his sister or his mother. Anyway, he said he'd handle her."

Alarm bells started to ring in my brain. Loudly.

Marla—Marla Todd. Jane Hamilton. English professor.

Strange address. Prison addresses *were* strange. "What was this man's name?" I asked, trying to stay calm.

"James." Maggie's sweet voice sent a shudder through me.

Marla Todd had been obsessive about James Todd. Obsessed to the point of unhinged. And I hadn't been able to get through to her at all.

James Todd had been a family member of Jane Hamilton's, all right. He'd been her husband. He'd been Lee Anne Todd's husband, too.

Until he'd murdered her.

While he was married to Marla.

The man was a bigamist who'd also been an abusive husband.

But Marla hadn't seen that.

She'd thought he loved her. For herself, not her money.

She adored James so she believed he adored her.

She'd stood by him during the murder trial that I'd been called in on as an expert witness.

Against James.

I'd been hired to get the truth out of Marla.

I'd gotten it out of the first wife, Jane Hamilton, instead.

And James Todd had gone to jail.

But it wasn't James Todd I was worried about. It was Marla Anderson Todd. She'd been willing to do anything to keep James. She had money, power. She was a strong, athletic woman. And the story about my release was all over the news.

And if she thought, for one second, that James was going to throw her over, as he had his first two wives, if he was going to make a fool of her after she'd made such a public display of standing by him, and if he chose me, whom she despised…

"And you let James think I liked him?"

Marla was obsessed with him to the point of mental illness. She— Suddenly I remembered that sound, the one I'd heard on the bike path before everything went dark. It was someone calling me. Marla. She was the one. Not Abrams. Or Lori Winston. Or any of the others. It had been Marla. And now she knew I was free….

"Yeah. But he's nice, Kelly. He'll understand when I tell him the truth. But he might want to talk to you, just in case you like him, after all."

Camy barked a third time.

And the glass behind my head broke.

"Don't move."

I recognized Marla's voice.

34

Clay took his time at the store. Partially to give Kelly some privacy with Maggie. They'd both been through hell, had so many emotions to work through, and now they had a stranger in their midst. And he took his time for his own reasons, too. Being in Kelly Chapman's home was knocking him for more of a loop than it had before.

It was…as if she cast a spell and it permeated everything she touched.

If he believed in spells. And magic.

And love-ever-after.

Clay believed in picking up one quart-bottle of beer and getting back to the job. He needed the night to pass swiftly and hoped that by morning they'd have put enough pieces together to nail Abrams for the Chapman kidnapping and he could close this case. Agents were perusing Abrams's phone records, his bank and credit card statements. They'd seized his cars and computers and were thoroughly searching his home and office.

JoAnne was at the prison interviewing Lori Winston again—regardless of the growing lateness of the hour. They needed answers.

Once she'd heard about Abrams's arrest, Lori had been willing to cooperate. At least enough to agree to meet with the federal agent without her lawyer present.

His detour around the block on the way home was standard. Habit. Securing the perimeter.

And...

A little red sports car was parked in front of a house on the block behind Kelly's. It hadn't been there before.

Clay slowed. The house was dark. At 9:30. It also had a three-car garage. And an empty driveway. Presumably someone who owned such an expensive car and lived there, or was an overnight guest, wouldn't leave the little car in the street all night.

And if the owner of the car was a guest just for the evening, lights would be on somewhere in the house.

And the car would most likely be parked in the wide, empty driveway....

The yard was fenced, but the wrought iron was decorative, not high enough to keep anyone out. And in the light from the street, Clay noticed something shiny on the hard, dead grass. Something that glistened.

He left his car running at the curb and stepped out. Walked over to pick up the shiny object that was out of place.

A set of keys. Adrenaline shot through him. They could be keys to the red car. Or not. They might belong to the owner of the house.

But they didn't.

Attached to the ring that held the keys were two little license plate luggage tags. Clay didn't need light to know that they were inscribed with two names. *Maggie* and *Kelly*.

Chandler, Ohio
Tuesday, December 7, 2010

My kidnapper hadn't been a professional. Or a *he*. She was a smart, determined, very deranged woman.

She'd climbed through the front window and was in the house. Directly beside me.

She had a gun.

And if it went off, Maggie would be caught in the line of fire.

"It didn't have to come to this. I went to a lot of trouble to make things as easy and painless as possible. I padded the utility cart. And I waited until you'd slowed down before I tripped you. You could've just gone to sleep and died slow and easy," Marla Anderson Todd said, her voice calm.

"Your plan was foolproof, Marla," I said, calm, too. "But if you shoot me now, you won't get away."

They didn't have much time, either. The woman had come in through the front window. Someone could have seen her. Or could drive by and see the broken glass. Could call the police. I listened for sirens and prayed not to hear them. Clay could return. I prayed that he wouldn't.

Because any disturbance now would set her off. I'd be a dead woman. Marla was at that point. A distraction would cause her to put that small bit of pressure on the trigger first, and look around second.

"I saw James today. I told him what I did. I saved those luggage tags just to show him, so he'd know I was telling the truth. I thought, after Lee Anne and all, he'd understand. That he'd be proud of me. That he'd know how much I love him. But no. He yelled at me. Because of *you*, because you have your hooks in him. He called me a stupid bitch. He said they'd blame him, and he'd never get out. He's probably going to turn me in. But you and he—you aren't going to get what you want. You won't be together. I'm planning to see to that once and for all."

Camy was barking frantically, and I gestured for Maggie to pick her up.

"Let Maggie go," I said, now that I'd gotten Marla to engage in conversation. I was facing death. Some part of me knew that. But I just kept focusing. "She hasn't done anything to you. She doesn't even know who James is. She's nothing to me. Not my daughter. I've only known her a few months." Maggie could easily be hurt in a perverse attempt to get at me.

"Why is she staying here?"

"Maggie's a client of mine. Her mother's in jail."

I didn't let myself feel the child at my side.

"That true?" Marla moved the gun a little closer to the side of my head, but she was looking at Maggie.

"Yes."

I recognized the voice. And yet I didn't.

"Then get," Marla raised her voice to be heard over Camy's menacing growls and high-pitched barking. "Lock yourself in the bathroom and don't come out. And take the yapper with you. After you hear the gun go off, call the cops."

She was methodical even now. And if Maggie called the police before Marla had killed me, it didn't really matter. It was only going to take a split second for her to shoot. She could do it just as easily with them coming in the door as with them out driving around on patrol. Or sitting at the station eating doughnuts.

The bathroom door closed. The lock clicked. I flinched. And heard a sob.

Focus. If I kept her talking, I kept myself alive. "Where'd you get the utility cart?" I asked.

"Had it shipped from Minnesota," Marla said. "That's what gave me the idea in the first place. That and the map published by the Historical Society of those pre-Civil War slave hideaways. I knew where you went skating and when I found one near the path—and on public land yet—I knew I'd been given a sign." Her eyes were glassy and her hand tightened on the gun.

"Maggie wrote the letters to James," I said. "She thought he was the family member of a client. She wanted me to have a boyfriend so I'd understand about being in love. Because she was in love and I didn't like her boyfriend."

I wasn't begging. Or demanding. Neither was going to faze this woman.

She was going to pull the trigger any second. I had to focus.

"James killed Lee Anne. I guess you know that. It's why you're killing me. You'll have something else that you share."

"I'm killing you because you tried to take him from me. You tried to split us up during his trial. You wanted him even then."

"If I wanted him, why did I help Jane Hamilton?"

Marla didn't say anything.

"I helped her because I understood her," I said. Jane would be having her baby any day now. "She didn't want my help. Didn't think she needed it. But I knew."

"You think you know everything. You think you know people better than they know themselves. That's what you did to James. You worked your spell on him, got control of his head and made him think he wanted you."

"All I do is listen, Marla. I don't know any more than anyone else. I just listen. I didn't write those letters to James. A fourteen-year-old girl did that. I didn't even know he'd written to me. And in Jane's case—" *and Marla's* "—I understood some of what she was feeling because I recognized myself in her. It wasn't that I knew more than Jane did, it's that I was like her."

"Don't pull your psychobabble crap on me."

"I was like her because I was ashamed of who and what I was. Jane felt humiliated because she was a smart, successful woman who'd fallen for James's lies. She'd let him convince her that each time he'd physically hurt her, it had been an accident that was her fault. She couldn't stand to be the kind of woman who'd allow that to happen to her."

My head was still intact.

And out of the corner of my eye, I saw movement beyond the barrel of the gun. Way beyond.

I focused on Marla.

"I couldn't face who and what I was, either," I said. "I'm nothing fancy like you are, Marla. I'm not rich. I'm the daughter of a two-bit whore and the drug-dealer who was her pimp."

The shadow moved closer.

"James wouldn't have anything to do with me," I said, my voice calming me. "I'm nowhere near good enough for him. When I was three my father sold me to an adoption agency for two thousand dollars."

No sound, but movement.

"That's all I was worth to him. And just yesterday, he was willing to sell me again, for two million. You think James would settle for someone from that kind of background?"

Shadows. Closer. *Focus.*

"And if he'd settle for that, why would you want him, Marla? You're classy. You've got money and success. You come from a good family. You love fiercely and loyally and those are good qualities. It's not your fault James abused them."

"James did not abuse me, bitch! He loved me. He still loves me."

"Then why am I a threat to you?"

I heard the click as the gun went off.

The local police, headed by Samantha Jones, wanted to handle the crime scene and Clay turned over the Chapman file. It was no longer a missing persons case.

Marla Anderson Todd was already spilling her guts when they cuffed her and took her out to the waiting squad car. James Todd had confessed to her that he'd killed

Lee Anne. He'd done it for her, he said. Which was why, in her twisted way, she'd been willing to kill Kelly for him, because Kelly was trying to split them up.

The man might never be tried for the murder of his second wife. Double jeopardy prevented new charges. But if the prosecutor had a lot of energy, and he'd been told Sheila Grant did, she could move for a mistrial on the grounds that a key witness, Marla, had been coerced. Because Marla hadn't been legally married to James at the time the original charges were filed, so she might win that argument.

In any case, Clay didn't envy James Todd his final day of reckoning. He had a lot to answer for, ruining the lives of innocent women. Kelly Chapman was the fourth victim. After Jane and Lee Anne and Marla.

Clay had never worked a more grueling case.

"Thank you."

The voice. It had become a part of him.

He stood in a corner of the kitchen, watching while law enforcement personnel went about their business. Waiting.

"You could have died." He spoke without turning his head.

"But I didn't."

"I walked out of here and left you alone. For a beer, for chrissake. A fucking beer."

"And you came back."

"You're only alive because you had the wherewithal to keep the woman talking."

"I'm alive because you got to her just as she was pulling the trigger and managed to deflect her aim."

"It doesn't really matter who did what. I'm so glad you're both okay."

Maggie Winston seemed to be taking the incident in stride, better than either of the adults she stood with. But she was clutching Kelly's hand. She hadn't let go since the gun went off and she came tearing out of the bathroom to find Kelly still sitting upright on the couch.

Not even when they tried to get her loose so the emergency squad could check Kelly's vitals.

Or when she'd gone back to her room to pack up a few things. She'd insisted Kelly go with her.

Sam approached them. "That's it for now. The forensics team will do their thing. I've got to get down to the station. See you out at the farm?" The look she gave Kelly and Maggie spoke of the love she felt for the two of them.

Kelly nodded.

Kyle and Samantha had insisted that Maggie and Kelly stay at the farm for a few days—at least until the end of the week. Kelly's house was taped off at the moment. And when she was allowed to go back in, she'd get the front window repaired.

She hadn't decided whether Maggie would start school again the next week. Kelly might keep her out until the first of the year.

"You ready?" Clay asked Kelly as Samantha and Maggie discussed Kelly's sleeping arrangements. He was driving them out to the Evans farm.

She nodded again and said, "You and I, we make a pretty good team."

Instinctively, he resisted the idea. And yet…he couldn't argue the point. He picked up her bags and Maggie's and led the twosome, their hands joined, out to his car. Kelly sat in the back with Maggie.

Chandler, Ohio
Wednesday, December 8, 2010

I was back at my house for the day. The police were finished there. Samantha had told me, and then Clay had called. He'd offered to drive me over to help clean up.

And to sit with me while I waited for the window company to show up. Someone had taped cardboard over the shattered glass the night before.

I'd already called that morning and had a drywall guy coming out, too. And Maggie and I had decided to replace the living room furniture. Neither of us ever wanted to sit on that couch again.

Samantha had searched Marla's home. None of my belongings were there—but there'd been a recent fire in the fireplace. Marla Anderson Todd had almost committed the perfect crime. I believe that until James dumped her, she'd been unable to kill me outright, which was why she'd left me to starve. But once she'd lost James, she'd lost herself. At that point, she was capable of anything. Including murder.

I rubbed my finger over the hole left in the drywall from the bullet Marla had released. The hole was bigger now, because someone had dug the bullet out of the wall.

Thank God there was no blood. The only casualty from the night before was my right hand. The scrapes that had scabbed over were raw again this morning.

I didn't mind the pain. It was a result of Maggie's unrelenting grasp for hours the night before. She'd held on until she'd finally fallen asleep sometime after midnight.

And this morning, although she hadn't wanted to be alone, she hadn't been quite as insistent about keeping me in sight.

She'd called three times since I'd left the farm, though. I'd only been gone an hour.

"I have a question," Clay said as he wiped up fingerprint dust from the windowsill.

"What?" I was picking shards of glass out of the carpet.

"Why were you so loyal to your mother?"

"Why are you loyal to yours?"

"My mother's a little easier to be loyal to," he said. "She's sick, but she's always done her best for me."

"Mine, too." And this was a new realization for me. I'd learned my lesson. No more hiding. "And after all this, I think I was probably loyal to her because she saved me that day. I had vague memories about that time, but nothing concrete. I used to have nightmares…. Anyway, when I pushed her about it while I was in college, she did admit I wasn't imagining things like she'd always told me I was. She admitted the place existed and that they do sell kids there, but she said my father wasn't going to sell me, and therefore she hadn't saved me. Now that I know he's still alive, it all makes sense. She was scared to death that I'd go after him—and then he'd come after her. She said she'd been outside the agency the whole time. That they'd gone there together to see about a job for him. He'd taken me in to show that he was responsible around kids. She said she'd only gone in to pick me up because she'd heard me cry. I guess I believed her because I wanted to. But I remember now. I remember his words that day. He bargained with them. I remember him saying, 'It's a deal,' right before the lady grabbed my arm. I think my mother knew he was up to no good. She couldn't stop him from taking me—he'd just have hit her. But she followed him there. And arrived in the nick of time. I'm guessing the adoption people, protecting their legitimate business, prevented him from exacting any retribution. I have no idea what happened after that."

A piece of glass pricked my finger and I raised it to my lips, sucking on it.

Clay was on his haunches beside me in a flash. "Let me see that."

"It's okay," I said. "Nothing serious." But it felt good having someone there to care. To help. Even when I didn't really need help.

He looked at the tiny dot of blood. And he looked at my lips.

And he dropped my hand.

We were done within the hour. I gave the window people a key to the front door, which they'd leave with Deb at my office. I wasn't going into work for the rest of the week, but I didn't plan to move back home for a few days.

And then I was back at the farm, sitting beside Clay Thatcher as he pulled into the drive, afraid I was never going to see him again.

"I have a problem," he said as he put the gear into Park, but didn't turn off the car.

"What's that?"

"You."

"Me?"

"Yeah, you. I can't get your voice out of my head."

"I'm sorry. I didn't mean—"

"Stop."

I did.

"It's not your fault. And...I like it." He paused, tapped his thumb against the steering wheel. "When I don't hate it. You... I..."

I waited.

"You want to have coffee sometime?" he asked. And then he laughed. "Great, Thatcher, way to go. Invite a woman out for something you know she hates."

And just like that, a life that had almost ended less than a day ago now held the promise of a whole new world.

A better world than any I'd ever inhabited before.

I stared straight ahead.

"I'd love to have coffee with you sometime," I said.

"Tonight? After dinner and a glass of wine?"

"Yes."

"You think Maggie'll be okay without you?"

"As long as she's with Sam and Kyle. I don't want to

establish an unhealthy dependency. And I'll have my phone with me."

Now we were both staring out the windshield.

"Can I pick you up at seven?"

"Yes."

I looked at him.

And he looked at me.

We looked at each other's lips.

And I got out of the car.

Clay waved.

I waved.

And as I stood there, watching his car back down the drive, I had a delicious feeling of anticipation. I couldn't wait for this evening. And the one after that...

* * * * *

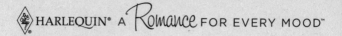

NEW YORK TIMES
AND *USA TODAY*
BESTSELLING AUTHOR

CARLA NEGGERS

The small town of Black Falls, Vermont, finally feels safe again—until search-and-rescue expert Rose Cameron discovers a body, burned almost beyond recognition. Rose is certain that she knows the victim's identity...and that his death was no accident.

Nick Martini also suspects an arsonist's deliberate hand. Now the rugged smoke jumper is determined to follow the killer's trail...even if it leads straight to Rose. Nick and Rose haven't seen each other since their single night of passion, but they can't let unhealed wounds get in the way of their common goal—stopping a merciless killer from taking aim straight at the heart of Black Falls.

COLD DAWN

Available wherever books are sold.

MIRA®

www.MIRABooks.com

MCN2824

REQUEST YOUR
FREE BOOKS!

2 FREE NOVELS
FROM THE SUSPENSE COLLECTION
PLUS 2 FREE GIFTS!

YES! Please send me 2 FREE novels from the Suspense Collection and my 2 FREE gifts (gifts are worth about $10). After receiving them, if I don't wish to receive any more books, I can return the shipping statement marked "cancel." If I don't cancel, I will receive 3 brand-new novels every month and be billed just $5.74 per book in the U.S. or $6.24 per book in Canada. That's a saving of at least 28% off the cover price. It's quite a bargain! Shipping and handling is just 50¢ per book.* I understand that accepting the 2 free books and gifts places me under no obligation to buy anything. I can always return a shipment and cancel at any time. Even if I never buy another book, the two free books and gifts are mine to keep forever.

192/392 MDN E7PD

Name	(PLEASE PRINT)
Address	Apt. #
City	State/Prov.	Zip/Postal Code

Signature (if under 18, a parent or guardian must sign)

Mail to **The Reader Service:**
IN U.S.A.: P.O. Box 1867, Buffalo, NY 14240-1867
IN CANADA: P.O. Box 609, Fort Erie, Ontario L2A 5X3

Not valid for current subscribers to the Suspense Collection
or the Romance/Suspense Collection.

Want to try two free books from another line?
Call 1-800-873-8635 or visit www.morefreebooks.com.

* Terms and prices subject to change without notice. Prices do not include applicable taxes. N.Y. residents add applicable sales tax. Canadian residents will be charged applicable provincial taxes and GST. Offer not valid in Quebec. This offer is limited to one order per household. All orders subject to approval. Credit or debit balances in a customer's account(s) may be offset by any other outstanding balance owed by or to the customer. Please allow 4 to 6 weeks for delivery. Offer available while quantities last.

Your Privacy—Harlequin Books is committed to protecting your privacy. Our Privacy Policy is available online at www.eHarlequin.com or upon request from the Reader Service. From time to time we make our lists of customers available to reputable third parties who may have a product or service of interest to you. If you would prefer we not share your name and address, please check here. ☐

Help us get it right—We strive for accurate, respectful and relevant communications. To clarify or modify your communication preferences, visit us at www.ReaderService.com/consumerschoice.

MSUS10R

MICHELLE GAGNON

When the world's foremost kidnap and ransom negotiator is snatched by a ruthless drug cartel, Jake Riley becomes ensnared in the effort to save him. But he's up against Los Zetas, an elite paramilitary organization renowned for their ferocity and skill, in the dark underbelly of Mexico.

After nearly losing her life on her last case, FBI agent Kelly Jones is determined to regain her confidence. She joins Jake on his mission—and quickly realizes she's in over her head. In the slums of Mexico City she has one last, desperate shot to prove herself—by taking down a killer.

KIDNAP & RANSOM

Available wherever books are sold.

MIRA®

www.MIRABooks.com

MMG2826

Try these Healthy and Delicious Spring Rolls!

INGREDIENTS

2 packages rice-paper
spring roll wrappers
(20 wrappers)

1 cup grated carrot

¼ cup bean sprouts

1 cucumber, julienned

1 red bell pepper, without
stem and seeds, julienned

4 green onions
finely chopped—
use only the green part

DIRECTIONS

1. Soak one rice-paper wrapper
   in a large bowl of hot water
   until softened.

2. Place a pinch each of carrots,
   sprouts, cucumber, bell
   pepper and green onion on the
   wrapper toward the bottom
   third of the rice paper.

3. Fold ends in and roll tightly
   to enclose filling.

4. Repeat with remaining
   wrappers. Chill before
   serving.

Find this and many more delectable recipes
including the perfect dipping sauce in

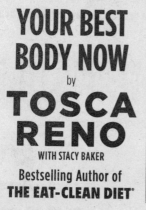

YOUR BEST BODY NOW
by
TOSCA RENO
WITH STACY BAKER
Bestselling Author of
THE EAT-CLEAN DIET®

Available wherever books are sold!

NTRSERIESJAN